ENDORSEMENTS

"*A Mother for Leah* is a story about finding love and joy again after an unexpected tragedy rocks an Amish family's life. Sweet, compelling, and filled with a charming cast of characters who will resonate with readers of all ages."
  - Suzanne Woods Fisher, bestselling author of *The Quieting*

"Miller's love for the Amish people and culture is evident in her story, *A Mother for Leah*."
  - Ruth Reid, Bestselling author of the *Heaven on Earth* novels

"*A Mother for Leah* is filled with charming characters and emotional moments that will touch your heart. Highly recommended for Amish romance lovers!"
  - Jennifer Beckstrand, author of *Return to Huckleberry Hill*

"Miller creates stories of faith, hope, and love that draw in the reader—and won't let go... I was captured from the start as I found myself weeping along with Leah."
  - Naomi Miller, author of the bestselling *Amish Sweet Shop Mystery* series

"Miller has penned an Amish tale guaranteed to captivate the reader. The story is rich with hope of new life and love. A well-written story for fans who can't get enough bonnet fiction."
  - Laura V. Hilton, author of *The Amish Wanderer* (Whitaker House)

"Miller's Amish novel, *A Mother for Leah*: Windy Gap Wishes Book One, is a comfortable read. It's a simple story of faith and the never-ending cycle of life amongst the Amish... a pleasant read, a story written with compassion."
  - Readers' Favorite [4 stars]

A MOTHER FOR LEAH

A MOTHER FOR LEAH

WINDY GAP WISHES
BOOK ONE

Rachel L Miller
WITH Naomi Miller

A Mother For Leah

Copyright © 2017 by Rachel L Miller

A Mother For Leah / Rachel L Miller, Naomi Miller

ISBN: 978-0998169262   (Paperback)
ISBN: 978-0998169279   (Paperback)
ISBN: 978-1386519379   (Ebook)
ASIN: B072FT6PJY

1. Fiction / Religion & Spirituality / Christian Books & Bibles / Christian Fiction. 2. Fiction / Romance. 3. Fiction / Christian Books & Bibles / Literature & Fiction / Amish & Mennonite.

2017938042

S&G Publishing, Knoxville, TN
www.sgpublish.com

Scripture quotations are from the Holy Bible (KJV)

This book is a work of fiction. Names, characters, places, and incidents are either products of the author's imagination or used fictitiously. Any similarity to actual people, organizations, and/or events is purely coincidental

Cover by: Expresso Designs

Second Edition 2018

Trust in the LORD with all thine heart; and lean not unto thine own understanding.

In all thy ways acknowledge him, and he shall direct thy paths.

~ Proverbs 3:5-6

For Mom

A NOTE FROM THE AUTHOR

Hello lovely reader,

Thank you for picking up my novel. I hope you enjoy reading about my made-up family as much as I have enjoyed writing about them.

Yes, as sad as it is and as much as I wish they were real, the characters and the communities in the following story are entirely fictional.

While there are Amish communities both in Cattaraugus county in New York and Holmes county in Ohio, I have created my own fictional communities within those areas so that I do not accidentally imitate any actual members of the Amish community.

Also please note that each community lives by slightly different rules and standards so I may have taken a bit of creative license in certain areas to make portions of my story work. Please understand that this is done, not out of a lack of research or respect, but strictly in the interest of the story itself.

God bless!

GLOSSARY

The German/Dutch dialect spoken by the Amish is not a written language. It is solely dependent on the location and origin of each settlement. The spellings below are approximations.

Ach = Oh (exclamation)
Aenti = Aunt
allrecht = all right
appeditlich = delicious
boppli/bopplin = baby/babies
bruder/bruders = brother/brothers
danki = thank you
Dat = Dad
daudi haus = house for grandparents
Dietsch = Pennsylvania Dutch
dochder/dochdern = daughter/daughters
eiferich = excited
Englisch/Englischer = non-Amish person
freind/freinden = friend/friends
frau = wife
froh = happy
gegisch = silly
Gotte = God
Gotte's wille = God's will
grandkinner = grandchildren
grossdaddi = grandfather
grossmammi = grandmother
Gudemariye = Good morning

gut = good
Gut nacht = Good night
haus = house
hochmut = pride
in lieb = in love
jah = yes
kaffe = coffee
kapp = head covering
kind/kinner = child/children
kumme = come
lecherich = ridiculous
maedel/maedels = girl/girls
Mamm = Mom
naerfich = nervous
nee = no
nacht = night
Onkel = Uncle
Ordnung = rules for Amish life
rumschpringe = running around time for youth
schmaert = smart
schpassich = odd
schweschder/schweschders = sister/sisters
sitzschtupp = special living room
verrickt = crazy
verhuddelt = mixed up/confused
Was iss letz = What's wrong
Wie geht's = How are you?
wunderbaar = wonderful

PROLOGUE

Leaning over the porch railing, Leah Fisher looked up at the sky. It was hidden behind dark clouds and thick rain.

There was a swooshing sound overhead, as the rain rushed down the tin roof into the waiting gutters below. Just beyond the edge, nearly everything was lost behind the thick curtain of water.

Leah wanted to step out into that rain—to wash the tears from her cheeks. Her eyes ached from all the tears she had shed in the past few days. She wondered if the rain would wash away a little of that ache along with the tears.

Before she took a step she remembered Anna, her elder *schweschder*, telling her to stay clean. She knew

Anna would not want her to get wet. . . not today. For certain, Anna would want her to look her best today—for *Mamm*.

Leah pulled her *mamm's* worn handkerchief from her apron pocket and rubbed at the tears on her face. She felt a strange tightness in her chest.

She wanted to say something to *Dat*, but he was so sad, she did not want to add her own worries to his load, so she kept them to herself.

Trying to distract herself, she looked back at the thick blanket of rain that was blocking the sun from view. She could not even see the dark clouds now.

Leah told herself it was better that the rain was hiding the sky. If she could see the sun, it would feel too much like any other day. And it most certainly was not like any other day she had ever experienced before. Leah could not imagine how it would ever feel like a normal day again. How could it . . . without *Mamm*?

Soon the rest of her family was hurrying down the steps to climb into the waiting buggies. Leah watched as her *bruders* and *schweschders* moved past her and filled first one buggy and then another. Leah stayed very still, almost hoping that no one would notice her.

Perhaps if we do not go, it will be like it did not happen.

Her heart felt like it was breaking. Still, she stood there waiting, not thinking about the cold. Instead, she was thinking about *Mamm*, and staring at the thick wall of rain all around her until she felt a hand slip into hers and heard *Dat's* voice at her ear.

"It's time, Leah. We must go now."

He gently tugged on her hand, compelling her to follow him as he turned toward the steps that would lead them down into the driving rain. They quickly moved down the steps to the buggy that was waiting. *Dat's* strong arms lifted her, swinging her through the air and into the buggy.

It took a moment for her eyes to adjust to the darkness inside the covered buggy before she saw Anna motioning her forward. She forced her feet to move and climbed onto Anna's lap as *Dat* climbed into the buggy behind her.

They were pushed back against the seat as the buggy moved forward. Leah held tightly to her *schweschder* as the buggy wheels went over large ruts that had appeared almost overnight from the rushing water.

She turned her head and looked out the small window as *Onkel* Josiah handled the team, but there was only the thick, dark curtain of rain in sight.

. . .

After sitting with her *schweschders* during the long church service, Leah was relieved to be back with her *dat*. They stood under a big, black umbrella at the front, so close to the simple pine box that Leah could have reached out and touched it. She held tightly to *Dat's* hand, as she stood beside him, thinking about *Mamm* in her pretty dress, lying in that long, wooden box. She tried to pay attention to the bishop, but the words were swirling around in her head as he spoke.

All around them, the heavy rain continued to fall. Leah could hear the steady thumps of fat raindrops hitting the umbrella over their heads, while the salty, wet tears ran down her cheeks.

．　．　．

Samuel heard the words of Bishop Beiler, but nothing truly seemed to penetrate the haze that had been his constant companion since his beloved Elisabeth had taken her last breath. He had prayed for so long to *Gotte*, but there had been no answers. Perhaps his prayers could not penetrate the haze, either.

He looked down at the soft pressure on his fingers and saw Leah watching him. Her sweet face was so like Elisabeth's; her eyes and her nose especially favored her *mamm*. It was like looking at his beautiful *frau* again. And it was nearly more than he could bear.

His little *dochder* looked up at the sky and then back at him before squeezing his hand again. Her fingers felt small and delicate, wrapped in his large, calloused hand. The feel of those tiny fingers reminded him of all the things that were facing them in the days to come.

He looked up at the dark sky, trying to see through the clouds for even a hint of sunshine, but there was not so much as a crack to be seen in the thick, gray clouds. Rain poured over his face as he closed his eyes and let it wash his tears away. As he did, he could see Elisabeth's face, her lips turned up in a sweet smile and the light of that smile dancing in her eyes.

Elizabeth had been his angel. Much too soon, *Gotte* had called her back to Heaven. He was grateful for the time he had enjoyed with her, but he knew it would never feel like enough. And what would they do without her? How would the *kinner* fare without their *mamm*?

Anna would be all right. She had stepped in to take over Elisabeth's duties as mother more and more each year. He didn't worry over David one bit. He had a *gut* head on his shoulders. He would miss his *mamm,* Samuel was certain of that, but he would go on the way he knew he must.

Miriam was more difficult to figure out. She was so quiet, always keeping to herself. *Of course, with Anna's shadow so tall, perhaps she is content to go unnoticed.*

Benjamin was already such a wild one. Samuel worried for how he would keep the boy in line without Elisabeth's strength and support.

And, of course, Ruth doesn't help one bit—always in the other children's business.

Elam and Caleb were in that difficult time. They would remember their *mamm* certainly, but Samuel was not at all certain they understood just how her loss would affect their lives.

Peter might remember his *mamm,* but what of Matthew and Lillian? They would never even know her. And Leah... his dear, sweet, delicate Leah. Samuel looked up to the heavens again, crying out silently to *Gotte* for help.

Dear Gotte, help me be a dat and mamm to the kinner.

Help me to give them comfort during the dark days ahead of us. Oh Gotte, help me to carry on . . . I don't know how to make it alone.

How would any of them go on without Elisabeth?

No winter lasts forever.
No spring skips its turn.
~ Amish Proverb

ONE

Leah felt a shiver skitter along her back as she looked through the lacy patterns of white frost that covered the window and saw *Dat* making his way to their large, sturdy barn. It was earlier than he normally left the *haus,* to be sure, but she knew he would be concerned about the animals, since the temperature had dropped to well below freezing in the *nacht* hours.

He knew even better than she how unpredictable the weather could be in their part of New York. If the wind was blowing steadily in from Lake Ontario, the weather could turn frigid in a matter of hours.

Watching the bounce in *dat's* step as he made his way across the snowy yard was a comfort to her though. He must not be worrying overmuch about the animals or anything else this fine, crisp morning.

Leah imagined she could almost hear the musical pattern of his steps as he crossed to the barn to begin his daily routine.

There were many cares on his shoulders, but you would never know it by watching him. Full of life and happiness he was. She was grateful for it, and for him. He was a rock in the storms that had raged through her life for nearly ten years now.

It was difficult sometimes to think that *Mamm* had truly been gone for so long. Many times Leah still expected to hear her calling up the stairs for the boys to go out and help *Dat* with the morning chores. Leah could picture her *mamm* standing in the kitchen by the sink, taking something *appeditlich* from the stove or sitting by the fire knitting—the rockers creaking quietly against the floorboards as her foot slowly moved her chair back and forth.

Guilt flooded her as she thought of it and she reached up to dash away the tears that escaped. She had *nee* right to feel sorry for herself. At least she had memories of *Mamm* to comfort herself with. Matthew barely even remembered her and Lillian had never really known *Mamm,* being just a few months old when the cancer had taken her from them.

Leah tried to tell herself that *Gotte* must have had a reason—it must have been in His plan for this to happen, for *Mamm* to be sick for so long and then to die, but it didn't stop her from wishing His plans were a bit easier to understand sometimes.

. . .

Samuel's thoughts were on his sweet *dochder* as his favorite old boots crunched over the frozen ground on his way to the barn. For sure and for certain, it was a worry for him.

Even after all this time, it seems like only yesterday. Has it truly been ten years?

It was nearly a shock to realize so many years had passed. There had been a time when the hours had moved so slowly, it seemed impossible for him to get through a single day—and now ten years had passed nearly in a blur. Yet, here they were—and the tiny *maedel* who had clung to his hand at her *mamm's* graveside was growing up into a young woman.

It might be difficult for Samuel to accept, but it was clear that time had sneaked away from him. It would not be long before the young men would come calling on her. And he was not at all prepared for that. She was still his little *maedel* in so many ways. But he knew the day would come—far too soon—when he would have to give her into the keeping of another man. It was a worry for him that she would not be prepared for that day.

Elisabeth had taken care to train up their *dochdern* well, but Leah had still been very much a *kind* when her *mamm* had fallen ill, and there were so many things Elisabeth had not had time to impart to their younger *dochdern*—Leah especially.

He did not worry so much for Lillian. Her sunny disposition made it nearly impossible for anyone to be sad when she was near. She was such a social *maedel*. Indeed, he often found himself wondering if Leah sent Lillian in her place as hostess when their neighbors came visiting.

Leah was clearly much too content to stay hidden from view of everyone. The more he thought on it, the more he realized that she made a point to stay inside whenever it was sunny outside. He could not remember the last time she had attended one of the youth singings.

One thing was for certain . . . she was not out doing the things a young woman was supposed to be about. Samuel knew he must do something—and quickly. He could only hope that it was not too late.

How have I missed it? My dochder is growing up and hiding herself from the world.

He stopped a few feet from the barn and looked up to the sky, sending a silent prayer to heaven. There must be some way he could help Leah, but Samuel had *nee* idea of where to begin.

He knew for certain that he must lean completely on *Gotte* if he was to have any hope of helping Leah find her way in this difficult world. They would both need *Gotte's* guidance in the time to come. Samuel feared he was much more ill-equipped than his young *dochder*.

It was several long minutes before he moved his feet again.

Just as his hand touched the wood of the smaller barn door, Samuel looked back to the *haus* he had built for Elisabeth and their family. She had been the most beautiful *maedel* in the entire community for as long as he had known her and he still had trouble sometimes believing that she had said *jah* when he asked her if he could take her for a ride in his buggy.

From there, it seemed they were mostly always together. For sure and for certain, they both had plenty of chores at home, but he made the trip over to her *haus* at least once during the week and on the Sundays when there was *nee* church service. One of his happiest memories was the day they took their vows to love one another till death. How could he have ever thought she would be taken in death so soon?

Nee more sad thoughts. I've got to get on past that— and be prepared for when Leah begins to take notice of the boys around her.

The thought that Leah would soon be in that same situation filled him with strong emotions that were a bit unfamiliar. He knew it was part of *Gotte's* plan for a young *maedel* to marry and raise a family, but he also knew that he was not yet prepared to let her go.

When he stepped into the barn, Samuel noticed the door to his shop was open and, after only a moment's hesitation, he pushed it open and stepped inside. Tools were scattered over the surface of the large workbench, but they were clean and free of dust. Leah and her *bruders* cleaned the barn regularly, but they never moved his tools. They sat there, still in the same position he had left them. Clearly, they were hopeful he would resume his woodworking someday soon.

He picked up the nearest tool. The feel of it made him realize that it had been more than ten years now since he had held this very chisel.

I cannot remember the last time I held a tool in my hand without a clear picture coming to mind. The last thing I carved was for my darling frau. Gotte, please bring back the desire to create something; if not for me, for the kinner.

As Elisabeth had become weaker and it was apparent she had little time left here, none of them wanted to be away from her for even a minute. The whole family had gathered around her in every spare moment to be found, crowded into the large sitting room where Elisabeth had spent her final days.

And then after she passed, he simply had not picked up the tools again. Always one to follow the Lord's leading, his woodworking *nee* exception, he stood there holding the chisel in his hand, rubbing his fingers absentmindedly along the well-worn handle. After a minute or two, he realized he was beginning to feel a hint of excitement. He could feel a familiar itch in his fingertips as he looked down at the tools laid out across the workbench.

A vague idea for a project began creeping slowly into his mind. It was elusive, an impression only, nothing solid yet, but familiar—as was the image spreading in his mind's eye.

Slowly, a warmth spread along his fingers where he held the chisel and excitement crept along his spine. Even after so long, he had not lost the gift *Gotte* had bestowed upon him.

He bent over and plucked a piece of wood from the box under the table and looked at it for a long moment. He could already see the shape it should be as clearly as if he had already carved it. With the chisel in one hand, he laid the wood on the tabletop, picked up a small hammer and began to shape the wood.

He worked slowly, carefully, and was comforted to find that his fingers still knew just what to do after all this time. As he stood there, slowly working the piece of wood, he thought again of his relationship with his dear Elisabeth.

They had been deeply *in lieb*, but he knew there had been too many times he had taken that love for granted. After it had become clear to them all that she would not be getting well again, he made a strong effort to show her just how much she meant to him. He was deeply ashamed it had taken such extreme circumstances to awaken him.

He thought about how empty his heart had felt for so many years. The image of Leah with tears in her eyes, standing in the doorway to their sitting room where her *mamm's* empty rocking chair sat, crowded into his mind as well. Sometimes it was hard for him to remember that losing Elisabeth had not only been a difficult time for him, but they had all suffered through it.

Nee matter the hurt that came with Elisabeth's death, Samuel knew he would not change one thing about their life together. Even a life without her was to be appreciated, because every moment of the time they had shared was precious and he still had eleven pieces of her. Each of his *kinner* was a part of her and he saw her in them every day. He was grateful to *Gotte* for each one of them.

He wanted that for Leah. He wanted her to catch the eye of a young man who would appreciate her the way she deserved. Samuel wanted Leah to know the happiness he had known with her mother, but she needed to be prepared for it.

There were things his own *Dat* had taken him aside to discuss privately when he had finally shown an interest in courting. There must be something the young women needed to hear about courting as well, but he had *nee* idea of what it might be. Would her schweschders think to speak with Leah about such things or did it fall entirely to him?

He simply did not know.

He could only pray and lean on the *gut* Lord to provide someone who could help his sweet little *maedel* ease into her adult years with as little fuss as possible. And he knew prayer was the answer. *Gotte's* ways certainly could be mysterious. And prayer was the only way anyone could begin to understand them.

It felt like *nee* time at all had passed when Samuel heard the loud pounding of boots. They went right past him and on into the barn. He could hear laughter and he easily pictured the boys playfully shoving each other as they went to feed the animals. He felt a smile spread across his face as he studied the piece of wood he still held. He'd left all the work to the boys, but the wood *nee* longer resembled the rough scrap he had picked up earlier.

Much of the morning was already gone so he took a moment to tidy the area before stepping out of the workshop. The barn door stood open and he could see the sky overhead. It was filled with an amazing range of color as the sun slowly moved from behind the hills that stretched as far as the eye could see.

He marveled, as he always did, at the beauty of *Gotte's* creation. And he wondered how anyone could miss the beauty here, especially looking at the breath-taking morning sky. How could anyone question *Gotte's* existence when they were faced with such a majestic view? He felt blessed to live in such a place, on the farm he and Elisabeth had purchased, in the home they had built for their family.

His thoughts went again to Leah and it made him realize just how much responsibility had settled on her young shoulders when Ruth married. There was much work to be done every day for sure. With all of his older *dochdern* now taking care of their own families, Leah handled all of the cooking and cleaning here at home, which left Samuel and her *bruders* free to care for the farm. He was so grateful for her spirit of helpfulness.

He and Elisabeth had been blessed with a large family and they all worked hard alongside him. Even little Matthew did his share. They were *gut* boys. And Leah was a *gut maedel*.

But the more he thought on it, the more he worried. Leah handled more than her share of the work, but he never heard a word of complaint. She had watched her *schweschders* for years so he was certain she had slowly taken over for them as they married and become responsible for their own households.

He had always thought she worked so hard to hide her loneliness, but what if it was something more? What if she was not simply trying to keep busy? What if she was afraid to step out into the world? Had Leah's devotion to the family kept her from growing, from doing the things that a *maedel* needed to be doing or from becoming acquainted with others in their community?

Was it too late? Was there hope for her still?

TWO

After breakfast, Dat thanked Leah for the *gut* meal.

"*Dochder*, I'll be heading out this morning to do some visiting. I should be back by suppertime. If not, I would be obliged if you would put back a plate of food for me."

"Of course, *Dat. Jah*, I will do that." Leah wanted to ask where he was going, but said nothing. It was a cold day for traveling. She was surprised that he had not said anything about it at breakfast.

Her *dat* usually kept to his routine and this was not a day he would normally be going out visiting. He usually asked Leah if she'd like to go along with him, but he didn't ask today.

Once he had gone, Leah chased her *bruders* out so she

could put the kitchen to rights before heading upstairs. There was always lots of work to be done and Leah wanted to have a *gut* supper ready for her *dat* whenever he returned.

Sometime later, a loud knock at the front door sounded, pulling Leah from her thoughts. She got to her feet and carefully made her way to the stairs, wondering who could be at the door.

She wasn't expecting anyone today, which was why she had chosen to clean the upstairs bedroom floors.

As she descended the last few steps, she brushed a hand over her apron and reached up to set her *kappe* to rights. Since she was not expecting anyone, it must be a stranger. Their neighbors would not feel a need to knock. And they would use the side door and *kumme* right in to the kitchen.

Perhaps someone has gotten lost and needs directions.

That happened often in their small community. Someone visiting the area would get turned around on all of the narrow country roads and lose their bearings.

Leah had just reached the bottom step when the knock sounded again. And she might be imagining it, but there was something about the sound that was urgent, worried, frenzied.

Perhaps someone needs help . . .

Fear gripped her and lent speed to her feet. As she moved closer to the door, she looked out the windows that faced the porch. She could see a young man standing in front of the door, but she did not recognize him.

He was turned away from the door, looking toward

the barn, perhaps questioning his decision to knock at the *haus*. But after only a moment, he turned back to the door and knocked again, loudly, insistently, before turning away again.

Leah reached the door and took a deep breath before opening it. When she did, she discovered her elder *bruder* Benjamin on the front porch with the stranger.

The young man was standing there, turned slightly away from her. She couldn't help but think that he seemed very *naerfich*, shifting from foot to foot. His head turned quickly, as he looked toward the barn; a moment later, he looked back toward her *bruder*.

Long, thin fingers held a crumpled, black felt hat. He was turning it around and around in his hands, despite the cold wind that was blowing.

He had a full head of shaggy, brown hair and it looked as if he had been running his long fingers through it. She could only see one side of his face; his cheek was red from the cold and there looked to be a bit of snow-burn on it.

I do hope he is not frostbitten.

She stood there in the doorway, as he continued to speak to Benjamin. His words were tripping out so quickly, Leah only caught a few, not even enough to determine what the young man was there about, but somehow her *bruder* must have understand enough of what the situation was, because a moment later he headed for the barn at a jog, motioning for the young man to follow.

The young man turned to look at her for a moment before following and Leah had to stifle a gasp of surprise.

His eyes had to be the deepest green she had ever seen. The color reminded her of the Norway Maples that dotted the edges of their property.

The leaves had always been her favorites. Her *bruders* and *schweschders* could never tell them apart from the sugar maples, but she'd always had a soft spot for the special, deep green color only found in the leaves of the Norway Maples—a cousin to the sugar maple trees.

The young man slapped his black felt hat onto his head and nodded at her, before turning to follow Benjamin. She watched the two of them disappear into the barn and shook her head at the strangeness of the situation.

Why would that young man affect me so? Could it simply be the tension that was flowing through her veins at the worry over whatever had brought him here this morning?

That must be it, she told herself. *Why, I don't even know what it is that's going on.* She stood there; looking toward the barn another minute before the wind whipped the hem of her long, deep purple dress against her legs and reminded her that she was not dressed for being outside. She stood inside the doorway for another moment before shaking her head.

There is nee use letting the warmth out, especially for nee gut reason.

Closing the front door, she decided to check on the bread she had put in the oven earlier, before heading back upstairs to finish her cleaning. If anyone needed her, they would let her know.

Several minutes later, Benjamin walked into the kitchen. Leah was just closing the oven door and she quickly shooed Benjamin back out, admonishing him to go back out the way he came in.

"For sure and for certain, there is mud all over those boots, Benjamin Fisher, and I just mopped this floor. You get yourself back to the mudroom and take those filthy boots off before you come back in here."

Benjamin smiled at her and shook his head as he snatched a cookie off the cooling rack beside her. She gasped in surprise before swatting playfully at her *bruder*. "And stop sneaking cookies before lunchtime."

His laughter bubbled out as he made his way out of the kitchen. When he reached the door to the mudroom he turned, looking serious. "The young man had a buggy accident just outside of town; he needs help trying to get his rig back on the road."

At least a dozen questions came to mind, but before Leah could ask even one of them, Benjamin held up a hand and went on speaking.

"We will also be returning with his cousin. It was too cold for her to walk such a distance, so he left her in the buggy, wrapped in blankets."

Her . . . the thought struck Leah and her hand flew up to cover her mouth as a gasp of shock escaped. Benjamin nodded his head at her, looking none too pleased with the news himself.

Leah fought to swallow all of her questions. Now was not the time for them. It was a bitterly cold day. If the *maedel* was injured . . . she opened her mouth to speak, thinking that she might need to ride down the street to fetch their neighbor, but her *bruder* was a step ahead of her, which he usually was.

"Do not worry; she wasn't injured when the buggy slid off the road; neither of them was hurt. Jacob offered to walk to the nearest home to get help. Ours was the first one he came to."

Leah let out a breath of relief at Benjamin's words. The doctor would not be needed after all. That was a small mercy.

"He only left her there because he feared she could not make the long walk. He assures me he left her with plenty of warm coverings." Benjamin held up his hand as Leah started to interrupt again. "I plan to head out right away and fetch her. I will bring her back as quickly as I'm able to, little *schweschder. Then I'll go back and help him with his horse and buggy.*" And with that, he turned and tromped out of the room.

Leah followed and watched as Benjamin heaved a large toolbox into the back of their smallest buggy before turning to go back into the barn. She looked at the small buggy, thinking that three would be a tight fit, but that might indeed be a blessing if the young man's cousin had been outside for a very long time.

Only a minute or so later, Benjamin returned. He was leading Popcorn, their other horse, out of the barn. The young man swung himself into the saddle easily and Leah found herself looking at him more intently than was necessary. He sat in the saddle with an ease that made her think he had spent much of his young life in a saddle.

Where did that come from? What am I thinking? What is wrong with me?

Leah shook her head to try and clear her thoughts. Why was she paying any attention to the way this young man sat in a saddle when his cousin was somewhere along the road, cold and frightened?

Leah shook her head again, but watched them until Benjamin pulled out of the yard and head away from town, the same direction she had watched *Dat* go early this morning.

Dat must have just missed their accident. Otherwise, he would have returned with the young man's cousin. Most likely he would have also picked up the young man on his way back.

Or else he would have simply taken the two of them on to their destination. And Leah wondered why that thought made her sad. Why should it make her sad to think that she might never have had the opportunity to meet the young man?

Now stop this, Leah . . . she told herself. *You are being gegisch.*

She turned deliberately away from the window, determined to find something to distract herself.

As she walked around downstairs, wandering somewhat aimlessly, Leah found herself curious about the age of the young man's cousin. Benjamin was the only one of her *bruders* so far who was dragging his feet about finding a nice *maedel* to settle down with.

Most young men in their community had at least one prospect by the time they were Benjamin's age, but he had shown *nee* interest in anyone. Leah was certain her *gut freinden* Ada would have noticed, and told her about it, if he had.

Looking out at the fat flakes that were lazily drifting down and adding to the thick layer of snow already covering the ground for as far as she could see, Leah thought of the *maedel* who was sitting somewhere out there in the snow, huddled under a mound of blankets.

Bowing her head, she sent up a silent prayer for the young woman; asking Gotte to keep her safe until help arrived.

THREE

As he traveled along the main road, heading toward their nearest neighboring community, Samuel thought of his *bruder* Josiah's advice. Then he thought about what his neighbor Elias had said at their last meeting—about waiting for *Gotte's* timing.

His *bruder* was worried for him; he knew that, for sure. He had certainly been vocal enough about it over the years. Samuel had been listening for *Gotte's wille* every morning for the past week while praying. This morning, he had woken up with a strong desire to visit the neighboring town—with the intention of looking for a *frau*.

Thinking of his conversation with Elias made him feel better about it all—even better than when he had finally made up his mind after visiting with Josiah. There was a strong sense of hope in his heart now; something that he had not felt in a long time.

With that feeling to guide him, Samuel had gone to the barn and readied their buggy and then hooked up Matilda. Now that he was on the road and alone with his thoughts, he began to feel *naerfich* about the whole thing. He began to wonder if he was being *gegisch*, thinking his answer was in the next town over.

He was ready to turn around and go back when he saw a small buggy that had somehow ended up almost in the ditch. He slowed his own buggy as he pulled up beside it.

He could see *nee* horse, but once he was beside the small buggy, he could see there was a passenger—a *maedel*, if he could judge by the black travel bonnet. She was wrapped in a mound of blankets. He doubted she could even see him as he pulled up beside the buggy, so he called out to her.

"*Hallo* . . . Is there anything I can do to help?" He sat there a moment, looking at the tall bundle of blankets on the front bench topped with a bonnet, and felt a moment's panic when he heard *nee* reply.

How long has she been here? The weather for sure is not fit for sitting in a buggy on the side of a road. If she has been here all nacht . . . surely someone would have seen her before now.

He set the hand brake on his own buggy and started to step down, just as the mound moved ever so slightly. He watched the thick black bonnet rise up over the top blanket and turn toward him.

The young woman's small, delicate features were nearly hidden within the depth of the bonnet, but he saw a grateful smile spread over her features and he felt his breath catch.

Seemingly unaware of the effect she was having on him, she smiled even wider and began pushing her way out from under the pile. For a moment she didn't say anything—she was still trying to untangle herself from the pile of blankets.

Samuel was not sure what to say or do. She was clearly alone, but as there was *nee* horse attached to the buggy, there could have been someone with her. Or else her horse had somehow become detached and run off.

He found that he wanted to ask if she had she been all alone—or if her husband was out there looking for help even now. He started to ask, but she spoke before he could form the words.

"Did Jacob send you?"

It's just as well, he thought. As *verhuddelt* as he was by her smile, he would not be able to make sense of anything. Samuel shook his head, but still could not seem to form any other words.

Now that she was out from under the pile of blankets, his thoughts from earlier returned and he found himself concerned about how long she had been out here in this cold weather. She was a tiny little thing—in her simple dress and apron, she looked more like a doll than a woman.

If not for the laugh lines around her eyes, he would

have taken her for a young woman, perhaps even the same age as his own *dochdern*. But the mouth that formed her brilliant smile was surrounded by tiny lines as well, so she must be nearer his age.

He sat a bit straighter in his seat and tried to give her all of his attention, but it was not easy. He found himself distracted by a tiny dimple that appeared to the left of her lips as she spoke.

"My cousin went to find help," She said, her voice full of concern. "But he has been gone a very long time."

Samuel looked up at her eyes then, and what he saw nearly stopped his heart. Her enormous brown eyes held him simply transfixed. In that moment, without any doubt, he knew that this was her! This was the woman *Gotte* had sent him looking for. He was exactly where *Gotte* wished him to be. He did not know how he knew this—but he did for sure know it. He felt it from deep within his soul.

This tiny woman with the enormous brown eyes was the one *Gotte* had sent him to find. He was suddenly very glad he had not turned the buggy around at his earlier feelings of foolishness.

Samuel quickly climbed down from his buggy and stepped over to hers. He was not at all surprised at what a mighty struggle it was to look away from her brown eyes.

"I have not seen anyone walking along the road. Is there any way that I can help?" He noticed her look of concern and he found himself wishing he had seen her cousin on his way here—if only to ease that concern.

He could see conflicting emotions flit across her features. She must be trying to decide whether to leave the buggy and risk worrying her cousin when he returned, or to stay here in the cold. He hoped common sense would rule and she would realize she needed to get indoors and near a *gut*, warm fire . . . and soon.

He was surprised she had been able to survive in her thin clothing—and in such cold—for any amount of time, especially being so delicate. But perhaps there was a simple answer; *Gotte* had kept her warm until Samuel could reach her.

She continued to stand there, clearly trying to decide what to do. Samuel was uncertain whether he should hurry her along or wait. Although if she waited much longer, for sure and for certain she would wish she had not. She would certainly not be able to withstand much more of the bitter cold.

He forced himself to look away from those warm, brown eyes and realized he was much closer to her face than he had thought. He could see every detail of each tiny line feathering out from the corners of her eyes and he found himself wishing he could place a kiss on that dimple that had appeared earlier at the corner of her mouth.

When he realized where his thoughts had wandered, again, Samuel forced himself to think of something else. He could not completely tear his attention away from her face, so he thought instead of the tiny laugh lines around her lips.

She was obviously someone who smiled a lot. That was a *gut* thing. If she was to be the *frau* for him, he was pleased to see she was a *froh* person. That thought took Samuel by surprise, but he was much more amused by it than anything.

"I think it would be best if you could deliver me to my *aenti*'s home," She said as she started to move forward, but her foot must have caught in the blanket because she began to tumble forward.

Samuel reached out and gently gripped her elbows to keep her from tumbling out of the buggy and a deep pink blush appeared and colored her small cheeks.

Her next words tumbled out in a rush, as if she were as affected by his closeness as he seemed to be to hers. ". . . if it would not be too far out of your way. That would be *gut*. She will not be expecting me and I have *nee* idea where Jacob has disappeared to, but certainly he can find his way home and . . ."

She stopped abruptly; sounding very uncertain and Samuel found he wanted to reassure her that all would be well.

He actually opened his mouth to tell her that *Gotte* had directed him to her, before the thought came to him that she might very well think him crazy. The words stuck in his throat as a thoughtful frown took over his features. If she noticed, she did not give any indication of it. She chewed on her lower lip a moment before she continued speaking.

"I will leave a note for my cousin Jacob. I would stay here, but it is very cold and he has been gone such a long time." She stopped talking as a violent shudder overtook her and another blush crept up her cheeks. Then she smiled tentatively at him before turning away to pull a small notebook from under the seat; moments later Samuel could hear a pencil scribbling furiously on paper.

He waited while she wrote her note and thought about how absolutely charming she was. Clearly he was not the only one who was feeling a bit *verhuddelt* and he was glad of it. *Gotte's wille* might be difficult to understand at times, but it could be wondrous also and he was very *froh* he had taken the time to listen.

"Your *aenti's* home sounds *gut*. When you are safely there, I will *kumme* back and help your cousin with the buggy. Perhaps together we can set it to rights."

She folded her note in half and laid it on the bench beside the small mountain of blankets and then she placed her tiny hand in his.

"That would be *gut*. He did not know what to do, which is why he went for help. He knew he could walk much faster without me—and with the freezing temperature, we both thought it would be better for me to stay here." She chattered away as Samuel helped her down from the buggy and then she stopped suddenly, nearly falling over him again.

"I forgot about my suitcase," she gestured to the back of the buggy and Samuel nodded his head.

"Don't worry yourself about it. I'll get it. Let's just get you settled first." He helped her up into his own buggy, before turning back to her cousin's buggy to retrieve several of the blankets she had been wrapped in. It was so cold; he knew she would need the extra warmth.

"How far away is your *aenti's* home?" He asked her as

he settled the blankets around her.

She tucked them even closer around herself as she answered, "Not far by buggy." She said it with a little smile, even as she shivered.

After that, she snuggled down into the warm blankets before adding, "But too far to walk in such cold weather. The *haus* is right outside of town, on the main road."

Samuel nodded as he went back for her suitcase. When he unstrapped it from the back of her cousin's buggy, he was surprised by how heavy it was.

Well, she is either coming for a long visit . . . or she is moving here. Samuel felt a thrill at the idea that she was moving here. *She is the one for me then. Praise be to Gotte!*

He set the suitcase in the back of his own buggy before walking back around, running a hand over Matilda's flank as he did so. Then he climbed up into his place on the seat, settling himself quickly and then they were off.

Nee matter how many blankets she had wrapped about her, Samuel knew she had been exposed to the cold for much too long. For now, the important thing was to get her to her *aenti's haus* quickly and inside where it would be warm.

FOUR

Leah turned her head, looking toward the door, at the sound of horse's hooves on the hard-packed ground outside.

So soon? For sure and for certain, they can't have gone more than just down the road.

She walked out onto the front porch, thinking that perhaps it was someone else she was hearing . . . perhaps one of their neighbors coming for a visit. But it was not a neighbor.

Leah watched as Benjamin pulled the small buggy into their drive, followed by another small buggy hooked up to Popcorn and driven by the young man who had *kumme* to the door earlier.

She turned and went back inside once they steered

both buggies toward the barn area. She knew Benjamin would take care of the horses before they told her any news. She also knew Benjamin would want some strong, hot *kaffi* to warm up with, so she went about the business of heating water for her tea, brewing *kaffi* for the men and preparing a warm snack as well.

They had not been away long, but certainly long enough to have worked up a hearty appetite.

. . .

She was just pulling a pan of biscuits out of the oven when she heard the side door open and then shut after a minute, followed by the sounds of boots stamping on the floor. She looked heavenward, hoping they were stamping the mud off their boots on the stiff rug she and Miriam had woven for just such a purpose.

Still, whether or not they were using the rug, she knew they would most likely be tracking mud into her nice clean kitchen—something she had finally, after all these years, begun to grow accustomed to—having so many *bruders* about.

She was grateful though, that *Dat* did not share the habit with her *bruders*. He removed his boots just inside the door every time he came inside. He used the mudroom most every time, unless he was escorting company inside or simply coming inside from the porch.

Once Ruth and Miriam were married and Leah had begun to help more with the everyday cleaning, she had started to pick up on many things she had missed before.

Whether it was due to her youth or simply that she was not often mindful of the floors because she had not been required to clean them she was not certain, but she had wondered how her *schweschders* stood cleaning the floor so often and she had told Miriam she intended to speak to *Dat* about it.

Miriam had taken the opportunity to show Leah how it was a blessing instead—which was Miriam's usual response to any complaint.

This time Leah was thankful of the memory, especially now, with two of her *schweschders* married and taking care of their own families. Soon David would be married as well—he was already spending a great deal of time in his new home, preparing it for his bride.

In *nee* time, their family would all be scattered about and Leah would have *nee* one left to take care of. And she was thankful for it right this minute.

Hardly any time passed before Leah heard boots on the kitchen floor behind her. They were talking quietly, already sounding like *freinden*. She shook her head at it. Leave it to her *bruder* to make *freinden* with someone over a broken down buggy.

She wondered where the young man's cousin could be. He had said she would be with them, but Leah watched as only the two men walked into her kitchen.

Fortunately, Benjamin's words answered her questions before she had to ask. ". . . just like something my *schweschders* would do. From what she said, it sounds like my *dat* was the one who stopped to help her. He will get her to where she needs to be and then head back to the accident." Benjamin laughed lightly as he said this last, almost as if he was enjoying a joke at *Dat*'s expense.

Leah tried not to take exception to what Benjamin was saying. She knew he must be talking about Lillian or Ruth when he said "one of my *schweschders*," especially since Leah was standing right there with them, but it was a puzzle how Benjamin could be so informal with someone he had just met.

"It was a *gut* idea you had, to leave him a note as well." Benjamin chuckled again and Leah could easily picture the pithy words he might have chosen to put in that note for *Dat*. Leah did not know of anyone who truly appreciated Benjamin's sense of humor, but he certainly seemed to enjoy making the rest of them the target of his jokes.

Leah's irritation with her *bruder* grew as she listened to him. But then the young man he had called Jacob earlier spoke, and she was distracted by his voice. It was clear and strong. She could not help but be amazed at how different he sounded when he wasn't *naerfich* and cold.

"At least he will not have to wonder where we've gone off to." He stopped and Leah found herself straining to listen for anything else he might say. Fortunately she didn't have to wait long.

"I do hope he got my dear cousin though, before she tried to walk home alone. She is such a little thing." Leah heard a low chuckle that could only have been his and was surprised at the feelings that skittered up her spine at the sound of it. ". . . But I can't see her sitting still very long either."

"I thought she would insist on going for help herself when the buggy slid off the road. At first she did . . . it took everything in me to convince her to stay put. And then Midnight ran off when I unhooked him. I wrapped Naomi up in the extra blankets in the buggy and rushed off to find help."

He still sounded a bit *naerfich* when he spoke of his delicate cousin and Leah found herself wishing that she were the object of that concern.

How delightful it would be to have someone other than Dat worry for me so.

She reached up and tried to cover the cheeks that had suddenly warmed at the thought.

She should be thinking of his cousin; the poor, delicate *maedel* could have been half frozen and she was standing here wishing things about this mysterious young man that she had *nee* right thinking.

Of course, from what her *bruder* said, it sounded as if *Dat* had found the *maedel* and rescued her from the cold so she would be inside soon enough. Leah wondered if *Dat* would be bringing her here.

Nee, that makes nee sense, either. He will certainly take her on to her family. That is where she should be. Leah scolded herself for being so *gegisch*. She must be *verhuddelt*.

"I am grateful I found someone at home and that you were able to help so quickly. If your *dat* had not found her and taken her on to our *haus*, she certainly would have been half-frozen by the time we returned." His low, smooth voice washed over her again and Leah struggled with the large tray that weighed heavily in her hands, nearly dropping it.

Definitely verhuddelt.

She had filled the tray with fresh *kaffi*, a bowl of biscuits, honey and several different jams she and her *schweschders* had put up in the fall. When they looked over at her standing there with a large tray, laden with food and warm *kaffe*, they seemed to move into the kitchen a bit quicker.

The young man rushed over and took the tray from her hands, his fingers brushing against hers as he did. The heat that raced across the tops of her hands took her by surprise and it was all she could do to smother the gasp that sprang to her lips. She looked up and found herself staring into his eyes, which were much too close—due to the fact that he'd had to bend down to take the tray from her.

There was a strange itch in Leah's hands; she wanted to reach up and run her fingers through the mop of hair that was dangling over his forehead as he bent toward her.

Behind them, Benjamin cleared his throat and Leah felt heat creep up her cheeks again at the smile that spread across Jacob's features.

Leah turned away and rushed over to the counter, looking for anything she could do that would keep her from having to return to the table.

Her resolve only lasted a moment though, when she spotted the stack of napkins she had forgotten to put on the tray. She picked them up and turned, only to bump solidly into Jacob.

He took her by the elbows and kept her from falling backward. Heat filled her cheeks again as she looked up into those deep, green eyes and could not form a single word.

After only a moment, he let go of her and Leah was comforted when the warmth where his fingers had touched her elbows did not immediately fade. He grinned at her as he turned back to the table and took a seat across from her *bruder*.

Even though he wasted *nee* time in filling his plate with biscuits and cookies, he kept sneaking glances at her and the warmth from her elbows spread down her arms and tingled in her fingers again. It was a mighty struggle to look away from him and over at her *bruder;* she immediately wanted to cluck her tongue at Benjamin's manners, but she remembered he had been out in the cold for quite a long time so she held her peace.

Leah looked back at Jacob and met his eyes.

The thought that he had been watching her sent heat back into her cheeks again. She found herself wondering if this was going to be something she would always be doing when he was around.

Well, that is just silly. I simply cannot continue to behave this way

She scolded herself as he turned to his food with a smile on his handsome face.

She watched as he took his first bite of the biscuits and felt such joy at the look of enjoyment on his face. He smiled up at her again as he chewed and nodded his head while waving the biscuit; then stopped waving it as a tiny piece flew off and landed on the floor behind them.

She lifted a hand to smother the giggle that burst from her lips. Benjamin, however, had *nee* such reticence. His laugh sounded from across the table and he leaned back to slap his knee.

Benjamin's laughter was very hard to resist and her own giggles were becoming harder to suppress so she turned to wipe down counters that really did not need wiping, forgetting all about the piece of biscuit that needed picking up.

There were so many new feelings rushing through her and it was a struggle to figure out what it all meant. She wiped down the last counter and looked around for something else she could clean as the side door opened. The sounds coming from the mudroom made it clear that it was *Dat*. She opened her mouth to speak, but before she could call out, Benjamin spoke up.

"*Gut, Dat.* You found our note?" Benjamin chuckled as he said it.

"*Jah,* Benjamin, I found the note. *Danki* for your thoughtfulness," *Dat* said as he walked into the kitchen.

Leah could hear the same dry tone in *Dat*'s voice that normally let Benjamin know that he did not appreciate his sense of humor, but *Dat*'s voice did not sound nearly so disapproving as Leah had expected.

That is schpassich. Dat does not usually enjoy Benjamin's sense of humor.

She thought over it and wondered what could have happened to put *Dat* in such a *gut* mood. She watched as he walked over to the table and sat down next to Benjamin before addressing the young man across from him.

"You would be Jacob, then. Do not worry. Your cousin is safe and well." There was something very different about *Dat*'s voice when he spoke of Jacob's cousin. Leah wondered if it was simply his way of reassuring young Jacob.

"I drove by and saw your buggy off the road, so I stopped to offer my assistance. I was quite surprised when I saw a woman alone in the buggy."

Leah noticed right away the use of woman and not *maedel* and wondered at her *dat's* choice of words. She had thought the young man's cousin would be about the same age as him or somewhere close.

Wouldn't an older woman travel with her husband and not a cousin?

Unless she is not married . . .

The thought came to her and she wondered about the difference she had heard in *Dat's* voice earlier.

"I felt it would be *schmaert* to take her on to your home, rather than wait for you to return, since she was mighty chilled already." *Dat* stopped for a moment before going on.

"I am glad to see you found her note." He was most likely thinking of Benjamin's note again when he said it. Leah found herself wondering why her *bruder* thought his jokes were so funny.

Certainly *nee* one else seemed to agree with him.

"She wanted to make certain I would tell you right

away not to worry for her. Your *mamm* immediately bundled her up by the fire and she was making tea when I left." He stopped there, chuckling a little. Jacob joined in so he must be familiar with his *mamm*'s ways.

"I only stayed a moment to introduce myself and explain, since your cousin was in *nee* condition to explain herself, what with her teeth chattering so. Then of course, I headed back to the buggy to find you."

Leah was puzzled as she watched *Dat's* face light up when he spoke of the young woman's teeth chattering. Why should such a thing bring a special sort of light into *Dat's* eyes?

FIVE

Naomi walked over to the ancient stove in her *aenti*'s kitchen and picked up the tea she had prepared. The kitchen was still quiet this early. *Aenti* Ida and her family were still sleeping.

So strong was the habit, after so many years of rising early, that Naomi still rose at the same time each day, even when she tried to sleep longer. She had begun using the time for special prayers over a year ago when her dear *mamm* had told her that she believed *Gotte* had another husband in mind for Naomi.

Naomi had long ago given up the idea of ever being someone's *frau* again and had simply been trying to get on with her own life, but she had to admit, the idea had begun to take hold of her heart and she found herself rising early as usual and using the time for prayer.

She prayed for her own *mamm* and *dat;* she prayed for sweet Rebekah, who was having such a difficult time in her young life. And this morning, for the first time in over a year, she did not have to pray for the husband her *mamm* had been insisting was out there somewhere. However, she did pray that *Gotte* would show her how to proceed with him.

Naomi was not certain how she had known *Gotte's* leading, but when Samuel Fisher had stopped his buggy and asked her how he could help, she had known this was the man *Gotte* meant to be her husband. Now she just needed to know how to go forward.

She remembered feeling a blush spread over her cheeks when Samuel had reached out to catch her to keep her from tumbling. Even now she was surprised by it. It had been many years since she had blushed and it made her feel like a young woman again. She had nearly forgotten what it felt like.

She had certainly forgotten how warm her cheeks would feel. For sure and for certain they had felt nearly like they were on fire after so long in the cold air.

She was not certain if Samuel had seen that first blush, but she knew he had seen the second. He had not mentioned either one though, bless him. He simply went about bundling her up for the drive to her *aenti's haus*.

She was still a bit uncertain whether *Gotte* had meant for her to say something to Samuel Fisher or not. By the time she had finally decided she must say something to him, he had been hustling her up to the door of the ancient, rambling farmhouse.

Then *Aenti* Ida had immediately bundled her up and rushed off to make tea. Naomi had made introductions as well as she could, with her teeth chattering and her body chilled by the freezing temperature outside. Samuel had taken over her broken explanation of the day's events. Then he had left to see to young Jacob and their buggy.

She had not seen Samuel again, but Jacob had been full of stories and news when he came in some time later. He told them of Samuel Fisher's family and there was a twinkle in his eye when he mentioned that Samuel was a widower.

Naomi did not dare reveal *Gotte's* message after such news, but she felt much warmer on the inside knowing that she had not gotten it all wrong.

She had also noticed how quiet Jacob became when he spoke of Samuel's young *dochder*, Leah. Naomi expected she was not the only one who had seen the look of hope on Jacob's face when he said the young woman's name and spoke of her kindness.

Aenti Ida must have seen it as well—she noticed everything.

Earlier that day, once Naomi was bundled up by the fire, sitting in the rocking chair that had been in their family for several generations and holding her warm tea, it had not taken more than a moment before *Aenti* Ida began to ask her a dozen questions about Samuel Fisher— and Naomi's feelings for him.

Aenti Ida had clearly seen the way Naomi was looking, as she sat by the fire and thought about the man who had rescued her.

Naomi had not known the answers to most of the questions her *aenti* asked, but she had told her a little about her own feelings—it was the best she could do. She had described her blush—both of them—and she'd described the feelings that had come over her when he touched her and the warmth that had flowed through her as he helped her out of the buggy and into his own.

She even told her *aenti* a little about how she had felt when she saw Samuel for the first time. She left out the part about knowing he was *Gotte's wille* for her, but she did tell *Aenti* Ida about the fluttering that had filled her stomach in that moment and how the words she tried to say had stuck in her throat when he spoke to her.

Aenti Ida, known for being a romantic, had simply lit up when Naomi told her all about it. And later, when Jacob had *kumme* in and told them about Samuel Fisher being a widower, she had lit up again and looked over at Naomi with such a hopeful expression that it was all Naomi could do not to laugh.

Still, she dared not tell her *aenti* about feeling it was *Gotte's wille* for her to become Samuel Fisher's *frau*—at least not yet. She carefully held that information close to her heart. It was precious to her and—for now at least—it was her own little secret.

Not to mention it was their way. She might not know much about how young people went about courting now, but she did remember that when John had been courting her, most couples kept the knowledge of their courtship secret for a time. She could certainly do that.

Ach, it may just be wishful thinking though.

She and Samuel were hardly courting, at least yet. She would have to find a way to talk to Samuel—and soon. There was *nee* easy way to go about that. She would have to pray very hard that *Gotte* would show her the words to use and the right time to broach the subject with him. She only hoped he would be receptive.

But what if I should not say anything at all to him? After all, it is the man who is supposed to approach the maedel.

If she said anything to him, he would certainly consider her too forward and not a *gut* choice for a *frau* since women were meant to be submissive to their husband's wishes.

But what if he does not have any special feelings for me and I do not say anything? What will I do then?

The thought was almost too much for her. She had come all this way with a very specific mission in mind and if it did not work out the way she planned, there was nothing else that she could do.

Go back to Ohio, I suppose.

Hope Springs was home, was it not? Shouldn't she be content to return to her haus—to their land—to family and *freinden* and her *dochder*?

She knew she should, but there was nothing in her that wished for in her former community. In fact, the last place in the world she ever wanted to be again was Hope Springs, Ohio. The only things she missed there, were her parents and Rebekah.

Naomi thought about the events of her visit until now

and it was simply astonishing. *Mamm* had given her the idea to visit weeks ago. She had told Naomi that it would be *gut* for her—and Naomi had known right away that this was her answer to the problems she faced in Ohio.

Aside from her journey having a somewhat difficult beginning, it was going very well indeed. It was *wunderbaar* to visit with relatives she had not seen in years and it was exciting to think about meeting people who were not aware of the things she had dealt with during the last ten years of her marriage. And meeting Samuel Fisher—well, she had certainly not expected to meet her intended so quickly.

She had been certain she would need to be here for some time and make continual excuses to *Mamm* about why she had not yet returned, without telling her that she had *nee* intention of ever returning.

Clearly *Gotte* had known better. He had known all along what his plans were for her and He had brought her here to show them to her. Now she just had to have the courage to follow His leading.

. . .

Jacob walked to the barn holding a lantern in front of him, even though he could have easily walked the path in his sleep.

On his way, he thought of the *maedel* he had met completely by accident. He was glad his dear cousin had looked as if she were praying when he slipped past her on his way to the back door.

Jacob wanted to figure out his plans for courting Leah before he had to answer questions from anyone—even his cousin, and Naomi had looked at him a bit strangely last *nacht* when he had mentioned her rescuer's *dochder*.

He thought about Leah's sweet face as he moved into the barn and went about the business of feeding the horses. He ran a hand up and down Midnight's neck.

It's a gut thing Midnight knows where the feed is. It did not bear thinking on what *Dat* might have had to say about Jacob's foolish actions if the horse had not found his way home.

Of course, it wasn't as if I wanted him to run away. The thought was still a bit painful. He should have known better.

I should have realized he would be spooked after the accident. Midnight is still in training. Just like me. Well, it is probably best, since I still have so much to learn about the business of training.

Of course, if Midnight had not run off, Jacob would have ridden on to their *haus* with Cousin Naomi and he would never have met the lovely and quiet Leah Fisher.

Perhaps it was all part of Gotte's plans, after all.

If he was not mistaken, his cousin seemed quite taken with Leah's *Dat* as well. Her cheeks had colored just as Leah's had several times the day before, when Jacob had mentioned Samuel Fisher at dinner last *nacht*.

Behind him, Jacob heard the unmistakable clomp of his *Dat* as he came into the barn—followed closely by the quick, *eiferich* steps of Jacob's seven-year-old *bruder*. Levi was always so *froh* to help out their Dat with anything; be it mucking out stalls or repairing fences.

Jacob sometimes envied his younger *bruder* that innocence. He did not yet have to worry about a job, making money—or the thing that weighed most heavily on Jacob's mind of late—being able to care for a family.

His reaction to Leah Fisher had made Jacob very much aware of how far he still had to go before he would be able to present himself as a suitable husband. A husband needed to be able to take proper care of his family.

Shaking his head at the serious turn his thoughts had taken, Jacob turned his attention back to the horses.

Still, it won't hurt to see if Leah is as interested in courting as I am . . .

There's plenty of time until I have to be able to support a family. After all, courting season has barely begun.

SIX

Leah sat on her bed, snuggled up under the quilt *Mamm* had made for her when she had been just a young *maedel*. She could remember sitting at *Mamm's* feet while she stitched, playing with small scraps and trying to make them into a quilt like the one her *mamm* was working on.

Leah was glad *Mamm* had used such quality materials and done such fine work, but she had also been careful to take exceptional care with the quilt so that it would last many years. Still, Leah did not sleep with it, but kept it tucked away in her hope chest with other things that were special to her.

Nearly a year ago, Leah remembered Miriam and Anna deciding Leah needed more than a few keepsakes in her hope chest. They had opened the lid one day, with *nee* warning, and Miriam had nearly had a fit at the emptiness that met her gaze. She and Anna had gone on about it all afternoon. Since then, the chest had slowly began filling up and Leah worried that she would soon need to find a different place to put her keepsakes . . . which might be part of Miriam and Anna's plan.

For as long as Leah could remember, Anna especially, had told her that it was not *gut* to hold on to things. Leah had long ago given up explaining to Anna that it was not the things themselves that she was holding onto, but the memories of *Mamm*. As Leah had grown older, those memories were slowly fading and it broke her heart a little more every time it took more than a moment to bring *Mamm's* face to mind.

Her *schweschders* simply did not understand. They had so many more years of memories, they had been so much older when *Mamm* died—they remembered her easily. Leah wanted to be angry with them, but she knew they were only trying to help her. They truly did love her and she felt *gut* knowing that—but she missed *Mamm* so.

She worried about herself too. Now that *Dat* was beginning to move on with his life and look for a new *frau*, Leah felt nearly like he was betraying her. It made *nee* sense and it made her want to cry at all the confusion stirring within her. She had been praying for a new *mamm* for many years now, so why would she be hurt to think about *Dat* marrying?

Shouldn't I be froh that Dat will soon be giving me the answer to all those prayers?

Even worse, while it made her want to cry, it also

made her angry. The thought of another woman coming into their *haus* and doing the things *Mamm* had done, or the things Leah had taken responsibility for now, made her want to scream and stomp her feet. She knew it was *lecherich*, but she couldn't seem to stop the emotions from filling up inside her.

Yesterday when she had thought of where *Dat* was going, the anger had risen up in her. She had spent the morning trying to empty herself of the unwanted anger, by vigorously scrubbing every floor in the *haus*. Then she baked bread and muffins and *cookies*. Baking always put her in a better mood, and the family had certainly enjoyed the fruits of her temper, but that was small consolation for Leah.

Only a stranger knocking on their door had managed to distract her from the anger this morning. Thinking of Jacob brought heat to her cheeks. Leah put a hand up to her lips at the strange tingling feeling that appeared with the heat.

She could not help wondering about him. Had he thought her *gegisch* to have blushed again and again every time he had spoken to her or brushed her hand? Was he sitting somewhere thinking of her right this moment?

Ach! It's lecherich. I'll never understand boys. I'm never going to get married. Who could possibly want me?

Leah felt the despair that always came when these sort of thoughts creep in and settle in the pit of her stomach. It didn't seem to matter that Ruth told Leah that her quilting stitches were just like *Mamm's* or that Miriam had remarked on more than one occasion that Leah was the only one who had mastered *Mamm's* canning recipes or how many times their *freinden* and family told Leah her pumpkin bread was the best they had ever tasted.

When despair crept in, Leah felt as low as the rocks at the bottom of their frozen pond. There was nothing and *nee* one who could change her mind until she managed to shake off the mood that had dragged her down.

She might have gone on like that for half the *nacht* had it not been for the strange light that appeared at her window.

She jumped off the bed and rushed over to the window to see what the light was, thinking that perhaps someone was hurt or lost and she might be able to help. But the sight that met her on the ground below was not at all what she was expecting.

Jacob stood on the snow-covered ground just below the empty branches of her favorite maple tree, moving his flashlight a tiny bit back and forth at her window. He stopped when he caught sight of her and motioned for her.

The emotions that filled her, as she slid the window open as quietly as possible, were overwhelming and questions were rushing through her muddled brain.

Was he coming here to court her? What was she supposed to do? Should she go out to meet him or just talk to him from her window? Wasn't this what Ada had told her the other young people did when they were courting?

Is this what David does with Catherine, what Anna did with Daniel, and Miriam with Joshua?

Thinking of her *bruder* and his *fiance* and her

schweschders and their husbands, she felt the urge to laugh.

It was a struggle, but she quickly smothered the urge. She just couldn't picture Ruth's David waving a flashlight into her window; it seemed easier to picture it other way around. It was definitely something her stubborn *schweschder* would do.

Ach! If only I had someone to ask about these things.

"Jacob, what are you doing here?" She whispered as loudly as she dared and hoped her voice carried down to him, but she cringed at the words that had come out. That was not at all what she had meant to say, but Jacob only smiled up at her.

"I should think it is obvious. I've come to court you, Leah Fisher." His strong, clear voice floated back up on the crisp, cool, *nacht* air to her and sent the warmth that had spread across her cheeks a few minutes ago rushing all through her, making her feel as if she were standing in the heat of late July, instead of the frigid air of early November.

She opened her mouth to speak, but stopped and bit her lip. What should she do? The emotions were pulling her in so many different directions.

"Can you *kumme* down? I have a warm brick for your feet and hot cocoa to warm your insides." His smile was so warm, Leah could not imagine needing anything other than that to keep her warm and toasty.

"I brought my courting buggy, but we can go slowly so you don't get too cold." The plea in his eyes was too much for her to resist.

Heaven help me if this is the wrong decision.

She threw the prayer up to *Gotte*, hoping that he would stop her if it was the wrong thing, but also wishing fervently that nothing stopped her from going down to Jacob.

"Can you give me five minutes?" She asked and cringed when she realized her voice was a bit too loud.

"Take all the time you need. I will be right here."

Leah flew away from the window, glad she had not gotten dressed for bed already. All she needed to do was to pull her shoes back on, pin up her hair and grab a warm coat on her way out.

She grabbed her warmest boots and moved quietly down the hall to the bathroom. It was tricky to pin her hair in the dark, but she didn't want to take a chance with a lantern. Lillian might be a sound sleeper, but Benjamin was not and he would certainly notice a light.

Once she was satisfied with her hair and *kapp*, she crept down the stairs, careful to step over the one that creaked. Rushing through the back hall, she actually slid into the mudroom in her stocking feet and had to stifle the gasp that tried to sneak past her lips. She pulled on her boots and laced them tightly before pulling her coat and scarf off the peg, then worked to open the door as quietly as possible.

The hinges creaked twice as she pulled and each noise sliced through the sound of her own pounding heartbeat and seemed as loud as a gunshot in her ears. She slipped through the door as soon as she could fit and then nearly laughed at how soundlessly it shut behind her.

She turned and nearly screamed when she bumped solidly into Jacob. He caught her before she could tumble backward and hit the door, which would certainly be loud enough to wake someone.

"We have to stop meeting this way." His breath tickled her nose as he whispered the words and she was glad to hear a hint of laughter in his voice as he helped her gain her footing again and then slowly let her go before stepping back.

The instant he let go, Leah found herself wishing he hadn't. She fought back the sound of disappointment that rose to her lips. It was a struggle, but she certainly did not want to give him the wrong idea about her.

He smiled and took her hand, leading her off the back porch and down the lane, careful to walk across the snow-covered grass, avoiding the rocks—which would certainly crunch with every step.

"I parked at the end of your driveway. I hope that isn't too far for you to walk in the cold." He looked back at her and it was all she could do to nod.

She began to worry about someone waking up and not finding her there, but the excitement of the moment was too strong. All this time, worrying about whether or not a boy would ever like her and now she was about to go on a moonlit ride with one. She was not about to back out now.

I would not miss this for anything. I can worry about the rest of it tomorrow. Besides, isn't this what I wanted? For Jacob to come courting?

She knew it was and she was determined to enjoy every second of it, for as long as it lasted.

. . .

Jacob sat beside Leah on the blanket-covered bench and thought about *Gotte's* plans. Who would have thought that a buggy accident could be the thing that brought the two of them together? He felt immeasurably blessed. And though he knew his *freinden* would think him *verhuddelt*, he was already thinking of Leah in terms of the rest of their lives.

He had never met another *maedel* who affected him this way. He felt certain it was *Gotte's* way of telling him that Leah was the one for him.

Now I just have to convince her of that.

He turned into a small field that was brightly lit, pulling just far enough off the road so they would not be the way of the *Englischer's* cars, but not so far that Leah would feel uncomfortable.

"Would you like some cocoa? It's *Mamm's* secret recipe."

"So your *mamm* knows we're here?" Her eyes widened when she asked him and he nearly laughed at the sound of worry in her voice.

"*Nee, Mamm* hasn't any idea." He shook his head and then added, "but I know her secret." He grinned, hoping to put her at ease.

As they sat there, he could see that Leah was more *naerfich* than he had originally thought.

Is it even possible that she has not been courted by any others? If that is the case . . . his thoughts trailed off and he realized what it must mean for her to have come with him.

Why she must have feelings for me, if she has come out —having nee experience.

He knew he must find out so he asked as gently as possible.

"Leah, there is a question I must ask you."

She turned to him with such wide eyes, he felt he knew the answer already. "Have you been courting previously?"

She ducked her head immediately and he nearly felt as if he were being cruel to this gentle soul beside him. Clearly she was concerned he would not wish to spend any more time with her if he knew the truth.

"Leah, I do apologize. I did not think. I was certain that I would be competing with many of the young men in your own district." He reached a finger down and gently tipped her chin up so that her wide eyes met his again.

"I should not have made the assumption that you knew what you were about. I do apologize if this has all been too sudden." When she still said nothing, he added, "Am I mistaken? Is there another young man who holds your heart?"

Could I have been wrong? It made *nee* sense.

She still didn't speak, but her head slowly moved back and forth as she continued to stare at him with such wide eyes.

So she is simply overwhelmed.

The feeling of relief that spread through him at that knowledge was overwhelming. Clearly his feelings for her were bigger than even he had suspected.

I must be cautious. I certainly would not want to frighten Leah away.

"I am very glad you came out with me tonight." He purposely used a quiet voice, trying to infuse his words with shyness. He would have to find a way to make her more comfortable or he would never get the chance to see if she shared his feelings even a little.

Her head came up with his words and he thought he could see a hint of a smile in her eyes.

Gut. So maybe she is at least glad she came.

They sat there in silence for several minutes before Jacob remembered the thermos full of hot cocoa he still held. He reached under his seat and pulled out the insulated mugs he had bought just for this occasion.

After pouring the hot liquid into the first mug, he handed it to Leah and watched as she wrapped her hands around it. Even with gloves on her hands, she must be cold. Suddenly Jacob found himself wishing he had brought the closed buggy, even though it was proper to use the open cart-style buggy.

"Are you too cold?" He asked as she blew lightly over the surface of her cocoa.

"*Nee,* I'm *allrecht.*" She took a tiny sip of the cocoa and then another one, sighing a little after the second one. "This is *gut* cocoa. Would your *mamm* consider sharing the recipe?" She looked up at him from under her lashes and he thought he could see mischief in their depths. "Or would you?"

He laughed out loud. Here he had been worrying over her shyness and clearly he had *nee* reason to. She was comfortable enough to try and get him to spill his *mamm's* cocoa recipe—a secret she had guarded his entire life. He had only learned of it this past year. She had told him that it was a family secret and she would only pass it on to him if he solemnly promised to keep it within the family.

Suddenly a very *gut* idea came to him and he struggled to keep from smiling too widely.

"I would be *froh* to share it with you Leah. However . . ." he let his words hang, watching her face. Did she realize how expressive her eyes were? Every emotion was right there for anyone to read.

I could sit here all nacht, just looking into her eyes.

A man would for sure and for certain be blessed to look into those eyes every day for the rest of his life.

He had to swallow the words that leaped to his lips. After another moment, he decided she had waited long enough for him to answer. He also knew he might say the wrong thing and frighten her if he didn't answer playfully.

"I can only share the recipe with a family member." He watched those eyes of hers and nearly wanted to kick himself for the sadness he saw reflected in them, but it was *nee* more than a moment before it changed to what looked like hope.

Perhaps she does share my feelings.

He cautioned himself though. She was a full three years younger than he and it would not be a *gut* idea to push her too far too fast.

. . .

A slight chill went through Leah when Jacob said it was a secret only meant for family, but as she thought about it a thrill replaced the feeling. Was he saying she might one day be a member of his family? She was quick to try and smother the grin that was attempting to work its way across her features.

It would not be a *gut* idea to appear too eager.

And what if I am wrong? What would Jacob think of me if I jump to that conclusion and it is nothing like what he is thinking? Suddenly she felt *nee* reason at all to smile.

She looked at Jacob over the top of her cup as she took another sip of the *appeditlich* cocoa.

For sure and for certain he would not be sitting here in the cold if he had nee interest in me. I must leave this in Gotte's hands. He will know what is right for me and for Jacob.

Leah nodded her head a little as she came to this conclusion. It made the most sense.

She determined right then to enjoy the beautiful *nacht* sky that was filled with the light of so many brilliant stars as she sat here beside a very handsome boy, drinking such *wunderbaar* hot cocoa.

It was several minutes before either of them spoke, and when they did—they both spoke at once. They looked at each other and both of them started laughing at the same time. Leah looked around, feeling a bit *naerfich* when she realized how loud they were laughing, and clamped a gloved hand over her mouth to muffle the sound.

Jacob was still laughing and Leah took a moment to appreciate his deep laugh. This was certainly not the laugh of a *kind*; this was the laugh of a young man. It reminded Leah of her *dat*.

SEVEN

Samuel sat at the small kitchen table with his Bible open in front of him, but the words were not holding his attention. He was looking at the book, but the thoughts in his head were of brown eyes—Naomi's brown eyes.

Her small face was looking back at him from his memory and he could see nothing except her big brown eyes as she looked out sweetly from under impossibly long lashes. He could see the corners of her eyes lift. He was certain the corners of her mouth were, too, and the light of that smile was shining almost like stars.

Those eyes had distracted him for days. He found himself wishing he could find a reason to drive over to her *aenti*'s home so he could see her again.

If only it could be so simple. But Samuel knew that

nothing about this was simple. For so long he had prayed and asked *Gotte* to show him what he was to do. He had listened to his *bruder*'s advice. He had opened his mind and his heart to *Gotte's* leading. And now he had an answer. The only problem was that His answer presented even more questions for Samuel. He knew now that *Gotte* had a *wunderbaar frau* for him, but she didn't live in the next town, like he had thought. She lived in Ohio.

He had learned that bit of information from her *aenti* when he explained the events that brought them there with Naomi shivering from cold and exhaustion. Her *aenti* had told him Naomi was visiting from Ohio and the news had left him feeling *verhuddelt*, but he reminded himself that *Gotte* knew the plans *He* had for Samuel's and Naomi's life much better than they themselves could.

And if *Gotte* knew the best plan for them both, who was Samuel to disagree? He would simply keep praying and wait for *Gotte* to reveal His *wille* for this turn of events in Samuel's life.

He looked up at the sound of someone walking down the stairs and knew, before he saw her, that it was Leah. She was the only one of his *kinner* who did not make a point to skip the step with a creak when she went up or came down the stairs.

Looking at her, he found himself wondering what Leah would think of Naomi. Would she be glad to know that Samuel had found the woman he felt *Gotte* intended for him to marry? Would she welcome Naomi into their home—into their family? Would the rest of the *kinner* welcome a new *Mamm*? And how would Naomi react when he told her of his eleven *kinner*?

Should he have mentioned it already?

Nee, that is gegisch, he thought. *I should at least speak to her about Gotte's plan for us first.*

He looked up at Leah as she crossed the room and moved toward him. Whether or not she would welcome a new *Mamm*, clearly she needed someone to talk to. Lately, she had begun keeping secrets from Samuel and it worried him. He had *nee* idea what to do about it. All he could think to do was pray, so he prayed.

He asked *Gotte* to show Leah His *wille* for her life the way He had shown Samuel. He asked *Gotte* to comfort her in the time to *kumme*.

Samuel could only pray—and hope that his sweet *dochder* would be able to handle all of the changes he was about to put her through. He prayed for *Gotte's wille* in all of their lives and he prayed for peace and understanding with his family and for himself.

And he prayed for *Gotte's wille* to be done with him and Naomi Yoder. Just because he felt that she was part of *Gotte's wille* for him did not mean Naomi would agree. He would have to pray about that as well, pray that *Gotte* would give him the right words when he spoke to Naomi next.

He had a lot of work ahead of him and he was curiously *eiferich* to get started. He would have to find a way to convince Naomi to give him and his large family a chance and he would have to do it soon—before she went back to Ohio.

. . .

Leah walked into the kitchen and saw her *dat* sitting at the small table with his Bible open in front of him. She knew he must be communing with *Gotte* so she tried to be as quiet as she could. For sure, she did not want to disturb him. She had almost turned around to go back upstairs before she'd remembered the squeaky stair.

Since she had hit it on her way down, she felt certain he had already been disturbed enough. So she went about the business of preparing breakfast, trying to make as little noise as possible.

Dat had already put on the *kaffe,* so Leah went about putting together the batter for pancakes. There was nothing like pancakes on a cold day and one look outside was all it took to see that it would be a very cold day.

As she gathered the ingredients, she thought of her late *nacht* ride with Jacob. He had been so thoughtful. He could have made her feel *lecherich* about her lack of courting, but he had not.

She still remembered the glow of his smile—one that could only have been called triumphant—when she had told him there were *nee* other boys she was interested in.

The warmth that had spread through her when his smile bloomed and spread across her face had been very pleasant indeed. She found herself hoping he would come shine his light in her window again . . . soon.

"*Gudemariye,* Leah." She heard from behind her.

She had not expected to hear *Dat*'s voice so close behind her and she let out a loud gasp and almost dropped the large bowl of batter she had been stirring. Guilt filled her over what she had just been thinking of and she felt color creep up her cheeks. It was a struggle to push the guilt down; she could do nothing about the color.

I can only hope he thinks it is due to my hard work.

She turned to find him smiling broadly at her. She could see he had not startled her on purpose. She was grateful to see that he clearly had *nee* notion of where she had been last *nacht* or what she was thinking of this morning.

She felt her lips curl in response to the mischievous smile tugging at her *dat's* mouth. Still it took a moment to calm her speeding heart so she could answer.

"*Gudemariye, Dat.*" The words had *nee* more than left her tongue when she found herself catching her lower lip between her teeth to keep from laughing as she said it. Relief had rushed in to replace the guilt and with it had come such a desire to laugh, she knew he would think her *gegisch* if she were to let it loose.

She turned back to the stove so that *Dat* wouldn't see the grin that had spread across her face, replacing her blush. Behind her, she heard his chair move, followed by footsteps as he crossed the kitchen.

His words were loud in the stillness of the early morning hour, but she could hear laughter in his voice.

"Pancakes this morning; what an unexpected treat. Are you trying to spoil us?" He sounded as if he was struggling with laughter and Leah wondered at the reason, but didn't get a chance to ask as he went on.

"You have to be more careful *dochder*, or Benjamin

will never move out and find a *frau* with such *gut* meals right here at home."

Leah turned to defend Benjamin, but stopped when she realized *Dat* was teasing her. She was *eiferich* to see him in such a *gut* mood. He had not looked so *froh* in such a long time.

For just a moment she thought of Jacob's cousin. *Dat* had found her at the side of the road and taken her on to her *aenti's* home.

Which would also be Jacob's mamm.

Dat had not brought her back here to find her cousin. He had taken her on and left Jacob to fend for himself. Was it possible that *Dat* had been a bit *verhuddelt* after finding the woman at the side of the road? Could he be feeling—for Jacob's cousin—what Leah found herself feeling for Jacob?

Could that explain his gut mood?

Leah thought it might. She found herself feeling more *froh* than she had in a long time. She had not thought nearly as much about her worries over *Dat* or the possibility of a new *Mamm*. She felt certain it must be because of Jacob. There was nothing else that could explain it.

If Dat has feelings for Jacob's cousin, he will certainly be courting her as well.

The thought came to Leah that she was very blessed indeed that *Dat* had not been heading out himself last *nacht* to shine a light in Naomi's window—if, in fact, older people did that sort of thing, too.

While she wondered about it, she heard her *bruders*

and young *schweschder kumme* down the stairs. Young Lillian was the first into the kitchen. Her cheerful face was the first thing Leah saw when she turned to offer them a *Gudemariye*.

"*Gudemariye*," Lillian sang out as she skipped into the kitchen.

Leah felt her smile light up as she looked over at Lillian. *Nee* one could be angry with her around. She was like a ray of sunshine, always so *froh* and sunny. There were times Leah knew she had given Lillian a difficult time due to her own turbulent emotions, but this morning it was easy for Leah to respond with a smile and a sweet "*Gudemariye*." in return.

Their bruders were not so *froh*. Leah had never been able to figure out how they kept from running into the walls because their eyes were hardly open. They staggered into the kitchen looking more like they were still sound asleep.

Leah and Lillian looked at each other as the boys came into the kitchen. In a rare moment, they shared a *gut* laugh as they watched the boys stumble to the table and drop into chairs. Clearly their *bruders* had *nee* idea of how *gegisch* they looked early in the morning.

Leah went back to making the pancakes as the rest of the family gathered around the table, smiling to herself. She was feeling very contented this morning—to be here, taking *gut* care of her family.

Dat seemed to be feeling much more himself as well, which made her *froh*. The kitchen felt warmer this morning than it had in some time . . . especially when

Lillian skipped over next to Leah and offered her another mischievous smile.

Thoughts of Jacob floated through her head again and Leah found herself smiling even wider—while thinking about her *wunderbaar* evening—as she and Lillian sat down to breakfast.

EIGHT

Leah sat beside her bruder Matthew and tucked a warm blanket around the both of them. She held two large loaves of bread, wrapped tightly against the weather, on her lap. She was thankful for the heat coming from the bricks on the floor of the buggy, under the bench they sat on. The blanket helped even more, creating a warm little cave around them.

Only a moment later, *Dat* settled himself in the buggy beside her and took the reins in his gloved hands. Leah took a moment to make certain her warm bonnet was firmly tied before the buggy moved forward.

She held tightly to the wrapped loaves as the buggy bumped over the rise of pavement at the end of their driveway. The main road might provide a smooth ride, but the lack of trees would lend strength to the gusts of wind that rocked their buggy as it moved along.

As they wound their way slowly through the maze of roads leading to the neighboring community where *Onkel* Josiah lived, Leah found her thoughts wandering to Jacob. She couldn't help thinking about when she might see him next. He had told her he would *kumme* soon to see her, but she'd had *nee* idea *Dat* would spring this visit on them so suddenly.

He had walked into the kitchen after the mid-morning chores were finished and announced that they would need to pack up for an overnight stay. Lillian had been the first to ask where and *Dat* had answered that they were leaving that very afternoon for his *bruder's haus*.

Leah thought about how long it had been since they had visited *Dat's bruder* and his family. She wondered what could possibly be the reason for them to go now . . . and so suddenly . . . but she didn't ask *Dat* any of that. She just went to work, preparing what they would need for the trip.

Onkel Josiah had never made any secret of his concerns over Leah's *dat*. She had strong suspicions that *Onkel* Josiah's habit of voicing those concerns—and the way he went about it—might be the reason behind the long space of time between their visits.

She could still remember clearly their last visit. *Aenti* Ella had asked her to take fresh *kaffe* out to *Dat* and *Onkel* Josiah.

Leah had not intended to overhear anything not meant for her ears, but when she had reached the barn door and heard raised voices, it had shocked her. She had never heard *Dat* raise his voice. Even when her *bruder* Peter had slipped on the ice and broken his arm, *Dat* had been the picture of calm. He had scooped up Peter, who was yelling right at the top of his lungs, and headed straight for the barn. All the way to the barn *Dat* had given her *bruders* instructions, but he had never once raised his voice.

So that was the reason why, Leah had told herself, she hadn't pushed on through the barn door. She had simply been shocked. She had told herself it must have been shock; it could not have been anything else. She would not have listened in on *Dat* and *Onkel* Josiah's conversation for any other reason.

Onkel Josiah's voice had been very hard and he sounded angry as he said, "You are being stubborn, *bruder.*"

"*Jah*, I suppose I am . . ." *Dat* sounded much more calm than his *bruder,* but still loud. "If you will remember, it is my family, my life, and my decision you are speaking of."

"That may be true, but they are my family as well; my nieces and nephews, and they need a *Mamm.*" *Onkel* Josiah's voice cut through the air as if he was standing right next to Leah and she had jumped.

His words had helped her to understand what the argument was about. *Onkel* Josiah had been saying for years that *Dat* must move on—and *Dat* had always put him off.

Leah could remember *Onkel* Josiah saying time and again that *Dat* needed to marry again, but she had never heard them arguing so fiercely about it before.

"Josiah, I appreciate your concern for me and for the *kinner, but* we are doing just fine."

"Fine, *bruder*? Truly? How can you say you are fine? Your *kinner* do not have a *Mamm*. It has been eight years. How much longer will you wait?" Josiah stopped for a moment and Leah found herself pressing herself closer to the wall of the barn.

"They are growing up, Samuel. All of them will be grown before you know it . . . and then they will be gone and you will be all alone."

Leah had been surprised to hear *Dat* let out a short bark of a laugh.

"Is that what you're really worried about Josiah, that I will be all alone? I have three *grandkinner* already, and with nine more *kinner* to marry, I cannot imagine there will ever be a time I will be completely alone. Even if only half of them follow in their *Dat's* footsteps and have large families, I will be surrounded by *grandkinner.*"

"It is not the same." Leah nearly hadn't heard *Onkel* Josiah's words that time, because they were so quiet.

She had waited for what felt like a very long time, but neither of them said anything else. While she waited, Leah thought about what they both said and had found that she agreed with every word *Dat* spoke . . . but she'd agreed with *Onkel* Josiah, too.

She had worried about the same thing many times. Anna and Miriam were already married at the time and Ruth would have been married soon. Now it would be David next, followed by Benjamin and all too soon it would be time for her, Elam and Caleb to consider courting.

She clearly remembered thinking it was all too much. Thoughts and emotions had swirled around in Leah's head as she'd thought of everything she'd heard and all of the new and confusing feelings she was experiencing.

Even though *Mamm* had been gone more than eight years then, the very idea that *Dat* would marry again and bring someone else into their home to perform *Mamm*'s duties had been hurtful to Leah.

She could well remember the pain that had shot through her at the idea. Leah had made her way to a small bench that sat against the wall only a few feet from her and waited a very long time before getting up and walking to the barn door. Without even thinking about the argument she had overheard, Leah had opened the barn door and walked right in.

Neither man had shown any sign that they had fussed at all, so she had deposited their *kaffi* and hurried back to the main *haus*, thinking all the way about what she had heard.

She had not heard them arguing about it again though she still wondered how *Onkel* Josiah could be so angry with *Dat*. Why, if it had been *Aenti* Ella who had died, Leah could not imagine *Dat* speaking to his own *bruder* in such a way.

Even now, not one bit of it made any sense to her.

Could that be why they were visiting now? Surely *Dat* would not want to be forever at odds with *Onkel* Josiah.

Thinking again of Jacob, Leah was reminded of his

cousin. Was *Dat* attempting to mend fences with his *bruder* or could it be something else? Could *Dat* be ready to consider *Onkel* Josiah's advice?

It had been ten years now since *Mamm's* death . . . and nearly two years since that visit to her *onkel's haus*. Could so much have changed in so little time? Could *Dat* be ready to open his heart to someone now?

The thought of it sent a sharp, stabbing pain through Leah's heart. Determined not to think about it too much, she focused her attention on the snow-covered fields they were passing and tried to turn her thoughts back to Jacob.

A thick blanket of clean, white snow covered everything she could see . . . fields and houses, barns and bushes, trees and fences. Leah had always enjoyed the beautiful sight of snow. There was just something about it that made the whole world look like a different place—one she was delighted to be a part of. Even her worries could not distract Leah from the beauty of *Gotte's* creation all around her.

Thinking of the snow and the cold reminded Leah of sitting in an open buggy with Jacob. Even though she had been very *naerfich,* she was *eiferich* to think about the next time she would see him.

Ach! I hope he does not kumme tonight and think I do not wish to see him.

She was distracted by that for most of the remainder of the drive.

. . .

Leah looked over at her cousin as they rolled out dough for more bread.

"*Ach*, Emma! I'm so sorry. I should have been holding on better to the bread."

"*Nee*, Leah. You are not to blame. My *bruder's* pup has knocked more than just bread out of my hands." With a laugh she added, ". . . too many times to count."

"But I should have been more careful." Leah felt as if she might cry.

"We can be thankful it was just the one loaf and that *Mamm* had extra dough ready to be made up." Emma said as she brought out a large bowl from the cool room. "Now we can have more bread and rolls, too!"

She set the bowl down between the two of them with a smile. Leah took enough dough from the bowl to shape into another loaf of bread. Emma stood beside her preparing dough for rolls, singing quietly with a smile playing at the corners of her mouth as though none of it had happened.

Leah sneaked another look at her cousin, as Emma's small hands deftly rolled and shaped the dough into the tiny rounded squares that would bake into *appeditlich* rolls. She watched her sweet cousin working the dough, and she suddenly wondered if Emma had ever spent an evening out with a young man.

Should she ask? Weren't the youth supposed to keep the secrets of courting to themselves? Did that mean they spoke to none of their *freinden* about it . . . or cousins?

Just when Leah had finally decided to ask Emma about it, her cousin chose that moment to speak and distracted

Leah from her resolve.

"Are you enjoying your *rumschpringe*, Leah?"

Emma was asking her about *rumschpringe*—what better time would there be to ask her cousin about her own experiences with courting? But as she began to form the words, she felt embarrassment creep up her neck and spread out over her cheeks.

"Do you go to many singings?" Emma asked when Leah didn't say anything.

"Actually Emma, I have not been to all of the singings lately, but my *freind* Ada has managed to get me to several of them." Leah laughed as she said it. Thoughts of her *freind* Ada always made her laugh . . . or cringe.

"Do you not like the singings, Leah?" Emma asked after a moment.

"*Ach,* Emma, that is not it at all." She searched for the right words to give her cousin. Was this the right time to ask about whether Emma had been out courting yet or not?

"But you are seventeen," Emma's voice had dropped to a whisper. " . . . Is there *nee* one you are courting? She asked in a voice so small, Leah almost couldn't hear her.

Now is my chance, Leah thought. *If I am going to say anything to her about it, it must be now.*

"Actually..." Emma turned from the rolls she was shaping, with eyes that were suddenly wide and intent on Leah's face. It was all she could do not to laugh at the look on her cousin's face.

"There is a boy who wishes to court me." She was quick to add, "but we have only been out together once."

"Does your *dat* know?"

"*Nee,* Emma. The youth keep courting to themselves for a time." They were both talking in whispers now. Leah nearly laughed at the picture they would make if someone walked into the kitchen.

"Is he very handsome?" Emma asked in almost a breath of a whisper. Leah could tell it had taken some courage for her younger cousin to ask such a question.

"*Jah,* he is handsome." And Leah knew her eyes lit up as she said it. "He is handsome and kind—and funny as well."

"Leah Fisher, you have all the luck."

At that, Leah laughed. For sure and for certain, 'twas not luck that had Jacob shining a flashlight in her window.

"Leah," Emma bumped Leah with her elbow, pulling her from her thoughts. "You have to tell me more."

Leah let out a laugh before turning serious again. She shared with her cousin as many details about the evening as she could remember.

As she and Emma chatted about Jacob, Leah forgot all about being irritated with her *bruder* and the ruined bread.

NINE

The last pan of rolls had just been placed in the oven when *Aenti* Ella walked into the kitchen. She walked up behind Emma and sniffed the air appreciatively.

"Something smells *wunderbaar gut*." She looked over at Leah with a mischievous smile. "I wonder what it could be."

Emma giggled at her *mamm*'s obvious teasing. *Nee wonder she is always so froh*, Leah thought to herself—she came by it honestly.

Aenti Ella put her hands on Leah's shoulders and squeezed lightly. The gesture was both comforting and loving and Leah wanted to lean into it, but she was afraid it might make her *aenti* ask questions—questions that Leah had *nee* answer for, so she stayed right where she was and enjoyed the contact as best she could.

"You have both done such a *gut* job. *Danki* to both of you. And I know the men will be saying *Danki,* too. You have saved them from a mighty disappointment." Ella smiled as she said it and there was a twinkle of mischief in her eyes again.

Just then Leah's young *bruder* Matthew came barreling through the kitchen with Mark right behind him —and the pup on their heels.

Aenti Ella and Emma were laughing as they ran through and Leah found herself laughing with them. It was still a mystery to her how her *aenti* and cousin were so calm with such chaos all the time, but she didn't feel so bothered by it as she expected.

Maybe I am growing up—finally.

.   .   .

Samuel walked into the barn, looking to the right and left as he entered. Ella had told Samuel that her husband was out here doing chores. It was a bit late for chores so Samuel thought it was possible Josiah was hiding out. Not to mention, the tone in Ella's normally sweet voice told Samuel that he needed to go out and find Josiah—to try to clear the air.

Thanks be to Gotte, that's one of the reasons I came.

He turned the corner and spotted Josiah mucking out stalls. The pitchfork in his hand was moving through the soiled hay with rough, jerky movements. Clearly Josiah was not only hiding; he was upset over something . . . and it was most likely something to do with his *bruder*.

Samuel walked over to the stall Josiah was working in and leaned against the post at the end of the long wall, crossing one booted ankle over the other.

"If I did not know better, I would say that you are hiding . . ." he purposely let his words hang in the air, giving Josiah room to answer or not.

Josiah looked back at his *bruder* and then turned back to his work, shaking his head.

"Josiah, if you've something on your mind, I do wish you would just say it."

After what seemed like an eternity, Josiah turned and stood the pitchfork straight in front of him, placing one gloved hand over the other as he looked thoughtfully at Samuel.

"*Bruder*, I have tried not to put my nose into your business," he stopped for a moment, but Samuel chose not to say anything. Instead, he waited for his *bruder* to go on. " . . . You know that."

Josiah stopped a moment and then took a deep breath. When he spoke again, it was with a sound of resignation; as if it were the last thing he ever wanted to say. But his words were not the ones Samuel expected from his *bruder*.

"Ella has been telling me that I need to speak with you." Another pause and a deep breath followed.

"I know it's been difficult for you, moving on. But you must think of your *kinner*. Leah especially, is going to need guidance. Ella would be more than *froh* to try and help out, but she is convinced that Leah does not want her help."

At that point, it was all Samuel could do to keep from laughing. Here his *bruder* had been losing sleep over the very thing he *nee* longer had to worry about. However, it would certainly not do for Samuel to laugh, so he struggled to keep himself under control.

Trying to distract himself from the incredible irony of the situation and the desperate need to let loose of the laughter he was working so hard to suppress, Samuel picked up a pitchfork and studied it thoughtfully as his *bruder* continued.

"She has *kumme* to bed late many nights and spent much time in prayer. We have talked over her worries." Josiah held up a hand as if Samuel was intent on arguing, but he had *nee* such desire and he happily waited for his *bruder* to continue.

"Ella is convinced that Leah is struggling. She is very concerned . . . about all of the *kinner*. So she pressed me to speak with you."

Josiah didn't say anything for several minutes, but he did let out what Samuel was certain to be a sigh of relief. He had done what his *frau* asked of him and now he could tell her he had spoken to Samuel about it. Samuel felt another smile tugging at his mouth as Josiah turned to continue to muck out the stall he was standing in.

Samuel moved to the stall next to Josiah. They worked in comfortable silence for a long time, while Samuel thought of the best way to tell his *bruder* the news—and relieve his mind about it all.

He was a bit surprised when Josiah stopped working

and spoke again.

"I know you want to do what is best for your family. And it is my duty to help you all that I am able. You have said before that there are not many women near your age in your own community. And you don't want to marry a young woman." He said the words with a voice so full of defeat, Samuel almost broke in, but his *bruder* just kept going, so Samuel let him speak.

"Perhaps you would be interested in meeting some of the women from our own community. Ella has many *gut freinden* who would be *froh* to meet you." There was just a hint of hope in his voice. He fell silent again and continued to work.

Samuel was glad when his *bruder* stopped that time. He had nearly let out a bark of laughter when Josiah suggested meeting the young women in his own district. The whole thing had gone far enough.

"That will not be necessary, Josiah." Samuel said the words with a bit more finality than he intended, because he was still fighting the urge to laugh at how *lecherich* it all was.

"Samuel, now . . . you are not being fair. You must at least consider it. There are some mighty fine women in our small district." Josiah's voice was full of consternation and it was increasingly difficult for Samuel to hold back his laughter.

"You misunderstand, *bruder*. It is not at all what you are thinking.

Samuel took a moment to think how he could tell his *bruder* what had happened to him, when Josiah started speaking again.

"Or you could travel to other communities near us. I am certain there is a *wunderbaar* woman in one of them for you. I know *Gotte's wille* for your life includes a *froh* marriage," and he stopped, realizing what he had said and how it must have sounded to his *bruder* . . . because he quickly added. "Another, I mean."

Samuel found himself laughing even as Josiah said the words. After only a moment, Josiah joined in with him. As they laughed, Samuel realized how wunderbaar he felt. It was *gut* to be putting things right with his *bruder*.

Still, he could not help but enjoy a bit more of Josiah's discomfort.

"*Jah, bruder*. I believe it is *Gotte's wille* for me to have a *froh* marriage. Of course, I have already had one so that must mean another marriage need not be the same. Perhaps I shall simply marry for convenience. In that case, I may consider one of the young women in my own community."

Josiah stopped laughing and looked at Samuel, who flashed his *bruder* a wide smile to show he was teasing.

"That is not what I meant—and you know it, Samuel." There was a familiar twinkle of mischief in Josiah's eyes that Samuel was all too *froh* to see again. They laughed together for several more minutes before the moment of levity passed.

Samuel leaned back against the wall of the stall where he had begun spreading fresh hay.

"*Danki, bruder*. You do not know how long it has been since I have enjoyed a *gut* laugh."

Josiah suddenly looked very serious.

"*Jah, bruder,* that is what has me worried. I am glad to hear you laughing again, but I worry that you will be needing much more than one *gut* laugh to get you back to your old self."

Josiah turned to go back to work, but Samuel stopped and was staring at his *bruder*. What would he think if Samuel told him he had met the woman he intended to marry? Would Josiah think Samuel was simply trying to put him off?

Or worse, would his *bruder*, who had been telling him for years that he needed to move on and find a new *frau*, think that Samuel was moving too fast? Would Josiah tell him that he needed to take more time? The very thought made Samuel smile.

Imagine that . . . my bruder actually telling me to slow down. Why, it is lecherich to think it.

He looked over at Josiah, hoping his *bruder* would be *froh* for him and finally be satisfied that Samuel was taking his advice seriously. Josiah had finished with the pitchfork and hung it on the wall.

"*Bruder,*" Samuel began, "I truly appreciate your concern. I want you to know that."

Josiah held up a hand, stopping Samuel.

"Samuel, now I know you think I am pushing you, but it has been ten years. Elisabeth would not want you to do this to yourself."

Samuel listened while his *bruder* talked. When Josiah said Elisabeth's name, he expected to feel the familiar pain that had come every time someone mentioned her name, but it did not *kumme*. There was *nee* pain at all, only a very mild tug. Clearly *Gotte* had healed him.

Danki, Gotte. You know I will always remember Elisabeth, but I thank you for helping me to heal, for taking this pain from me and putting Naomi in my path.

If he had not been certain before, he certainly was now. Naomi was clearly the woman for him and it was as though *Gotte* had given them his blessing.

Samuel could not help himself, he laughed and his laughter stopped Josiah—who let out a growl of frustration at his *bruder*.

"Well, I can see you are not going to take me seriously, Samuel. But I have said my piece." He turned to go and Samuel reached out to put a hand on his *bruder's* shoulder.

"Josiah, I am sorry. I assure you I was not laughing at you or your concerns." Samuel tried to turn his *bruder* toward him, but Josiah was standing his ground and would not turn.

"I should have begun with this, I see that now." Still Josiah stood his ground.

"I have already taken your advice, *bruder*." And finally Josiah turned to look at Samuel, so he went on quickly. "I took the buggy out last week, with the intention of visiting a neighboring community."

Josiah was nodding his head at Samuel's words, a look of hope on his concerned features.

"While on my way, I came across a buggy on the side of the road," he paused only a moment before continuing, " . . . and inside the buggy was a woman." Samuel could see that he truly had his *bruder's* attention now.

"It had broken down and the woman's cousin had gone in search of help. In fact, I must have just missed him." He watched Josiah's face. It was clear that Josiah wanted to interrupt him, possibly to ask a hundred different questions, but he was holding his peace . . . for the moment at least so Samuel continued.

"I know it will sound crazy, but I knew the moment I saw her that she is the woman *Gotte* intends for me to marry." As his own words began to settle in, he realized what lay ahead for him.

He had been certain she was the *frau* for him, but what if she did not agree? He did not get the opportunity to follow that reasoning though because Josiah's laughter distracted him.

Josiah leaned over with his hands on his knees, and laughed so hard, Samuel could see tears in his eye. He was sputtering words in between bouts of laughter and though they were difficult to understand, Samuel got the general idea. Josiah was amused that all it had taken to change Samuel's mind about getting married again was the right woman.

With a noise that was half laugh, half growl, Samuel tackled his *bruder*, knocking the straw hat from his head. Then he trapped Josiah in a headlock and rubbed a grimy hand over his *bruder's* head as Josiah sputtered in shock.

After a moment, Josiah turned and hooked his arms around Samuel's waist and tumbled the two of them into the pile of fresh hay.

They were both laughing as they rolled across the bed

of hay and then onto the hard dirt floor of the barn.

TEN

After supper had been eaten and the dishes washed, Leah sat at the long table in the dining room and looked out the window, watching the snow as it floated softly down to add to large drifts, and as it filled in her *dat*'s and *Onkel* Josiah's tracks to and from the barn.

She could still see two rows of footprints that were straight and steady, but there was another pair of tracks alongside them and they were much messier.

There was a spot where the prints were scrambled around and overlapping each other in an absolute mess. It looked as though *Dat* and *Onkel* Josiah had been behaving like much younger men and since they had both come inside covered with snow, it was not hard to guess what they'd been about in the yard.

Away from the mess of tracks though, the sight was peaceful and serene. Snowflakes were drifting softly down across the brightly lit *nacht* sky. The moon hung low and large in that sky, the soft light of it spilling gently over everything.

It was such a contrast to what was going on inside of Leah's heart and mind. Now that she had time to sit and think, she was worrying over Jacob. What would he think if he showed up at their *haus* and she was not there? Would he think she did not want to see him?

Ach, why did I not leave a note for him somewhere? Of course, she knew the answer to that question already.

He would never have found it . . . but someone else might have. If only I had thought to find out where the nearest phone shanty for him was, I could have left him a message.

She thought on that for a moment before realizing that would not have been a *gut* idea either. There was *nee* way to know who else would have heard the message . . . *or that he would have received it in time.*

She had eaten her supper and done her best to join in the boisterous conversation going on all around her at the long table, but talking about Jacob with her cousin had only made her more aware that she would not see him this evening and her heart was miles away . . . along with her thoughts.

So here she sat, looking out the windows that faced the road that was her only connection to Windy Gap at the moment. Jacob was most likely doing his evening chores and thinking ahead to the evening before him.

Leah found herself wiping away a tear that slipped down her cheek. It simply would not do for her to start crying. Emma would probably be along any minute to suggest they head up to bed and she would want to know why Leah was crying. It would not do to tell her young cousin that she was crying over not being able to see the young man they had been excitedly talking about only hours ago in the kitchen.

Only because she was so intent on getting her emotions under control, did Leah miss the sound of footsteps as her *aenti* came in to the room.

"It is beautiful, *jah*?" Ella moved quietly into the room behind Leah, but did not sit down.

Clearly she was waiting for Leah to speak. And Leah knew she should, but she wasn't sure what to say. She did not want *Aenti* Ella to realize that she was sitting here feeling sorry for herself.

Nor do I want to explain why.

She was certain that her voice would give away the fact that she had been sitting here crying.

However, it would be much more suspicious if I say nothing. She told herself so she spoke very quietly. "It is beautiful, *Aenti*."

Leah was glad to hear that her voice sounded normal, but her relief was short-lived. Something obviously had given her away because the next thing she knew, her *aenti*'s hand settled lightly on her shoulder and she said, "*Was iss letz*, Leah?"

Leah wanted to answer. She wanted to pour her heart out to her *aenti;* to tell her all of the things that she was worrying over and then to ask all of the questions that were crowding into her head this very minute . . . but the words caught at the back of her throat.

She tried to force them out, but they simply would not come.

"*Wie geht's* Leah, truly?" *Aenti* Ella asked—and Leah wanted to cry again, in frustration.

Ach, if only I knew what to say.

Aenti Ella's small hand squeezed Leah's shoulder gently, but Leah still could not get any words to *kumme* out. After what felt like a long time, but was mostly likely *nee* more than a moment, her *aenti* pulled her hand away.

"I'd best get myself to bed." Silence hung in the air a moment before she continued. "You should be on your way soon, as well. Morning *kummes* early."

Leah could hear her *aenti*'s footsteps stop and shuffle a bit—almost as though she was hesitating at the door. Leah held her breath, not even daring to sniffle, even though it was a struggle. After another moment, she heard *Aenti* Ella once more.

Her voice was very quiet and there was a sound of defeat in it. "*Gut nacht,* Leah."

Leah heard her *aenti*'s steps retreat slowly from the room and felt fresh tears spring to her eyes. She might be wrong, but it sounded much like her *aenti*'s footsteps were much less *eiferich* leaving than they had been when she came in.

Leah felt terrible for bringing down her *aenti*'s *wunderbaar* mood, but there was nothing she could do to change it now. Feeling even worse, she laid her head down on the table and let the hot tears *kumme.*

. . .

Morning did indeed arrive early. Samuel woke earlier than usual; there was so much weighing on him. He had to figure out how to talk to Naomi. He had to find the right way to introduce her to his *kinner,* and then there was the matter of speaking to the Bishop in her own community. They would need his cooperation to be married here. With so much ahead of him, Samuel knew only *Gotte* could show him the way, so he prayed for *Gotte's* wisdom and guidance.

Gotte may know the plans He had for Samuel and his family, but those plans were a mystery to the people they were meant for. So Samuel spent extra time praying for *Gotte's wille* to become clear to him.

He offered his worries up to *Gotte* and he prayed for His *wille* in all their lives. And then, feeling lighter than he had in such a long time, Samuel rose to help his *bruder* with the morning chores, with a song in his heart.

. . .

Josiah was already in the barn feeding the horses when Samuel walked in. He was talking softly to one of the new mares he had shown Samuel the day before, her ears twitching as he spoke, almost like she understood every word he was saying.

"*Gudemariye,* Josiah." A smile was twitching around

Samuel's lips as he approached the pair.

"*Gudemariye, Bruder.*" Josiah said without turning.

Josiah was slowly pulling a brush down through the mare's mane while talking to her. Samuel watched in silence for a long time, admiring the patience his *bruder* always showed—brushing the horse as he spoke softly to her.

Josiah had always been clever about such things. He knew how to handle even the most difficult horses. Samuel had always admired the skill his *bruder* shared with their *dat.* The two of them were especially gifted with animals.

As Josiah worked his way around the mare, Samuel walked over to the long rack where his *bruder* hung his tools and lifted down a pitchfork.

In their scuffling last *nacht,* they had neglected a couple of stalls. Samuel figured the least he could do was to finish up the job he had interrupted.

He went to the first stall and began mucking it out. For a long time, Samuel worked, while he listened to Josiah talk to the skittish mare.

Occasionally a soft whicker or a snort would break into Josiah's words, but he never lost patience with her. After a time, Josiah appeared in the stall next to Samuel and they continued their work without speaking.

There was something about plain work that helped to calm Samuel and he wondered if it was the same for his *bruder,* as well. It was nice to work together in silence, especially now that they were *nee* longer angry with each other.

The work brought memories to mind of their younger days. Growing up, Josiah had always been quicker to wake fully in the early morning hours and they had always had an unspoken agreement that Josiah would give Samuel plenty of time to wake up before expecting conversation.

However, this morning Samuel was wide awake and, even though he had woken up with worries on his heart, his prayers had lifted that burden from him. He was feeling better than he had in a very long time. Last *nacht*, he and Josiah had cleared up much of the hard feelings that had grown between them and it was a relief to be on *gut* speaking terms again.

He sneaked a glance at Josiah and saw that the tightness that had been there in his shoulders whenever Samuel had visited him the last few years was gone. He felt his own shoulders relax as he thought back to their talk from the *nacht* before.

Josiah truly does have my best interests in mind.

The thought made Samuel wonder how he had ever been angry with his *bruder*.

When Samuel had finished the stall he was in, he moved to the other side of the barn to finish the stall on that side—one they had missed last *nacht*. Since Josiah was in the last stall on the opposite side of the barn, Samuel didn't speak again until his *bruder* joined him on that side of the barn.

"Did you get a *gut nacht's* sleep, *bruder?*"

Josiah didn't answer right away, but his lips twitched.

"I do hope you told Ella that we spoke. I would not want to be responsible for another late *nacht*." The sudden cough that came from the stall next to him made Samuel wonder if Josiah had indeed enjoyed a late *nacht*, but for a very different reason.

One look at his *bruder* and he knew he was right. Samuel felt a smile tugging at the corners of his mouth as he thought about what Josiah and his lovely *frau* had been up to last *nacht*. A moment later however, his thoughts turned to his own *nachts*.

Dear Gotte, I do miss being married.

He realized that he was looking forward to being married again. He truly had waited long enough. Elisabeth would never have expected him to mourn her this long. It was time—and Naomi was the one. Now he just had to convince her of it.

ELEVEN

At the sound of a knock, Leah looked up from her position on the kitchen floor. She waited a few moments, hoping someone else had heard and would come to answer the door. After several long moments— and another gentle knock, she decided it was not likely, so she pushed herself up and walked to the door.

Her feet slipped a bit on the wet floor as she moved quickly out of the kitchen and through the hall, but she managed to keep moving and regain her footing.

She reached the front door just as her older *bruder* David came bounding down the stairs. He laughed when he saw her, but a look at the scowl that ruled Leah's features had him smothering his laughter. He carefully schooled his face into a more somber expression as Leah reached for the doorknob.

Leah struggled to conceal her frustration at the sight of Catherine on the threshold. The smile on her face, already near as bright as the sun, brightened at the sight of David—who was standing just behind Leah.

"*Wie geht's*, Catherine," Leah responded, trying to smother the irritation in her voice.

"*Wie geht's*, Leah . . . David." Although Catherine spoke to Leah, she only had eyes for David.

Looking at the two of them, Leah was certain she could feel the love flowing between them. It was so thick in the air all around her, she could almost feel it pressing in on her. She fought the tears that were straining to be freed.

She had not heard one thing from Jacob since they had returned from *Onkel* Josiah's *haus*. *Nee* notes. *Nee* messages. Not a word—and she was not sure what to think. Had all of her worst fears come to pass?

Had he arrived to find them not at home and determined that she was not interested in seeing him again? Or had he not bothered to even *kumme* by because he had had a change of heart... or had found another *maedel* to pursue?

Looking from David to Catherine, it was clear they were only interested in each other, so she moved away from the door and turned back toward the hall.

As she walked slowly back to the kitchen, there were many thoughts rushing around in her head. All three of her elder *schweschders* were happily wed now. David and Catherine were to be next, and she was certain Benjamin would soon follow.

Was everyone around her destined to be lined up two by two? Would she ever feel the sort of love she could see in the faces of her *schweschders* when they looked at their husbands? Or the love she had just seen and felt flowing between Catherine and David?

Or would she always be the one who was left behind, taking care of everything and everyone? She gave herself a little shake. She knew those kinds of thoughts were not a *gut* idea. If it was in *Gotte's* plan for her, she would do well to be *froh* with it. At least she would always have a home with her family.

She moved toward the kitchen, moving as silently as she could, while listening to the soft voices of David and Catherine. They were speaking of wedding plans. Confusion and feelings of sadness were nearly too much for Leah.

Catherine's voice was so full of hope and love. David's voice sounded so sure and strong, and their laughter was full of delight.

They will make such a wunderbaar couple.

Leah felt certain there would be news in *nee* time at all that their family would be expanding again. That made her think of *Dat*. Of all their *bruders*, David was the most like *Dat*. He would make such a *gut* papa. And Catherine would be a *wunderbaar gut mamm*—she had such a peace about her.

Leah was certain Catherine would be calm and sure of herself in everything. And Leah would have more new *bopplin* to hold and cuddle. It was one of her most favorite things in all the world.

With *nee* warning at all, she felt a desperate need to make a trip to town. She moved quickly, dashing tears from her eyes as she went. In the kitchen, she wrote a note for *Dat,* knowing that David would never notice she was gone, and then she rushed out to the barn to hitch up Matilda and the small buggy.

. . .

There was a new quilt in the window of *Sew Nice.* It held Leah's attention, while she parked the buggy and tied up Matilda. She was so distracted, she nearly bungled the knot.

As she fought with it, she was surprised to hear Zeke Hershberger's voice next to her.

"Do you need some help with that, Leah?"

Leah knew she blushed right to her *kapp* at his words.

Ach dear Lord, why is Zeke here now, when I am making a fool of myself?

She threw the words up to heaven like a silent prayer, but she knew *Gotte* had a reason for everything and she could never hope to understand what it might be. She turned the corners of her lips up and tried to laugh a little as she answered him, hoping it might cover the hitch of tears still in her breath.

"*Jah, Danki,* Zeke. I am all thumbs today, it seems."

He gently took the lead rope from her hand and tied a *gut* knot around the hitching post. When he stepped back, there was *nee* hint of amusement on his face, which was a relief. Zeke was a nice boy and he was not likely to make fun of anyone, least of all her.

"*Danki,* Zeke. Truly I do not know what is wrong with me today." She thought to say something more to him, but changed her mind, closing her mouth with a little "hmm".

"Leah Fisher, there is not one thing wrong with you, today or any other day." He was looking at her when he said it, and there was an *schpassich* expression on his face.

As Leah watched, a fine line appeared between his eyes. Silently she prayed he would not ask more about what was going on with her. After a moment, his forehead smoothed out and his lips thinned out into a tight line, but he didn't say anything else.

Whatever the reason, Leah was glad. She had grown up with Zeke and they had always been *freinden*, but she had *nee* idea of how to explain her feelings to him.

After a moment more, he touched his fingers to the brim of his hat and ducked his head slightly as he said, "*Gut* day to you then, Leah Fisher." And he was gone before Leah could say a word in return.

She watched his retreating back for several seconds, before shrugging her shoulders and turning toward the shops again.

Who could understand boys . . .?

Looking up at the names of the shops in front of her, Leah smiled and began to feel better. Next door to *Sew Nice* sat the bakery that Abigail Stutzman's *schweschder,* Ruth Yoder, had named *Sew Sweet*.

Leah remembered asking why and Ruth had laughed

and told her that anyone new who stopped at the Bakery would stand outside looking at the name for at least a minute or two before going in to ask about the spelling—and the *wunderbaar* smells would entice them into purchasing something.

With a smile, Leah turned to *Sew Nice* and pushed through the door.

. . .

The tinkle of tiny bells announced Leah's entrance to her favorite store in Windy Gap. She raised a hand in greeting to Abigail Stutzman, who was presiding over a group of quilters at the back of the shop, and in *nee* time at all, Ana Hershberger joined Leah as she was walking along the rows of fabrics.

"*Gudemariye,* Leah. What brings you in today?"

Ana's voice was full of such joy. It seemed to Leah that Ana was always full of joy. Given what Leah knew about her, it was a wonder. Immediately Leah felt guilt wash over her. Here she was feeling frustrated over David and Catherine and worrying over Jacob and her dear *freind* Ana was just as *froh* as she could be.

"I am sorry Ana. I just—" she tried to put a smile on her face. " . . . just had to get out for a bit."

But even as Leah spoke, Ana nodded her head. Some days it was almost as if she could read Leah's thoughts. "David and Catherine are planning their wedding, *jah?*"

Leah nodded in return, but kept her head ducked, trying to keep Ana from seeing the look on her face. Ana would know Leah was not telling her everything, and Leah truly did not want to explain.

In an attempt at distracting her, Leah added, "I am *froh* that my *bruder* has found such a *gut maedel*. She will be a *wunderbaar frau*." She stopped a moment before going on, " . . . and most days, I can handle it."

Ana lightly laid her hand on Leah's arm as she spoke. Leah immediately felt guilty again for even the small deception.

Ana was nodding her head again as she slipped her hand into Leah's and began pulling her toward the back of the store.

"*Kumme,* you must see the new quilt."

Leah felt a little *verhuddelt* as Ana pulled her along She was certain the quilt in their window must be new, but Ana was headed to the back of the store. She pulled Leah with her as she moved between rows of fabric and past Abigail's class through the door marked Employees Only *Please.*

Leah laughed when she noticed the word "please" was written on a piece of paper and taped to the bottom of the sign. It was just like a plain shopkeeper to add the word to a store-bought sign.

Finally, Ana stopped pulling her hand. Leah noticed they were standing in front of a very large quilt frame, but the work that was stretched out on the frame was far from complete. She turned to Ana, ready to ask what quilt she meant, but Ana spoke before Leah could even open her mouth.

"*Gut.* Now that we are away from all those

busybodies, you can tell me what is going on with you, Leah Fisher."

Leah struggled not to laugh at the sight before her. She was not a large woman—she might even have some growing to do yet—but she had accepted that she might never grow much taller. In the meantime, she had resigned herself to being short, but Ana was several inches shorter than Leah and had a much more delicate build.

It was a struggle, to be sure, for Leah to control the laughter that was bubbling up in her chest at the sight of Ana standing before her, hands on her hips, with an expectant look on her tiny features.

It was nearly a minute, before Leah felt confident she would be able to speak without laughing.

"Nothing special is going on with me, Ana. Truly, I simply needed to get away from home for a bit." She quickly added, "and I need to purchase a spool of thread for the quilt I am piecing. I ran out this morning."

Leah was not surprised to see that Ana clearly was not fooled, but she didn't push for a more truthful answer. They stood there a few more seconds, before Ana let out a little huff and turned back to the door.

"Very well. I suppose I cannot make you tell me." She hadn't taken two steps, before she whirled back to face Leah. "Just you be sure you know that I am here for you, if ever you feel the need to speak up."

Leah did not trust her voice in that moment, so she simply nodded. She was truly blessed to have such a *gut freind.*

Ana shook her head a little, turned back around and pushed through the door.

Leah spent half an hour in the store. Every few minutes she would look at Ana and her *freind* would just shake her head. Leah purchased the thread she had planned to buy and had a *gut* conversation with several of the ladies from Abigail's class, while she moved through the rows of fabrics, looking aimlessly.

When the last of the women had left and Abigail busied herself with little things in the store, Leah knew she could not find any other excuses to stay here. She would have to go next door and hang about until Ruth found an excuse to send her away. She pushed open the door, sending Ana a last wave.

She had *nee* more than stepped a foot out the door when someone collided with her. A very hard, heavy body slammed into her from behind, and then she felt herself falling to the ground.

But before she hit the sidewalk, a strong arm snaked around her waist and pulled. Suddenly she was on her feet and pressed up against what felt to be a wall.

It was several seconds before the strong arm let go of her and the person stepped away. She looked up into beautiful, green eyes that seemed very familiar.

"My apologies." A smile was tugging at the corner of Jacob's mouth as he spoke, but Leah could see he was truly concerned about her. "I should have been looking where I was going."

They stood there for several seconds, just staring at each other, before Leah recovered her voice.

"*Nee* harm done." She could not stop the smile that spread across her own features, nor would she have wanted to.

"Leah, are you . . ." Ana's voice distracted Leah from staring up at Jacob. "Ah, I see that you are fine." Ana smiled at the two of them before turning back to the door she had just come through.

Before going inside, she whirled back to them and wagged a finger at Jacob. "Mind you watch your step, young man." And then she was walking back into the store, leaving them both to wonder just exactly what she had meant.

Jacob looked down as color flooded his cheeks. Leah struggled to smother the giggle that leaped to her lips at his discomfort. After a moment, he scuffed his shoe against the ground before looking back up.

"So, I came by your *haus* the other evening."

Leah's hand flew up to cover the gasp that escaped. "*Jah*, I was worried about that." Before he could misunderstand her reaction, she went on. "*Dat* announced rather suddenly that we would be going to visit his *bruder*. We left that very afternoon and we spent the *nacht* there."

A moment later she added, "I did not know how to reach you . . . and I thought about leaving a note, but..."

"But if you had left a note, someone else may well have found it; for sure and for certain I would not have . . . in the dark." He said, with a smile.

They both laughed and Leah felt some of her nerves disappear. She tried to think of something else to say, but nothing came to mind.

"Do you have to get right home?" He asked, his voice sounding almost timid.

"*Nee.*" Her words sounded very small and quiet to her, but he seemed to hear her. When she looked up at him, his smile could have melted the snow that covered the ground all around them.

"How would you feel about some hot cocoa? Or *kaffe*?"

"Hot cocoa sounds *wunderbaar gut.*" She turned toward *Sew Sweet* and waved a hand absently toward the sign. "Have you tried theirs?"

"*Nee*, I've not been there before. Is it *gut*?"

"It is. I make it a point to go in every time I am in town."

"Very well. I trust you know best then . . . shall we?" He moved to the door and opened it for her, stepping into the busy cafe behind her.

She heard a tiny sigh behind her and turned to smile at him. It was *gut* to know he enjoyed the *appeditlich* smells as much as she did.

"What is that *wunderbaar* smell?" He asked, his voice full of wonder.

"Ah, that would be Ruth's hot cocoa." Leah replied. When he looked at her with wide eyes, she added. "The recipe is top secret. She won't tell a soul; I do not believe even her own *schweschder* knows it." She said, with a little giggle.

He looked at her a moment, before he realized she was teasing him.

"You are having a joke at my expense, aren't you?"

"*Jah*, I am. I simply could not help myself. You looked as if you were taking it all so seriously." She worked to smother her giggles. It would not be *gut* for her to laugh at him.

"It is really Ruth's little joke. She tries it on people at times, just to see who will fall for it." And before she could say anything else, Ruth stepped in front of them.

"Leah, it is *gut* to see you. And you've brought a *freind*." Leah could see the interest in Ruth's eyes, but she was uncertain what to say, so she did her best to distract Ruth.

"*Jah*, Ruth. We are going to find a table. We would like two mugs of your . . ." she sent a little wink at Ruth as she said it, " . . . super-secret hot cocoa."

Ach, I hope that distracts her enough . . .

Ruth did not even hesitate; she answered exactly as Leah had hoped, with a knowing smile and a slight wink when Jacob happened to look over at Leah. Then she was off to get their hot cocoa.

Leah breathed a sigh of relief. She turned to see Jacob motion for her to walk ahead of him. They wound their way through the busy cafe and found a small table for two near the back wall.

"Is it always so busy here?" Jacob asked, leaning toward Leah to be heard.

"Not always quite this busy, but *jah,* it is usually busy. The hot cocoa is not the only thing that is so *gut*. You should try the pecan pie. Ruth makes it fresh every day." Leah sighed, just thinking of how *wunderbaar* the pie tasted.

"It sounds *gut* and I would love to try it, but it would not be a very *gut* idea, because I am allergic to nuts."

"*Ach,* I am sorry. I should not have mentioned it." Leah felt so very *gegisch* now. "Is it *allrecht* for you to be near them, or could you have an allergic reaction just being here?"

"*Nee,* Leah, please do not worry. As long as I do not eat anything with nuts in it, I will be *gut.*" He laid his hand over hers on the table as he was speaking and Leah was immediately distracted by the strange feelings at the light contact.

She didn't even look up when Ruth stopped next to their table with two large mugs of hot cocoa. Only when Jacob moved his hand away, did she look up and realize Ruth was standing there. And her smile was more than a little mischievous. Leah was surprised to see such a look on the older woman's face.

Why, it makes her look like a young maedel, Leah could not help thinking.

Then she looked across the table at Jacob and realized that his smile was very much like Ruth's, and she could not help herself—she laughed.

.   .   .

Samuel did his best to remove his boots without dropping dirt and mud all over the little room just off the kitchen. Elisabeth had called it their mudroom, but it had been one of her own little private jokes. That was a word the *Englischers* used. She would always laugh and say it was only called that because it was meant to keep the mud from the rest of the *haus*.

He had always enjoyed the joke. and in the years since, *nee* one had suggested they call the room anything else, for which Samuel was grateful. Their *freinden* and neighbors might think it a bit odd that they used an *Englisch* phrase, but they most likely remembered the word was used to honor Elisabeth.

Even the Bishop had never told Samuel he must call the room anything else, so it would always be the mudroom to the Fisher family.

His thoughts were interrupted by the sound of boots on the porch just beyond him. He had a moment to wonder who would come to the mudroom door, before it opened and Leah walked in, brushing snow from her skirt as she did.

When she looked up, she jumped in fright. Clearly she had not expected to see him close by. When she spoke, she said as much.

"*Dat*, I did not know you would be coming in so late from chores. Supper will be ready soon." She made to scoot past him, but he put out a hand to stop her.

"Leah, where have you been? Did you tell anyone where you were going?" He was concerned about the look of guilt that spread over her delicate features. What had his *dochder* been up to?

"I went into town." Leah answered, but she would not look up at him and he was having a great deal of difficulty understanding her muffled words. "I needed thread for the quilt I have been working on."

Still she looked down. Samuel was having a hard time understanding what there was about her words that could inspire such worry in her.

"*Dochder*, did something happen while you were in town? Did someone bother you or hurt you?"

She shook her head vigorously at that, which convinced Samuel that there was another reason for her hesitance. He put a finger under her chin and lifted her face so that he could see her eyes.

"Leah, I do not understand. If *nee* one bothered you while you were in town, what has happened to make you so fearful?"

She answered him, but her voice was so quiet, he could not understand them and when he dropped his finger, she lowered her head again.

He considered demanding an answer from her, but he was certain he would not get a proper answer until she was ready to give it. She was clearly not hurt in any way, so he decided to let it go until he could figure out how to convince her to confide in him.

TWELVE

Leah tried not to rush as she moved past *Dat* and headed for the kitchen. She did not even bother to put away her purchases. She had much to do before the evening meal would be complete and she must get to it before *Dat* could pin her with any more questions about her activities this afternoon.

As she worked, she thought about her afternoon with Jacob. He was such *gut* company, the time had flown by and when she had walked by Sew *Nice* and seen that it was closed, she had panicked a bit.

She had been gone much longer than she intended. Someone would have noticed her absence for sure and for certain. She had reluctantly said her goodbyes to Jacob and he had helped her into the buggy—and waited there as she moved out onto the street.

She could remember well the feelings that had rushed through her at the sight of him as he watched her move away from him. He had raised his hand in farewell and she had looked back at him as often as possible as she maneuvered the buggy along the streets.

It gave her a warm feeling to think that Jacob had *kumme* into town today simply on the chance of seeing her; hoping that she would also have some reason to *kumme* into town as well.

. . .

A knock sounded at the front door, just as Leah was pulling a batch of pumpkin bread from the oven. Her first thought was that it was late for visitors. Who would be away from home after suppertime had *kumme* and gone?

It must be someone in need of help. She quickly set down the stone loaf pan she held and reached into the oven for the other one. Just as she set the second pan on the stove top, she heard the front door open and *Dat*'s voice as he spoke to someone.

A minute or so later, she heard *Dat* calling to her from the *sitzschtupp*. She looked down at her apron. Noticing that it was covered in flour, she dusted it off as best she could, before closing the oven door and leaving the kitchen.

When she turned into the hall, she was shocked to see Zeke Hershberger sitting on their sofa. He shot to his feet as soon as his eyes met hers. She watched him as he stood there, twisting his felt hat in his fingers—like a small boy who had been caught with his hand in the cookie jar.

"Leah, you did not tell me there was a gathering tonight. You were planning to go, *jah?" Dat* asked, but did not wait for her to answer. He nodded at her and then looked back at Zeke with a smile before looking back again to Leah.

"Zeke has come to drive you there. Is *gut, jah*? Now you will not have to worry with hitching up Matilda."

Leah could hear the excitement in her *dat's* voice and she felt as if she were torn in two. How could she destroy the hope she could hear in *Dat's* voice?

But what about Jacob? I cannot tell Dat or Zeke about Jacob now. I must wait until I am certain there is something to tell. Thoughts went back and forth in her head, as she argued both sides of the conversation with herself.

If I do not go, it might break his heart.

If I do go, will Zeke get the wrong idea? Will I be able to explain it to him in a way that keeps our secret, while not hurting his feelings as well?

What if I do hurt his feelings? I will have destroyed a life-long friendship over a young man I have only spent time with twice . . .

And if I do go, Dat will begin to think perhaps that I am courting Zeke Hershberger. That thought stopped her internal debate. If *Dat* were to think she was courting Zeke, he might be less curious about the things she was doing when she disappeared for periods of time. He would certainly ask fewer questions.

I cannot lie to Dat. However, it would not truly be a lie. It would simply be allowing Dat to decide what he wishes to believe anyway.

The sound of someone clearing their throat pulled her from her debate. She would go; and she would think on the situation later. There was plenty of time to decide how she would make things *kumme* out right.

"That is sweet of you Zeke. I'm afraid I am not ready yet." She raised her hands and put a little half smile on her face, almost hoping he would be in a hurry and decide to go on without her. But before the last words left her mouth, he was nodding his head.

"It would be my pleasure to wait for you." He looked up at *Dat* with a look of question. "If it is *allrecht* with your *dat?*" he left the question hanging in the air.

Dat scratched his bearded chin with a look of deliberate consideration on his face and after several heavy seconds, he finally nodded his head.

"That would be *gut, jah?*" He settled himself into the chair across from the sofa and turned his head toward Leah. "You best get ready, *dochder.*"

Leah looked once at *Dat,* then turned to look at Zeke and shook her head at their identical grins before turning on her heel to go upstairs and change her clothes.

She turned the corner at the top of the stairs before she realized she'd been muttering under her breath all the way up.

She crept back to the top of the stairs and looked over the rail, with her ear turned toward the *sitzschtupp*— straining to hear what was being said. *Dat* and Zeke were speaking of the weather and *Dat* was saying he hoped to have more rain, instead of snow, in the coming weeks.

She breathed a sigh of relief and turned back toward her room. She caught sight of herself in the small mirror that hung in their hallway and had to stifle a gasp. Her face was liberally coated with flour and what looked like bits of pumpkin—and her prayer *kapp* had come loose from nearly all of its pins.

Ach, I cannot show up to the singing looking like this. Ada will have a fit.

Going quickly to the small upstairs bathroom, Leah turned on the tap and waited for the water to heat. She had a moment to think of how thankful she was that theirs was not a primitive district like Cousin Ella's.

Many a time Leah had shuddered over Ella's stories of slipping on ice as she made her way to their small outbuilding late at *nacht* or even first thing in the morning.

Even *Onkel* Josiah's district was more primitive. They allowed the indoor plumbing, but were not allowed to heat water with a gas heater like the members of Leah's district. It might be nice in the heat of summer, but Leah could not imagine using icy water during the long winter months.

Finally her fingers felt warm water running over them and she used one of the clean cloths stacked beside the sink to scrub the flour and whatever else there was off her face, before she attacked the apron that had been white earlier today.

It only took a minute to see that it was a lost cause.

She would have to change it.

She rushed to her room, thinking it was fortunate the apron had protected her dress. She whipped it into place and hurried back to the bathroom to straighten her *kapp*, hoping Zeke would not notice the new apron and think it was for his benefit.

When her hair had been tamed back into the *kapp,* she took several deep breaths and headed toward the stairs.

.   .   .

Leah had scarcely stepped a foot into the Beiler's barn before her *gut freind* Ada Stoltzfus rushed up to her, gave Zeke an odd look and pulled Leah away with a giggle. Her eyes were full of questions and Leah sighed quietly to herself. Ada would surely talk her ear clean off before the *nacht* was out.

"Did you come here with Zeke Hershberger? Are you two courting? How long have you been together? Why didn't you tell me?"

The last was said with great indignation and Leah felt the urge to defend herself, but she smothered it. She had *nee* reason to defend herself. She certainly had not asked Zeke to show up at her *haus* and offer to bring her here tonight.

"*Jah*, I came here with Zeke. *Nee*, we are not courting. He showed up at my *haus* this evening and invited me to come tonight. *Dat* looked so *froh*, I could not tell him *nee*. I had not even planned to *kumme* tonight—you know that. There is nothing else to tell."

She was very careful with her words. She did not wish to tell her best *freind* anything that was not true, but she had not decided if, or when, she was going to tell Ada about Jacob.

Leah felt guilt descend over her as she saw the *froh* expression on Ada's face crumble and disappear. She should not have been so sharp with her dear *freind*. Ada could not help her nature. It was common knowledge that Ada and her *mamm* were the most curious women in the district.

"I am sorry to be so touchy, Ada. It has been a long day and I am exhausted, but it is *nee* excuse to treat you poorly."

Leah could see that she was already forgiven. Ada might be quick to get her feelings hurt, but she was also very quick to forgive. In Leah's estimation, that was one of Ada's best qualities. There were even times Leah did not feel she deserved such a *gut freind*. With that in mind, she worked to put a smile on her face as she tucked her arm through Ada's again.

"Let us go see what fun we can get into." And she pulled Ada further into the barn, toward the group of young people, comforted—more than she could have expected—by the smile that lit Ada's face.

. . .

Leah sat beside Ada in the Beiler's barn, listening to the singing all around her. It looked as if every young person from their community had shown up tonight and perhaps quite a few from their neighboring communities had as well. After a moment, she realized that she was looking around the barn with a certain young man in mind.

And how would he know about our gathering? She asked herself. *He wouldn't.*

It was not as if she had neglected to mention it on purpose. She had not had any intention of coming this evening so it had never occurred to her to mention it to him while they walked about town earlier.

Ada interrupted her thoughts by whispering furiously into her ear; and her voice was full of excitement. Her voice always got higher and a little squeaky when she was *eiferich*.

"The Hershberger boys brought their sleigh. Are you going to take a turn?" Leah found herself wondering if the excitement she heard in Ada's voice was a sign of interest in someone. Was it possible Ada was interested in one of the Hershberger boys?

Miriam's *gut freind* Clara had married Timothy Hershberger just a month ago. His *bruder* Thomas had recently had his twentieth birthday. Since Ada was only sixteen, Leah didn't think she could be interested in him, but perhaps in Tobias or even Zeke.

Zeke was Leah's age, but Tobias was a year younger than her, so he was probably the perfect age for Ada. Leah was surprised to realize that she felt a little disappointed. She couldn't help thinking it would have worked out so well if Ada had been interested in Zeke.

Ada nudged Leah a bit harder this time.

"Well, are you going to *kumme* for a ride or not? If we do not go soon, we may not get a turn." Leah watched her *freind* as she spoke. Ada was clearly *eiferich* about something or someone. Leah thought she had better go along to see what or who it was, so she nodded and rose from the bench to follow Ada outside.

Many of the young people had already ridden in the sleigh and they were drifting back inside the barn to warm up by the wood stove or begin new songs. The younger Muller *bruders* were busy throwing snowballs at their *schweschders* and several of Ada's *schweschders* as well.

While she and Ada waited for their turn, they laughed about Ada's little *schweschder*, Elsa. She might be only six, but she had a frightfully direct aim. Leah watched her fling the snowballs with a surprising strength and knew that she must already be helping her *dat* in their dairy, to have such strength.

Ada laughed when one of Elsa's snowballs hit her *bruder* Caleb in the back rather unexpectedly. He had not even been involved in the snowball fight, but it had not stopped Elsa from aiming at him.

He was laughing as he ran off to join the Muller *bruders'* side. Leah couldn't help thinking that they were still going to get creamed. Boys always thought being bigger gave them an advantage, but they always seemed to underestimate the *maedels*.

Leah was glad the Stoltzfus family was not so fussy about keeping Ada's *bruders* and *schweschders* from the fun of the evening. Leah knew all too soon, their *mamm* would *kumme* calling for them to find their beds, but until the singing actually began, they could join in on the fun.

When the sleigh came into view, Leah felt a strange fluttering in her stomach. She wasn't sure why; perhaps it was the excitement of riding in a sleigh for the first time in a long while. The fluttering persisted as she stepped into the sleigh and sat in the back next to Ada.

As the sleigh moved forward, she was distracted before she could think too much about it. The sleigh seemed to be moving very fast and the snowy landscape around them seemed to fly by.

The wind was making the strings of her prayer *kapp* flutter and whip around and it made her eyes water a bit, but she was enjoying herself too much to be bothered by any of that. The wind was exhilarating as it flew by her. She was quickly becoming fond of the movements of the sleigh under them. It was so smooth a ride, it was like none she had ever experienced before. She found herself wanting the ride to go on all *nacht* long.

Beside her, Ada whooped with joy and Leah joined in. Thomas Hershberger was at the reigns of the sleigh and his *bruder* Zeke sat beside him.

Their laughter carried on the wind and echoed off the trees around them. Leah was glad Ada's family had such a large piece of land for them to use. It was *wunderbaar* not to have to worry that they would bother their neighbors as they flew by in the sleigh.

Much too soon for Leah, the sleigh came to rest slowly beside the barn and it was time for someone else to have a turn. She and Ada climbed out and Leah discovered that she felt a little funny when her feet touched the ground, almost as if she were still moving with the sleigh. She and Ada clung to each other, laughing as they made their way back into the warm barn. They dropped onto the first bench they reached, still laughing. Leah looked over at Ada.

"Ada, *danki* so much for asking me to join you on the sleigh ride. It was *wunderbaar*! It has been years since I have been in one and I did not remember sleigh rides were so much fun." She watched Ada's face light up and wondered if she had misjudged Ada's intentions. Maybe she had only wanted to go on the sleigh ride.

"I'm so glad you came! It was such fun. We should wait until everyone has had a turn and see if we can go again." Her face was glowing as she said it. Maybe she really was only *eiferich* about the sleigh ride. Leah knew that she would indeed enjoy another ride.

"*Jah,* that is a *wunderbaar gut* idea. Until everyone has had their turn, we could go find something to eat." She pulled Ada with her as she headed to the large table that held several trays filled with sandwiches and cookies.

There was a large cooler for water at one end of the table and a cluster of mismatched mugs. Someone had brought a small wood stove and there were several large pots full of hot cocoa and a large *kaffe* pot on top of it.

They each took a sandwich and a cookie, but they didn't take a plate. They both knew what a task washing up after so many young people was and they wanted to help out in any way they could. They did both take a mug of hot cocoa. Leah sighed as she took a tiny sip. Mary

Stoltzfus made the best hot cocoa in Windy Gap.

Perhaps only in Windy Gap, though.

The thought came to Leah and she felt heat climb her cheeks as thoughts of Jacob rushed into her head. Twice now they had spent time together over hot cocoa. She wanted to giggle, but knew her nosy *freind* would want to know why.

Leah followed Ada as they made their way over to the group of young people standing by the large wood stove. Almost everyone had a mug of hot cocoa. Leah sipped hers slowly. It was almost too hot to drink, but it tasted so *gut*, she could not wait for it to cool. She noticed several others doing the same. She chuckled a little to herself; she was glad not to be the only one.

Ada did not take a sip and Leah didn't expect her to; she had always possessed patience that Leah did not have. Even when they had been young *kinner*, Leah could remember Ada's patience being limitless.

Leah had asked Ada many times as they grew up how she had such patience, but Ada truly did not think her patience was anything unusual. However she almost always turned it around on Leah, pointing out that Leah had a nearly uncanny perception for things that needed to be done. She was almost always a step ahead of everyone else with sewing projects and cleaning. Like Ada though, Leah did not see that as anything exceptional; it was just a part of who she was.

Leah looked over at Ada as they stood with the other young people. They had known each other their whole lives and Ada had never been anything but nice to her.

Leah found herself wondering why she had not come to Ada to share the thoughts and feelings that she had been worrying over all this time. She should have been comfortable enough with her *freind* to talk to her about her worries.

Perhaps it was something she could only share with a mother. She had *nee* difficulty sharing other thoughts and dreams and worries with Ada. They had shared those things as long as they had known each other.

Leah realized something else just then. Ada had not shared any of those sorts of thoughts with her, either. She had *nee* idea if there was a particular young man Ada was especially fond of or if she worried over her feelings when the certain young man was nearby. Ada had never said a word to Leah about anything of the sort.

Maybe she had not shared her own thoughts about young men because Leah had not shared with her. Or maybe she was simply worrying over the same things Leah was and unsure of what to think of her worries or how to talk to her own *mamm* about them.

This made Leah wonder if she should say something to Ada—or wait until Ada brought it up with her?

She stood next to Ada, sipping her hot cocoa, enjoying the *wunderbaar* cookies and the warm fire in front of them. She wished it were just a bit warmer, so they could have a bonfire, but she knew the snow that was falling outside would make it difficult to keep a bonfire going.

Just as Leah took the last drink of her cocoa, the boys next to her launched a new round of songs, this time some Christmas carols. It was the one time of year they actually sang a few *Englisch* songs and Leah always found herself wondering about some of the words in the songs.

Did the *Englisch* truly know what they were singing about or did they only do it out of habit? Could they truly appreciate the words about Jesus' birth and the message that the heavenly host had brought to the world that *nacht* or did they think of them just as pretty songs?

There was not much about the *Englisch* world that Leah had ever truly wanted a part in, but the church expected all of the young people to expose themselves to enough of the *Englisch* world that they were able to make a decision to join the church due to their own feelings and their faith and not because they knew nothing else.

Truth be told, she had never looked forward to her *rumschpringe*. Thinking of it, she was glad her running around time was over now. She had wasted *nee* time in letting the bishop know she wished to join the church, only spending enough time in *rumschpringe* to prove to herself that the *Englischer's* world held *nee* interest for her.

Ada gave Leah a mischievous grin just then, pulling her from her deep thoughts. A moment later, Leah nearly spilled her hot cocoa when she heard Zeke Hershberger's deep voice behind her.

"Having fun, Leah?"

She took a deep breath before turning to face him. By the time she had turned, Ada had moved to stand beside her; and she was ever so grateful. Then she felt her curiosity stir again when she saw that Tobias was standing next to his *bruder*.

So that's what Ada's grin was about. She does have an interest in Tobias.

Leah's soft heart compelled her to do whatever must be done to give her *freind* time with Tobias, even if it meant spending more time with Zeke.

THIRTEEN

Leah sat up and looked around the dark room, trying to determine what had woken her. Her eyes traveled to the closed door and back around to the small table beside her bed, but nothing appeared to be amiss.

She started to lie back down when she heard a strange noise. Reluctantly, she flipped back the quilt and climbed out of bed, gasping when her feet met the cold floor. Just as her searching toes found her second slipper, she heard the noise again. It was a strange clatter against her window.

She moved over to the window to see what was causing it and was surprised to see Jacob standing on the frozen ground below. His arm was raised over his head and a second later she heard the clatter again and realized he was throwing small rocks at her window.

He must have seen her because the grin on his face nearly matched the one he had worn earlier in town and she felt a little thrill when she realized why he was here. Waving to him, she held up both hands and mouthed *"ten minutes . . ."*

He nodded and smiled even wider—if that were possible—and she dashed off to slip back into her dress; a wide smile on her own face. She did not even stop for a *kapp*.

Having my hair down around my neck would certainly be warmer.

Her fingers fumbled with the pins in her hurry and she forced herself to stop and try to calm herself. It would certainly not be *gut* to stick herself with a pin. It was a surprise indeed when she realized how much faster she was moving once she calmed her rushing.

In less than ten minutes, she was creeping down the stairs, careful to avoid the creaky step. She slid a bit in her stockings on her way to the mudroom and had to stifle the giggles that burst out, but managed to keep herself from falling.

When she pushed open the back door, she was breathing so heavily, she didn't even notice whether or not the door was noisy.

Then she was outside and creeping as quietly as possible across the back porch. Jacob met her at the back steps and lifted her down so that she didn't even have to avoid the ones that made noise.

They were walking toward the driveway when Jacob

took her hand and a *wunderbaar* little shiver went through her. They moved quickly to Jacob's buggy and he helped her inside; then tucked a warm blanket around her.

She felt warm without the blanket, but knew the wind would put an end to that soon so she snuggled under its warmth and waited for Jacob to walk around and step up into the buggy himself.

He had parked a bit closer to the *haus* this time. Once he was seated, he sent the team down the remaining drive slowly. It was all she could do not to urge him to go faster. She knew they did not want to wake anyone, but she was impatient to be on their way.

Still, even when they were out on the main road, she was hesitant to speak first, so they rode along in silence for several minutes. For the first minute, Leah felt a little uncomfortable, but when she stopped to think about it, she realized she felt more comfortable than expected. It was nice to ride along like this, under a sky full of stars, with Jacob beside her on the bench, and a warm blanket tucked around her. It was a *gut* thing and she was glad to be here.

"So you never told me, did you have a *gut* visit with your *onkel* and his family?"

Leah was more than a little surprised by his question. It was true they had spoken a little about her visit when they had spent time in town, but she hadn't really told him much about the visit.

"*Jah,* we had a *wunderbaar gut* visit." She stopped for a moment, unsure of just how much to tell Jacob. Should she share the whole story or just tell him a little—and did he really want to know or was he just trying to get her to talk to him?

"Do you visit often?" He asked after a moment.

"*Nee.*" She stopped again, still unsure . . . and then the words began pouring out of her. "We have not seen them in years. After *Mamm* died, *Onkel* Josiah and *Dat* fought about when he should remarry. *Onkel* Josiah gave it several years before he said anything, but he thought *Dat* should marry again soon after *Mamm* was gone and *Dat* was not ready."

"They argued something terrible over it and we have not been back to visit since. I do not know what made *Dat* want to visit now, but it does seem that they have put aside their differences. I am real glad. I have missed my cousins so much over the years and I hope we visit again soon."

"It was *gut* to see everyone. There have been two new *bopplin* born since we saw the family and they have already grown so much, I can hardly believe it. Can you believe how fast *bopplin* grow?" She stopped talking suddenly and put a hand over her mouth; then looked over at Jacob to gauge his reaction. Had she said too much?

"They do grow fast. My little *bruder* is seven now and it is a wonder how fast he has grown. Truthfully, he is not so little anymore." He sounded almost sad when he said it and Leah reached over to gently squeeze his hand with her own.

He looked over at her and the intense look in his eyes

was difficult for Leah to figure out. She could feel the breath hitching in her throat at the intensity of it.

The loud blast of a horn pulled Jacob's eyes away from hers and he turned the team onto the side of the road quickly as the large truck bore down on them.

Leah looked behind them at the truck that was quickly approaching. The driver had plenty of room to go around them, why was he blowing his horn at them?

The buggy bounced as the wheels hit something and Leah found herself grabbing onto Jacob. She did not want to be bounced out of the buggy.

Jacob slowed the team more as the buggy moved onto the side of the road. The truck flew past with a sudden burst of speed; the driver blew the horn long and loud as he went by.

It was several minutes before Leah felt calm enough to disentangle her fingers from the sleeve of Jacob's coat. As she did, she realized that she was breathing in short, loud gasps and she could feel hot tears on her cheeks.

When Jacob had settled the horses, he turned to her. He looked into her eyes with such caring, she felt a bit of warmth come back into her.

"Are you *allrecht*?" He stopped and shook his head; and the next words were nearly under his breath. "Stupid question . . . of course you are not. That was horrible."

He looked at her again and she tried to think of something to say. She would have to say something or he would most likely turn around and take her right back home. She finally managed to open her mouth to speak, but what came out was not at all what she had intended.

"Is that what happened to you before?" It came out in a squeak, which made her want to jump down from the buggy and go hide somewhere far away. She did not get the chance because he took both of her hands in his as he nodded his head to answer her.

"*Jah,* it was the same kind of thing. I do not think it was the same truck though. Some *Englischers* seem to have *nee* patience at all."

Leah was surprised to hear how calm his voice was. He did not sound angry, only concerned and there was *nee* judgment in his words either, just a simple statement. She did not think she would have been so calm about being run off the road and having a wheel break.

And with that thought, she could feel panic wash over her. What if they had broken a wheel? How far were they from her *haus* now? Would they have to walk back in the dark? How would she explain everything to *Dat?*

"Leah," Jacob was saying; and she got the impression from the tone of his voice that perhaps he had said it more than once.

"*Jah?*" It was all she could seem to get out.

"Will you be *allrecht* if I get down and check the buggy and the horses?" And there was such care in his question; it nearly brought tears to her eyes again.

She couldn't seem to do more than nod to him, but he stayed right where he was until she nodded again and said "Jacob, I will be OK. I promise."

After another moment, he turned and jumped to the ground, walking first to the front of the buggy to check on the horses. They must have been fine because it was not very long at all before he moved back to the buggy, walking slowly around it and paying special attention to each wheel.

She watched him as he moved around the buggy; admiring the care he took in checking each part carefully for anything that could pose a problem when they were moving again.

After several minutes, he moved over to her side of the buggy, smiling up at her. She was glad to see him smile; for sure and for certain he would not be smiling if he had found a problem somewhere with the buggy.

He moved back to the front of the buggy. She knew he must be giving the horses a bit of attention. He was *schmaert* to do so. Even if the horses were not injured or frightened, they would be reassured by his attention.

It was only a minute more before he stepped back up into the buggy and settled himself beside her. He sat there for what felt like a long time. When she looked over at him, there was a twist to his features, like he had something to say, but was trying to figure out the best way to say it.

Leah waited without saying anything, hoping he had not found a problem somewhere after all, and was about to let her know that they would have to walk home in the cold and the dark.

He let out a deep sigh before finally saying "Leah, I think I should take you back home."

She looked back at him, trying to decipher his expression. Was he angry with her? Did he blame her for this? Would she ever see him again?

The sudden pressure of tears nearly choked her as she struggled to hold them back. She would not make this worse by crying. If there was any part of him that might still be interested in seeing her, crying hysterically would certainly do away with it.

She was so busy struggling to hold in the emotions that were determined to burst forth; she nearly missed the words he said next.

"As much as I would enjoy spending more time with you, I don't know that it's safe." He looked over at her and she bit her lip to keep herself from saying anything. She could hardly believe her ears.

He wants to spend more time with me, but he doesn't think it will be safe . . . truly?

"I have checked over the buggy as well as I am able, but it is very dark; if I have missed something . . ." he threw his hands up in a gesture of uncertainty before going on. "I would never forgive myself if you were hurt because of me."

She slapped a hand over her mouth to stop the sudden laughter that bubbled up in her at his words. He was worried about her and he was not angry with her at all. It was truly *wunderbaar* news.

"Leah, are you *allrecht*? You have a very *schpassich* expression on your face." And he placed his hand over hers and squeezed lightly.

It took another moment for her to get control of herself.

"I am fine, Jacob. I am just so relieved." And then she did laugh a little; and Jacob looked at her for several seconds before understanding seemed to dawn on him.

"You thought I blamed you for this. And you thought that was why I was going to take you home?" And then he reached over and folded her into his arms. "Leah, nothing could be further from the truth. My only concern is for your safety."

He stopped for a moment and moved her to arm's length, looking into her eyes with a sudden fierceness. "I would never blame you for something like this. There is *nee* part of this that could be your fault. Do you understand?"

All she could do was nod her head. The feeling of warmth that had begun to spread through her when he wrapped his arms around her was now burning through her whole body.

He cares for me; he truly does.

He pulled her back to him then, squeezing her shoulders gently before wrapping his arms around her again. He held tight to her and she realized that she had been shivering all this time because his warmth was stilling the little tremors that were shaking her whole body.

It seemed like a long time before he finally let her go again and when he did, he pulled the blanket tightly around her again before picking up the reigns and clicking his tongue at the horses.

They pulled out onto the road and he turned the horses slowly in a wide circle, pointing them back the way they had *kumme*. He drove slowly, looking over at her every few minutes; and each time he did, she felt a blush heat her cheeks. She felt like a *gegisch maedel* and tried to stop herself, but it was *nee* use, so she stopped worrying about it.

Returning to her *haus* felt as if it took half the time they had traveled before, which made *nee* sense because she knew he was not driving any faster. Perhaps it only felt faster because she did not want their time together to end. He turned into the driveway and went nearly all the way to the *haus* before stopping and pulling off into the grass.

"I know this is very close, but I did not want you to have so far to walk, after what you have already been through this evening." He spoke very quietly so his voice would not carry.

His words sent a little thrill through her. He was truly concerned for her. It was a *gut* feeling.

"I appreciate it Jacob; *danki*." She stopped, uncertain of what else she should say.

"Is this a visiting week for your district or do you have service on Sunday?" He asked suddenly, almost as if he had nearly forgotten it.

Leah panicked a little when she realized that not only did they have service this week, but it was their turn to host. Her face must have shown some sort of panic because Jacob reached over and squeezed her hand.

"*Jah*, we have service this week. And actually, it is our turn to host."

"*Ach*, so you will be very busy." He said this nearly under his breath. Then only a moment later, he turned to her and asked, "Will your youth be having a gathering

Sunday evening?"

"*Nee*, our gatherings are usually on a Friday evening." She answered, a bit absently—trying to think if she knew whether there was one the next Friday . . . and not thinking of Zeke Hershberger at all.

"Would you be interested in visiting our district? We have a gathering this week. It is a visiting week for us and the youth decided to have a bonfire and hot dog roast in the afternoon." Even though he was speaking very quietly, there was such excitement in his voice.

She thought over how she could make it work and only a moment later, he said, "There is a family who lives just down the road from you. Their *dochder* is *freinden* with my *schweschder* and she always *kummes* to the gatherings. I am certain she would not mind bringing you along with her if it would be easier to explain to your *Dat*." And Leah breathed easier then. *That would make it so much easier,* she thought, and nodded to him.

"I will have Beth set it up with her then."

"I may even know her already . . . what is her name?" Leah asked.

"Her name is Sarah."

He answered and Leah shook her head. The name was familiar, but there were so many young women named Sarah in the area, it was impossible for her to know who he meant.

Fortunately he went on. "Sarah is only fifteen, but she does have an older *schweschder* who is closer to your age; her name is Eliza."

Leah knew then who he was talking about. The Yoder

family lived on the same road, but quite a ways away. Eliza had always been very quiet and Leah had not had much chance to speak with her since neither of them went to many of the gatherings. When Leah did go to a gathering, her *freind* Ada kept her well occupied.

"I do not know her well, but I know who she is. Her family usually *kummes* to help prepare for service, so I may have a chance to ask her about it tomorrow. Does Eliza usually *kumme* with Sarah?"

He started to speak and then stopped, looking thoughtful a moment, before answering. "I was going to say *nee, but* now that I think on it, I do believe I have seen her there before. She is very quiet."

Leah was already nodding. "*Jah,* she is." Suddenly she had an idea, a *wunderbaar* idea. "Perhaps we can help her a bit. If she has some *freinden* there who are more familiar, she might not have a reason to be so quiet."

Leah tried to think who she had seen Eliza spending time with when they had kept the same company. She thought she had seen her most with Dora Kurtz and Cora Muller. Then she remembered that Cora had nearly stopped attending the gatherings almost a year ago when her fiancé had drowned.

Dora she was not sure about, but it seemed as if she had been absent from the few gatherings Leah had attended. She might have a lot to do if she was to convince them. But now she had a plan.

"Do not worry, Jacob. I have a plan. I will talk to them all tomorrow." She smiled at him and he returned the smile.

"As long as you are there." He squeezed her hand again—before letting go with reluctance that she could clearly see.

"I will be. It will all work out; you'll see." She smiled at him again and he nodded at her before climbing down.

He walked around the buggy and lifted her down, walking with her all the way up to the *haus*. He stood at the base of the back steps, while she crept carefully up the steps and opened the mudroom door as quietly as she could.

She stood there for several seconds, looking at him before a gust of cold wind blew around the side of the *haus* and she knew she must go in. She waved at him, before slipping inside and gently closing the door.

She removed her boots quickly and rushed through the hall and up the stairs, slipping only a little in her hurry, but when she reached her window, he was standing there in the yard, looking up at it, waiting for her.

He smiled when he saw her and waved as she did, before finally moving away and heading for his buggy. She sent up a silent prayer that *Gotte* would keep him safe on his way home, before getting ready for bed again.

He was very much in her thoughts when she slipped between her sheets again. She shivered a little at the coolness, but thinking of her time with Jacob helped to warm her and she soon drifted off.

FOURTEEN

Leah looked out the window just as *Dat* made
his way to the barn. As she watched for others to arrive,
he walked out the bay mare, harnessed and ready to hook
up to the small buggy.

She wondered where he was off to this morning. He
had not mentioned any special plans to her, but perhaps
someone needed a ride and he had volunteered himself to
get them.

Practically the whole community would be here,
helping in one way or another. There were many things to
be done today to get ready for the service tomorrow. It
had been nearly six months since they had held it at their
haus and their turn had *kumme* round again.

Leah thought about it as she washed the breakfast

dishes. It was one of the things she liked most about their community. Every other week, a different family hosted the Sunday services in their home and the other families in the community came together to help that family get ready. Why just two weeks ago, Leah's family had been at Ida's *haus*, doing their part to help prepare.

Sunday service required much hard work, so everyone pitched in. Leah considered it was a *gut* thing their congregation was only a dozen families now. Their community had split just last year, and their new district had ended up with a few less because of the distance some families had already been traveling. The twelve families that remained were the largest families among them though, so it balanced out nicely.

Leah looked out the window over the kitchen sink, watching for her *schweschders*, knowing they would be there shortly to help and that the other ladies in their community would arrive soon, as well.

She could not help letting her mind wander a bit as she washed the breakfast dishes. She thought back to the buggy ride she had shared with Jacob last *nacht*. Things had not gone at all the way she had expected them to, but still, she could hardly wait to see him again.

To think, I have worried for years that nee boy would ever show an interest in me. And now there is one at my window nearly every nacht.

The thought reminded her of Zeke Hershberger and with the reminder, came a feeling of guilt. She had not mentioned Zeke to Jacob, even when he had asked about their youth gatherings.

Of course, she had not mentioned Jacob to Zeke either.

It is not as if I have anything to feel guilty about, she tried to convince herself . . . but the guilt continued to tug at her.

She had not mentioned Jacob to Zeke because her mind had wandered the entire way to the gathering the other *nacht*. She remembered sitting there thinking of Jacob along the way. She had even been forced to ask Zeke to repeat something he had said to her . . . twice.

He had not said much to her on the way back.

At the time, she had been thrilled not to have to come up with things to say to him, but now she could see that she should have just told him what was going on between her and Jacob.

Of course, I really didn't know what was between the two of us until last nacht.

But thinking back over her conversation with Jacob last *nacht*, she realized there had been several opportunities to mention it to him as well. She had not— and she was not entirely certain why.

She had been somewhat distracted when he first mentioned the gatherings, but she could have said something later.

Yet again, I was distracted with making plans.

It was not as if she harbored romantic feelings for Zeke. It would have been so simple for her to say something to Jacob. She must find a way to remedy the situation, and soon.

As Leah was thinking about Jacob, Miriam came in the side door with her son John holding tightly to the back of her skirt. As she came into the hall, Leah rushed over to take the large crock out of her hands.

"Miriam, you should not be carrying such heavy things," Leah scolded as she took the crock from her *schweschder* and set it on the kitchen table.

"Leah, you sound just like a mother hen," Miriam told her, but she was laughing as she said it.

Ruth came in after Miriam, catching the last of what was said and her laughter made Leah turn toward her.

"Who's a mother hen? Leah?" Ruth asked, looking at each *schweschder* and then at the crock, sitting on the table next to Leah. She started laughing; after a moment, Leah and Miriam joined in.

"She will be a *gut Mamm* some day soon," Anna said, with a smile, as she walked on into the kitchen behind Ruth.

Leah watched as Anna jiggled little Isaiah on her hip. She turned away quickly, fussing with the dish Ruth had set down, trying to hide the blush that had unexpectedly appeared with the thoughts that were—if nothing else—a little premature.

She had *nee* business thinking of having a *boppli* all her own. She and Jacob had only begun seeing each other. There was a long way to go before she should even consider that possibility.

Nee one seemed to notice Leah's internal debate or the blush on her cheeks. They went on chattering, talking about everything from the neighbor's new pups to the bishop's nephew, who was apparently enjoying his *rumschpringe* just a little too much.

Ladies came and went throughout the morning and sometime later Leah heard their neighbor Beth in the *sitzschtupp* with Lillian and Daniel. Beth was directing the two of them and they were obeying her instructions, so Leah went back to the chores she'd been finishing up, shaking her head a little as she listened to everything going on around her.

One thing was certain—she was enjoying it all very much. Every few minutes, delighted laughter could be heard from one of the three in the *sitzschtupp* or from her *schweschders* in the kitchen. It sounded like Miriam had sat down at the table.

Leah looked around at her *freinden* and family surrounding her and thought what a *wunderbaar gut* thing it was to watch everyone interact and work together. Ruth had brought Miriam a bowl and some potatoes; Miriam was peeling them as she chatted with Ruth, not noticing how easily she had been maneuvered by her over-protective *schweschder*.

John was *nee* longer hanging onto his *mamm's* skirt and Leah peeked around the corner to look for him. Across the hall, he was playing happily with his cousins. Lillian was holding little Isaiah now and Leah could see Anna washing windows in the front hall.

"So Leah, tell us about this *maedel Dat* rescued from the snow." Anna's voice sounded from the hallway, surely loud enough for everyone to hear. It brought a blush to Leah's cheeks; thoughts of the young woman brought thoughts of her handsome cousin to Leah's mind.

"*Jah*, we want to know all about it. How did *Dat*

kumme to be there?" This was said with a small giggle before Ruth added, "And is she doing well?"

"Is she pretty?" This came from Miriam, the most romantic of the *schweschders*. Leah sat there, blushing and trying to get thoughts of Jacob out of her head, while she tried to decide which *schweschder* to answer first.

"Ohhh . . . so she is pretty, then," Ruth said from behind Leah, stretching out her "oh" in a way that made it sound as if she thought she already knew the answer.

The whole subject made Leah very *naerfich* and she dropped the plate she had picked up to dry. It splashed as it dropped into the water in the sink, sending a wave of suds over the edge and onto the floor.

Leah jumped back, trying to avoid the flood of water and nearly succeeded in slipping in it instead. Behind her, Anna and Miriam were both laughing.

"I think that would be a *jah*. Don't you, Anna?" Miriam said, between laughs. They laughed together while Ruth and Leah stood there looking at each other. It only took a few seconds before they too, gave in and started laughing.

It really is pretty funny. Leah thought.

They think I'm being sneaky and trying not to answer their questions and they have nee idea what I am truly thinking about, or trying not to think about.

It was several minutes before everyone's laughter slowed and Leah went to work cleaning up the water that had spread across the kitchen floor. When Leah stood, Anna put her hand gently on Leah's arm. "Truly Leah, we are interested, and not just in gossip." She aimed a look at her *schweschders*, who only started laughing again.

Leah found herself wondering if she should tell them about the young woman's cousin . . . or if she should keep that to herself for now.

"I am sorry Anna, but I don't really know the answers." Another blush made its way up Leah's cheeks, before she turned back to the sink. "I never met her. Her cousin Jacob came to the door asking for help. Benjamin went with him to help and they came back without her." She paused there, giving everyone a moment before going on.

"She had left them a note. *Dat* evidently found the buggy—and the young woman—and offered to take her to her *aenti's haus*." Leah was curious about that, but she was determined to leave it all in *Dat's* lap. "*Dat* is the only one of us who has seen her and he has not said much at all about her, other than to tell her cousin that she was safely at their *aenti's* when he arrived home soon afterward."

"And not long after, the young man took his leave, so I did not learn anything from him, either." She thought about her words as she said them. They were true, but only because she had made *nee* effort to ask Jacob anything about his cousin. She would have to change that soon as well.

Her *schweschders* were talking among themselves now, about things *Dat* had done since that morning, trying to decide for themselves if there was a chance he was pursuing the young woman.

"*Ach*, but if *Dat* is really thinking of her in terms of a *frau*, how young could she be? He couldn't be interested in someone as young as one of his *dochdern*, could he?" Anna sounded a bit worried about it.

Leah's *schweschders* grew quiet at the idea of having a stepmother her own age. They seemed to think Dat had been impressed with her and that he would be calling on her soon.

I watched him hitch up the buggy only a few hours ago. Could he—would he—consider such a thing? Nee, I can't even think of such a thing as that.

And then her thoughts turned to Jacob. She would have to ask him what he thought about all of this. Surely he would know if her *dat* had been calling on his cousin. And he could certainly tell her more about his cousin.

And that thought reminded her that she was supposed to speak with Eliza Yoder. Without giving herself time to forget again, she turned and went in search of her. Fortunately, she was easy to find. She sat in the *sitzschtupp,* reading to the small *kinner.*

Leah stood there for a long time, just listening to the story Eliza was weaving around what the book in her lap contained. Eliza's story telling was simply amazing and Leah found herself caught up in the story right along with the *kinner.*

When she finished, the *kinner* all begged for another and Eliza looked as if she wanted to agree, but she shook her head a little and stood up.

"I need a break . . . just a short one." She said in answer to the immediate sounds of disappointment. "I must get some water. A dry throat cannot tell a *gut* story. I will be back soon." And she made her way across the room. After a moment, the *kinner* turned their attention to the assortment of toys and games that were scattered all around the room. Eliza made her way out of the *sitzschtupp*, walking right past Leah, who turned to catch up with her as she went down the hall.

"Eliza, are you ill?" Leah asked. It would not be a *gut* idea to invite her to an outdoor event this time of year if she was ill.

She laughed before answering. "*Nee* Leah, I'm not ill, just dry. That is the fourth story they have talked me into and my throat is begging for water." She laughed again.

Leah nodded her head. "Well I can certainly see why they want you to tell them stories. You are a gifted storyteller. Even I was caught up in your *wunderbaar* tale."

Eliza blushed and ducked her head. Leah realized this was the most she had heard the young woman speak in a long time. Either she was coming out of her shell—or she was flush with the success of her storytelling.

"Eliza, I have a question for you." Leah waited a moment to see if her neighbor had any objections before going on, but she only nodded her head, so Leah went on.

"A *freind* invited me to the youth gathering that is going on tomorrow evening. He mentioned that your younger *schweschder* is *freinden* with his son and he suggested I could catch a ride with you."

Eliza's jaw dropped—it actually dropped—and Leah worried for a moment that she had said something wrong, especially when a tear appeared on Eliza's cheek. She started to apologize, but Eliza waved it away.

"Leah, that is so *wunderbaar* of you." And before Leah

had any idea about what was going on, Eliza had wrapped her in a tight hug. It was not hard to figure out then—that it was not something wrong Leah had said—but something right.

"*Nee* one has ever invited me to a gathering, even my own *schweschder*. Oh Leah, you are a *wunderbaar gut freind!*" Eliza's words were a little muffled against Leah's shoulder, but there was such a sound of joy in them, Leah felt even better.

Here she had only been thinking she would help Eliza open up a bit and she had given the shy young woman a *wunderbaar* gift as well.

Oh Danki, Gotte, for showing me what to do.

Leah sent the thanks up to *Gotte,* feeling better all the time about the upcoming gathering. It was sure to be quite a *nacht.*

FIFTEEN

Samuel pulled into the yard and looked up at the large white *haus*, trying to tell himself that he was not doing something *gegisch*. He remembered how difficult it had been for him to find the courage to court Elisabeth—and they had grown up together.

Though the two of them had not been *gut freinden*, their families had been, since long before he was a boy. He had played with her *bruders* and he had watched her grow up alongside them.

Then one day he had stopped looking at her like a neighbor or even the *schweschder* of his *freinden*. He had seen her as a young woman and he had known she was meant to be his *frau*. Still, it had taken much courage to speak to her, ask her permission to court her, to go and speak to her *dat*.

This was *nee* less difficult for him—even though he was certain that he was where *Gotte's wille* wanted him. And he knew, as hard as it was, he should follow *Gotte's* plan. He gathered his courage and stepped down from the buggy, saying a silent prayer as he went.

He managed to walk up the front steps, but between the top step and the door, he thought of ten different reasons why this was not a *gut* idea. When he finally reached the door, he reminded himself—again—that he was where *Gotte* wanted him. He reached out and knocked on the door, before he had enough time to talk himself out of it.

It was *nee* more than a few seconds before someone opened the door. He recognized Naomi's *Aenti*—and she obviously recognized him. She smiled when she saw him and she very nearly pulled him across the threshold.

"You have *kumme* to check on Naomi. That is *gut*. She is doing well." There was such joy in the woman's voice, Samuel could not help but relax and smile as she chattered on.

"We are so grateful you found her and brought her home. When I think what might have happened..." a little shudder went through the tiny woman standing before him, but she went on talking.

"You are a blessing, for sure and for certain. You must *kumme* and join us. We are just having tea."

She had moved slowly through the kitchen and down the hall while she'd been speaking so he'd had *nee* choice but to follow. She turned the corner and walked into their spacious *sitzschtupp* and he found his feet moving the same direction. He could see a rocking chair near the fireplace. In it a young woman sat, wrapped in a thick blanket and delicately sipping tea.

It only took a moment to see that it was Naomi, she was so slight, but clearly not a *kind*—and it all made sense to him then. And somehow, discovering that her *aenti* was clearly his ally, he was *nee* longer *naerfich*. He was calm; he knew this was *Gotte's wille*. And then he knew just what to do. He would simply tell her . . . everything.

Gotte, give me the words, he said in a silent prayer as he stepped into the room.

Naomi turned her head when her *aenti* came into the room and when she saw him, the most beautiful smile lit up her face and he could only stand there—staring at her.

"Samuel, you came to see how I'm doing?"

He could only nod.

"That is so thoughtful," her *aenti* said. "You have already done so much already. We are so grateful that you brought our precious niece safely back to us."

Naomi sat in the rocking chair, moving it gently back and forth. She turned her head to look at her *aenti*. Ida shook her head in return, then they both looked back at Samuel.

"Won't you join us?" As she spoke the words, she shook her head a little and then started again. "Actually, would you care to join me? I would be so glad of the company. *Aenti* Ida has been sitting with me, but if you wouldn't mind for a bit, she has so many things she needs to do." Naomi smiled again and Samuel could only seem to nod his head.

His feet did not feel as if they touched the floor even once as he made his way across the room. He sat down in the chair across from Naomi as her *aenti* bustled out of the room and disappeared in the direction they'd *kumme* from a minute ago.

He sat there, looking at her, trying to think of something to say to her, but the words wouldn't come. And then she saved him from having to say anything.

"I hope you will not think me too forward." And she took a deep breath before going on. "You are not married? Is that right?"

He nodded again, wondering how long it would take her to notice that he wasn't speaking.

"Jacob told us the other evening, after you . . . well, after you rescued me. Your son Benjamin helped him to repair the buggy. Jacob came home telling us all about his visit with your family. He told us your *frau*, Elisabeth, died several years ago." And then she waited.

Samuel knew he would have to say something now. He took a deep breath and leaped.

"*Jah*, that is correct. We discovered Elisabeth had cancer more than eleven years ago. She died before my youngest *dochder*, Lillian, was with us even a year." He thought a moment before adding, "and I do not think you are too forward."

"*Nee*, that is not why I say you will think me too forward." Naomi bowed her head for a moment and he wondered if she was praying. What could she possibly say that she needed to pray about? Before he could wonder too much, she looked back up and began. It quickly became clear.

"I am a widow. My husband was sick for many years and *Gotte* finally called him home just two years ago." He was surprised to hear the strength in her voice.

He had known she must be unmarried; if *Gotte* planned for them to be married, she would have to be. Somehow he had not truly allowed himself to hope, to hear what she had been through. It sounded much more difficult than what he had been through with Elisabeth and she had not yet told him the full story.

"My family is in Ohio . . . in Hope Springs. My *dochder* is there with my *mamm* and *dat*. They are looking after her while I visit with family here." She stopped again and took another deep breath.

"I feel that *Gotte* has brought me here to Windy Gap— to be your *frau*."

She said it as though it should be a great shock to him, but when he said nothing, she looked over at him.

He suddenly felt as though he had been expecting it all along. He certainly knew *Gotte* had brought her here. Now it seemed as if she were waiting for him to respond.

"I should perhaps be shocked," Samuel said. He was becoming more *verhuddelt* at everything she said, but he immediately regretted his words because whatever he had said made her smile disappear. He rushed on, determined to bring the smile back to her beautiful face.

"I know I *would* be shocked, if it were not for my own feelings." He paused there only a moment before going on. "I feel the same way that you do . . . or at least, I hope it is the same."

He watched her, hoping to see a smile and after a moment, he was rewarded with a hint of one, giving him the determination he needed to go ahead and get it all out.

"I have been praying for some time that *Gotte* would show his *wille* to me and I believe He has when He brought you here." He watched as her smile bloomed and become even more beautiful than the one that had tied up his tongue just a few moments ago.

He waited for her to say something more . . . but she did not. She just sat there, rocking the chair back and forth and smiling and he realized that he did not have to convince her.

He was surprised to realize that he hadn't really had to do much of anything. *Gotte* had done the hard work for him already.

And to think, she was worried about being too forward . . . the thought came to him and he laughed.

. . .

Naomi sat there in the rocking chair, thinking about what Samuel had just said. She had been worried that he would think she was too forward and have nothing more to do with her and all the time, he had been feeling the same things she was feeling.

I should have had more faith in Gotte's wille!

She knew her thoughts were right. Why had she questioned *Gotte's wille*? He meant for her to be with Samuel, so why had she thought he would not take care of the particulars as well?

"Where do we go from here?" She looked up at Samuel as she asked and found herself staring at his face, wondering why had she failed to see what a handsome man he was before now?

Was it stubbornness on her own part or was it that *Gotte* had chosen to wait and reveal those things to her in his own time? It was a puzzle indeed. She was so distracted; she nearly missed what he was saying to her.

"I believe *Gotte* means for us to marry."

When Naomi said nothing, Samuel went on. "I suppose the next thing we should do is take time to get acquainted with each other." He spoke as if it were a rule to be followed.

And that *verhuddelt* her. *Gotte* meant for them to be together. They would have the rest of their lives to become acquainted. And she found her tongue rushing ahead of her mind as she voiced her concerns.

"Is that really necessary? We know *Gotte* has decided we are for each other. We have many years to get to know each other."

.   .   .

Samuel smiled at her impatience. He had worried ever since that first moment that he was going to have to convince Naomi to marry him and that he would have to wait a long time before she felt like she knew him well enough. Clearly she was a woman of great faith, and practical as well. She truly would be the perfect *frau* for him.

He started to reply, but then he thought of his *kinner* and he knew they would feel that they would need time to get to know Naomi, even if their way of telling him would be to suggest he get to know her better.

He almost laughed as he thought of it and she looked at him with a quizzical expression so he shared his thoughts with her.

"We may have the rest of our lives to get to know each other, but I believe our families would like the opportunity." And he was relieved to see her nodding— they would suit very well indeed. Suddenly he could not wait for the rest of his family to meet her.

Ideas began rushing into his mind. He would have to speak with the bishop. They would need to make arrangements to transfer Naomi to his own district— Naomi and her *dochder* . . . and that thought stopped him.

Her *dochder* . . . she had a *dochder*. And then a dozen questions crowded into his head, pushing out everything else for the moment. How old was this young woman? Why only one *dochder*—that would certainly be something they would need to talk about.

Naomi's words interrupted his thoughts before he could go any further.

"You are right. My family will want to meet you, and I am certain they would want to be here for the wedding." She smiled as she said it, but then a shadow crossed her face.

Right away, concern filled him. What could upset her so? "*Was iss letz*?"

But she shook her head and went on. "I mentioned it earlier, but I am not sure if you truly caught it. I have a *dochder.*"

He was certain that was not what she had been thinking of only a moment ago, but he decided it would be better to let it pass for now. And then he remembered his earlier questions. "Only one?"

Naomi nodded her head slowly, but didn't say anything.

"Does she have any *bruders*?"

"*Nee*. It is only Rebekah." She said very quietly. "My husband was sick for a very long time."

Then she shook her head a little again and smiled, "I would imagine you have more than one."

Her words gave Samuel an idea about what the shadow might have been about. Well, he was still young enough to have more *kinner*—if she wanted more.

"I have eleven *kinner* and four *grandkinner* already. Three of my *dochdern* are married and beginning their own families. Anna has Daniel, Isaiah and little Elisabeth. Miriam has only John so far."

"My eldest son David will be married just before the new year. That leaves Benjamin, Elam, Caleb, Leah, Peter, Matthew and Lillian still at home."

When he looked at Naomi, he was relieved to see that she was smiling, but he was also worried to see that her smile did not go all the way to her eyes—there was still a haunted look in them that worried him.

"You have been blessed with such a *wunderbaar* family. You said your eldest *dochdern* are all married.

How old are the two still at home?" Naomi asked, but her voice was overly bright. "My Rebekah is sixteen and I am certain she would enjoy having *schweschders*."

He watched her, trying to decide if he should ask why she was upset. After a moment, he decided it would be better to let her tell him when she was ready to talk about it.

"Lillian is eleven now and Leah is nearly eighteen. I am certain Leah would welcome a *schweschder* so close in age, especially seeing that she is surrounded by boys." Samuel was watching Naomi as he spoke of his family; she was looking down at the floor now and he worried she might even be close to tears. Could it be she wanted another *boppli*?

"Naomi," and he waited a moment until she looked up at him, "I am not so old. I am certain Lillian would enjoy having younger *bruders* or *schweschders* . . ." He purposely left the thought hanging, trying to give her a chance to respond, but he was concerned to see tears on her lashes as he spoke.

By the time he had finished speaking, the few tears had been joined by many more, but her smile had spread across her entire face, so he hoped they were tears of joy by now.

.   .   .

It was a moment before Naomi could find her voice again. She had yearned for more *kinner*—to the point that she had even questioned *Gotte's wille*. If she was not meant to have more *kinner*, why did he allow her to yearn so?

Deep down she had always known *Gotte* had a plan for her, but there had been so many times she felt like her heart was breaking. Especially when her *freinden* had new *bopplin*. Now . . . she finally understood.

"When do I meet your family then, Samuel? When will we tell them of our plans? *Ach* . . . will they like me?"

Samuel laughed at that and she was suddenly distracted, thinking of how *wunderbaar* his laugh was—so strong and full of life.

She stopped to listen and let it wash over her. It was rich and warm, like a comforting blanket and she wished it were possible to simply curl up in the delightful sound.

She had missed hearing a man laugh. Her own *dat* had not laughed much lately. He had been worried for her for such a long time; now he could finally stop. Unexpectedly she felt laughter bubble up in her and it felt very *gut* indeed.

They stayed there, looking at each other for a long time until Samuel's laughter finally faded away. His eyes locked onto hers and he sat there for what seemed a long time, holding her gaze. Then suddenly he looked away.

"They will *lieb* you, I am certain of it. You can meet them today—the *maedels* anyway—and we can tell them of our plans." He shook his head a little before continuing. "I am certain they will want to get started right away with the planning."

Naomi nearly laughed at how pained his expression was. Clearly he did not look forward to planning the wedding; it didn't surprise her at all, since most men considered such things to be women's work. The thought didn't bother her at all because she hoped to have the help of his *dochdern*.

She felt much better about meeting them now. She'd been certain he would put her off for a while; actually she'd been certain he would think she was too forward, which would have left *nee* reason to meet his family, but clearly she had not trusted *Gotte's wille* near enough.

"Leah and her *schweschders* are preparing now for our Sunday service. It is our turn to host. The other ladies will most certainly be there soon to help. You would blend right in and you would have the opportunity to meet our neighbors as well."

Naomi marveled at his words; not only had he seen her worry—he had known what it was about and he had come up with a *wunderbaar* solution right away, easing all of her fears—well, almost all of them, she admitted to herself.

"Truly Samuel, you are a treasure. How is it you are still available for *Gotte* to maneuver?" She was surprised when he laughed again.

It was almost a bark of laughter and she found herself wanting to laugh with him.

"You may understand soon enough." And he continued to laugh.

. . .

Samuel watched the confusion flicker across her face

and realized what he had said. He had not intended to make it sound quite that way. He opened his mouth twice to speak, but nothing came out and the third time, he mumbled a bit before firmly closing his mouth as Naomi shook with laughter. She was certainly enjoying the joke he had made at his own expense.

He should have been bothered by it, but he found himself affected by her soft, feminine laughter. Soon he had joined in with her, shaking his head at how easily his tongue become tangled up whenever he spoke to her. There was something about this tiny woman.

After several minutes of laughing together, Naomi waved a hand at him.

"I will go and let my *aenti* know where I am going. When should I tell her to expect my return?" Samuel was surprised that he wanted to say her *aenti* should not expect her to return. Now that *Gotte* had brought them together, he did not want to be apart. Of course, the practical part of him told him that was not a *gut* idea.

"Perhaps you would like to join us this evening for supper?" He made his words a question so that she could have the chance to politely refuse . . . but again, she surprised him.

"That sounds like a very *gut* idea. There will be much to do today, preparing for the Sunday service. This will give me an opportunity to get acquainted with your family. Supper would be a *gut* time to do that. And I can help them prepare the evening meal, if they will allow me to help. . ."

He noticed the question in what she said as well. And

he knew his *maedels* well enough to know that they would never expect a guest to help prepare the evening meal. Perhaps it was a *gut* idea.

"I am certain they would appreciate the help. And they will want the chance to speak with you without me present, I am certain."

"*Gut*. I will go and let my *aenti* know I won't return until this evening. Then, I think I had better bundle up a bit more." And her smile returned with her words.

Samuel was glad to see it. And he was thankful for her clever wit. He *nee* longer had any doubt that she was part of *Gotte's wille* for him. Clearly *Gotte* knew much better what Samuel needed in his life. The thought occurred to him that *Gotte had* been moving them both into place for quite a long time. It was a very humbling thought.

SIXTEEN

Leah happened to look out the window when *Dat's* buggy came into the yard. She noticed that he did not head for the barn, but instead pulled up next to the porch and she wondered at the reason for it.

She watched as he climbed down and walked around the buggy to help someone down. The person he helped was very small, but she was not someone Leah recognized.

"Ruth, Anna, Miriam, *kumme*," Leah called to her *schweschders*, "*Dat* has brought someone back with him."

Her *schweschders* joined her at the window and the four of them stood there, watching their *dat* help the person down.

"Did *Dat* say anything to you about bringing someone back with him, Leah?" Ruth asked, not taking her eyes off of the scene just outside the window.

Leah shook her head, but didn't say anything.

"Could it be the widow Yoder, *kumme* to help prepare for Sunday services? See how careful *Dat* is with her. The widow Yoder is very frail indeed." This came from Miriam —certainly the most tenderhearted of them.

"If I were you, I would not let the widow Yoder hear you refer to her as frail, Miriam," said Anna, giggling as she said it.

"*Dat* did not say anything to me about bringing anyone back with him," Leah finally found her voice to answer Ruth, "He did not even tell me where he was going when he left this morning."

Dat and the person turned toward the *haus* and the *schweschders* could see it was definitely not the widow Yoder with *Dat*.

"She looks so young." Miriam was the first to speak, with a glimmer of hope in her eyes. "Perhaps she is new to the community. How wunderbaar; a new *freind*."

Miriam sounded so *eiferich,* Leah couldn't help herself —she laughed—and after a moment her *schweschders* joined her.

Anna spoke up then, shushing her *schweschders.* "Ruth, if that were it, he would have brought one of us with him to fetch her." Ruth was nodding even as Anna said the words.

They all knew she was right. *Dat* would not want to do anything that could be considered improper—especially with someone who was a new neighbor. And that could only mean one thing. He must be planning to court this young woman—a *maedel* who looked to be very close in age to his own *dochdern*.

Leah felt a strange panic rising up in her chest. What could have given *Dat* the idea that they would want a new *Mamm* who was the same age as them?

That was something *Englisch* men did. They married women young enough to be their *dochdern*. How could he even think of such a thing?

She could feel tears burning hotly in her throat at the thought.

.   .   .

Samuel turned to Naomi just before they stepped onto the front porch. He would have used the side door if it had just been himself, but he felt it was important to show as much respect to Naomi as possible. Using the side door would extend a bit too much familiarity than was proper.

"*Wie geht's,* love?" asked Samuel. "Are you *naerfich*?

Her tiny hand had been squeezing his arm tightly. He had thought it was so she would not fall, but he could see there was *nee* ice, so he knew it must be that she was feeling *naerfich* about meeting his family.

"We do not have to do this now." He stopped and turned toward her, waiting until she looked up at him before going on. "I want you to be comfortable. My family will *lieb* you; I am certain of it." He watched as she closed her eyes, took a deep breath and nodded.

"Then I want to meet them now. I want them to know me. I want them to like me. If I wait, that will just be time

I do not have with them. Besides, we are already here." She added as she smiled up at him. A warmth spread through him at the brilliance of her smile.

He was lost for a moment in her beautiful smile, but then he remembered they were standing in the cold and she was not used to their weather, so he turned back to the porch and moved forward, helping her up the steps.

As they stepped up onto the porch, he thought he saw a flash of dark blue fabric at the window and he thought he remembered Leah wearing a dark blue dress this morning.

Has she been at the window watching us?

What would she be thinking, seeing her *dat* escorting a young lady to their home? And he laughed to himself a little.

He remembered when he had first seen Naomi. She was so slight and she had such youthful features, he had thought she was much younger. *Would Leah think the same?*

He was certain she would. And her *schweschders* would be here, too. *Was she even now rushing to tell them that their dat was bringing a maedel to their home? Oh, what would they be thinking?*

"Samuel, what is it . . ." Naomi asked, giving him an oddly quizzical look.

"I am just thinking of what may await us on the other side of this door. I don't know why I didn't think of it earlier. *Ach*, what they are surely thinking right this minute." He stopped for a moment, still struggling with the urge to laugh.

It was a *gut* feeling, but it certainly was not the right time. He turned back to Naomi and was relieved to see that she was beginning to enjoy his mood as much as he was—even if she had *nee* idea of the strange thoughts in his head.

"I remember when I first saw you in that buggy. I thought you were the same age as my young *dochdern*. You are so slight and *Gotte* has blessed you with such youthful features." He watched as light dawned in Naomi's eyes and she laughed with him.

"*Ach,* Samuel, *kumme;* we must hurry. They will be thinking the worst of their dear *dat*." She stepped up to the door as Samuel opened it for her, ushering her in ahead of him as he called out to his *dochdern*.

"Leah, Anna, Miriam, Ruth, Lillian, *kumme* please. I have someone to introduce you to." He called to the girls, knowing that his sons would be in the fields or the barn—doing chores and trying to avoid the mass of ladies inside.

He closed the door firmly behind him and waited for his *dochdern* to appear. Beside him, Naomi still held his arm tightly, but he thought her grip had loosened a bit and she was smiling more fully now, too.

Together they stood in the front hallway as Anna and Ruth slowly approached them, then Miriam, Lillian and finally Leah appeared.

. . .

Leah looked at her *schweschders* standing in the front hall, facing *Dat* and his guest. They all looked perfectly comfortable and welcoming. Then she stepped into the hall and looked at this *maedel* her *dat* had brought here.

For a moment, all she could see was the very young woman she had expected, but then she looked a bit closer and she could see the tiny creases at the corners of the woman's smile and more creases at the edges of her eyes.

They were crinkled up because she was smiling at them all, so they were easy to see. Suddenly Leah felt ashamed of herself. This woman could not possibly be near her age or even close to her elder schweschders.

She was clearly a tiny woman who looked quite youthful. She had greatly misjudged her *dat*. She ducked her head and she could feel tears of shame burning her throat.

"Leah, *was iss letz*?" She heard *Dat* ask her, but she couldn't seem to find the words to answer him. Fortunately, Anna came to her rescue.

"Are you going to leave us guessing then, *Dat*?" asked Anna, showing a bit of impatience.

"*Nee* Anna, I am not going to make you wait one more moment for this *gut* news." He tucked Naomi's hand in the crook of his arm and pulled her forward so that they stood together.

"This is Naomi, and she has already agreed to marry me."

Leah looked up in surprise. She had expected him to say that they were courting. She had not expected him to announce an engagement. It was too much . . . too fast, especially for *Dat*. She had to wonder what was going on, but before she could ask, *Dat* was speaking again.

"I know you are all thinking that we are moving too fast. We have both prayed about this and we both feel that we are in *Gotte's wille*. I do hope that you will be *froh* to have Naomi and her *dochder* Rebekah join our family."

For a second, *nee* one else said a word and then all three of her elder *schweschders* were talking over each other, offering congratulations and asking how it had all happened. Miriam walked over and wrapped Naomi in a hug.

"Welcome to the family." Miriam's words were warm and sweet, but the hug was a bit awkward. Of course, everyone could see the clear evidence; she was about to bless the family with another member.

Anna and Ruth did the same in turn and then Lillian stepped forward. She didn't say anything—which seemed *schpassich* to Leah—but instead threw her arms around Naomi's waist and held on as if Naomi were a raft in the midst of a vast ocean.

Leah watched with her *schweschders* as Lillian snuggled up to Naomi; it made Leah feel even more ashamed of her behavior. If they could all accept this woman, so could she.

She stepped forward and stopped, surprised to see that she was precisely the same height as Naomi. It took a moment for that to sink in before Leah moved forward again.

Naomi even seemed to sense Leah's reluctance— holding out her tiny hands to Leah in entreaty.

"Leah, my Rebekah is only a year younger than you, but I do hope you will welcome her as you have welcomed me. I just know she will feel blessed to have so many *wunderbaar schweschders*."

Leah looked at the tiny woman who still held tightly to her hands. She thought she could detect a hint of trembling in them.

Could she truly be naerfich about meeting us? Leah looked at her and what she saw then was a very different picture than she had seen through the window. She knew then that her fear had blinded her.

Naomi had such a kind, sweet face—a mother's face. Finally, Leah felt she had found the confidant she had been praying for. And with that in mind, she let go of Naomi's hands to throw her arms around her, the woman who would soon be her new Mamm.

SEVENTEEN

Leah watched Naomi as she visited with the other ladies in their community. It was truly amazing to see; they all talked with her and laughed like they had known her for years.

Even the widow Yoder, who had shown up with Benjamin about ten minutes after *Dat* introduced them all to Naomi, was showing a level of welcome that Leah had never witnessed. She and Naomi had been together much of the afternoon, talking like old *freinden*.

Naomi looked perfectly comfortable. She may have been *naerfich* about meeting Leah and her *schweschders, but* she was obviously enjoying the company of the other ladies in their community.

Leah had tried to keep an eye on her; to make certain

she did not get overwhelmed—she truly did look very fragile—but she never appeared uncomfortable in the slightest.

She was in a different room each time Leah saw her. She also made strides to include Lillian, suggesting Leah's young *schweschder* help them in the kitchen. The next time Leah saw her, Lillian was wearing the biggest smile Leah could ever remember seeing on her face. She was clearly enjoying being treated more like an older *maedel*.

After she completed the task they'd given her, Lillian followed Naomi around the kitchen, carrying things Naomi handed her and chattering away about a dozen different things. She asked questions so fast, Leah was amazed Naomi could even understand them.

The other ladies were not bothered by this at all. They smiled as Naomi and Lillian walked by them and a few of them even laughed to themselves or to each other. Soon they were each taking Lillian off this way or that way, showing her how to do all of the different things they were doing.

Leah wondered why she had never noticed how much Lillian needed the extra attention. She had always made it a point to include Lillian as much as she could, because she was the only *schweschder* at home that Lillian had to teach her things, but Leah had never seen just how much Lillian needed the attention— and the affection.

But Naomi had.

Leah closed her eyes at the sudden rush of tears and lifted up thanks to *Gotte* for bringing Naomi here. Clearly she was exactly what this family needed and He had known that all along.

.   .   .

Naomi looked around the kitchen at all the *wunderbaar* ladies she had met and now considered *freinden*. She was comforted to find that she would enjoy spending time with her new neighbors and the other community members.

They told her of their families, of their husbands, of the work the new bishop was doing in the community. Not one of them said that she was *gegisch* for rushing into marriage with a man she barely knew.

And not one of them was pressuring her to marry a man she did not love the way a woman should love her husband.

The widow Yoder was clearly intrigued with her story. She had actually asked Naomi to repeat it for her. The first time through, the widow had sat there quietly rocking, while Naomi talked.

Now she found herself telling the wise old woman the whole, long story, about her husband John and how he had been sick for nearly ten years before passing away.

She told her about her *dochder* Rebekah. It was difficult to speak of, but Naomi told about how she had always wanted more *kinner* and that Rebekah had yearned for *bruders* and *schweschders*. Possibly the most difficult story was about her *bruder*-in-law, who was expecting Naomi to marry him after his *bruder* had died. Of course it was tempered by how *wunderbaar* her parents were when

Naomi told them she did not want to marry someone she did not love that way.

Naomi talked about praying every day and sitting quietly, listening for *Gotte's* answer, about coming to visit her *aenti* in the next town over; then she talked about Samuel finding her in the broken buggy and how considerate he was to take her on to her *aenti*'s home so she did not have to sit there and freeze.

She even talked about Samuel coming to speak with her about his feelings about *Gotte's wille* for them and how her own feelings were the same so they had decided to get married.

The second time Naomi told the story; the widow Yoder stopped her in several places to ask questions. Naomi answered them the best she could; she didn't understand all of them, but she answered them.

And when Naomi had gone through the entire story twice, Ella Yoder just smiled and said, "*Gotte* certainly does work in mysterious ways—does he not?"

Naomi nodded and waited for the wise woman to say something else, but when she just sat there in the chair rocking calm and quiet, Naomi decided the conversation must be over and excused herself to get back to helping the others. The wise old woman rose just as gracefully as a cat from the rocking chair and walked with Naomi to the kitchen.

Once in the kitchen, Naomi realized that the ladies had all been listening to her when she shared her story. So now they all knew her history, her background. She waited to see if they would judge her for it. They didn't seem to be, as they were all going about their tasks as if nothing was unusual.

And then Ruth broke the silence. "Naomi, you might as well know right now, Ella Yoder is our resident story-teller. If we had not heard you telling her all about yourself and your family, we would have heard it in a day or two, anyway." She smiled when she said it and several of the other women laughed quietly.

Naomi could also see heads nodding around the room and the knowing smiles, one or two of them even looked a bit chagrined. It looked like she was not the only one who had fallen victim to the widow Yoder's curiosity.

It was not much of a surprise. She remembered the widow Kurtz in Hope Springs had been much the same. She was surprised though, when one of the younger ladies spoke up.

"I am sure you might not think so, but it sounds like a very romantic story. You have been terribly brave."

"*Jah,* I cannot even begin to imagine what I would do if I were to lose my Stephen." The words came from a *maedel* standing at the counter, kneading dough and Naomi realized she must be getting older because the young woman looked far too young to be married.

"I truly hope you never have to find out. If you did, I am certain you would do what you must. You have a *wunderbaar* community here. They would help you as well." After only a moment, she added. "Our community was most helpful to me."

And it was true. Naomi was still very grateful for her own community. Without all of them, she might never have been able to move beyond John's death.

Of course, without their insistence that she marry John's *bruder*, she might not have felt the need to escape.

Which would mean I would never have kumme here. I never would have met Samuel, or his family, or any of these wunderbaar ladies.

Meeting all the ladies here today had been such a blessing. She was thrilled to see this community was just as close-knit as her own, albeit a little less pushy.

"If I had chosen to stay on at our farm, I am certain there would have been many volunteers to take care of the work I could not handle." She stopped a moment, thinking of all she had left behind and was surprised to realize that she did not miss it even a little bit. After another moment, she finished her thought, ". . . but it seemed more sensible to allow Joel to take it over and to move back in with my *mamm* and *dat*.

"Rebekah was not so lonely then. It has been *gut* for her to be with them." There were other reasons, too. Things she was hesitant to tell any of these *wunderbaar* women, things she had not been able to move beyond as yet, but the one she stated was truth enough for now.

She thought about all of the obstacles that lay ahead of her. She would most likely have to meet with her own bishop before she and Samuel married. Her parents would support her in that meeting at least.

She prayed fiercely that her own bishop would allow her to leave the past behind her, and move here with her church standing in *gut* stead so that she and Samuel could be married with as little delay as possible. Now that *Gotte* had brought the two of them together, she found she was anxious to get started living again.

As she stood at the kitchen counter, surrounded by new *freinden*, Naomi knew she had never enjoyed an afternoon more.

She had been so lonely for fellowship since John passed, but she was hesitant to tell the ladies here the true reasons she had missed out on so much of it back in her own community; mostly due to how sick John had been and for so long.

. . .

Samuel stepped out of the barn and looked toward the *haus*, thinking of Naomi and wondering how she was faring with their neighbors.

He had walked out to the barn earlier to see if Benjamin had left him any chores to do and was not a little surprised to see that he had not.

The more he thought about it, he was certain his *bruder* must have had a talk with Benjamin about the chores. Even little Matthew was always busily working away now, helping Elam and Peter with mucking out the stalls.

He and his *bruders* had been helping their *dat* with chores for a long time, but in the last few weeks, they had taken over most all of them—which left Samuel with far too much time on his hands to do nothing but think.

The first few days he had come out to the barn to find that all of the chores were done—or almost done, he had been at a loss for what to do with himself.

Until he had made up his mind to pursue Naomi, which had most likely been his *bruder's* intention all along. When he really thought on it, Samuel realized that he was grateful to the boys. Since he had begun seeing Naomi, it was *gut* to have them helping out so much.

As he stood there, he thought back to his earlier questions. He had been so overwhelmed then by the wonder of Naomi accepting his *schpassich* proposal and the thoughts of all they had before them, but now he stopped to think about Rebekah.

He had not truly considered the idea of adding another *maedel* to their family. He wondered how Rebekah was going to feel about having them for her new family.

Samuel loved all of his *kinner*, but he knew theirs was a large household and at times, the noise within their walls overwhelmed some of their neighbors. How would she feel about joining a large, loud family, filled with people she did not know?

Naomi had told him she was certain Rebekah would fit right in and be pleased to suddenly have so many *bruders* and *schweschders* for company, but Samuel was not so sure.

Rebekah had grown up with only herself and her *mamm*, and he was certain it would be quite an adjustment. Perhaps he should talk with Naomi about bringing Rebekah out here before they were too busy with wedding arrangements.

He certainly did not want Rebekah to feel that they

were excluding her. He wanted her to feel welcome and like she was part of the family. He did not want her to feel that they were pushing her too fast; she would need time to become acquainted with all of them and, more importantly, she would need time to get used to all of them.

With that in mind, he headed for the buggy he'd left parked in the yard. He knew the ladies would be busy for most of the day so he would have plenty of time to go to town and check on prices for a train ticket and a driver to get Rebekah here from the train station.

Or perhaps he and Naomi should go and pick her up at the train. Then maybe she wouldn't feel as if they were dumping everything on her all at once.

. . .

Leah stood at the sink and washed dishes as the ladies finished with them. Miriam sat on a chair beside her, drying each dish and then handing them to Lillian—who was either putting them away or putting them aside for the ladies who had brought them.

The bread had been baked and the chickens roasted. There were several casseroles that could be served cold and at least two dozen pies on the large dining table. There were several large containers of tea in their gas-powered refrigerator and two insulated canisters of milk in the cold room.

The ladies had helped clean the *haus* from the top floor down and the men had brought in all of the benches and set them up earlier. Leah was thankful their *sitzschtupp* was large enough to accommodate their entire church body. Otherwise, they would have had to set up the benches in the barn. Body heat might help make it bearable, but they were due for a very cold *nacht*.

Leah was only a little bit surprised at how big a help Naomi had been. She had not stepped in and just taken charge—instead deferring to Anna and the ladies from the community—but she had made herself helpful wherever needed.

She even seemed to have got over her embarrassment about her personal conversation with the widow Yoder being overheard; Leah did not believe she could have been so quick to let it go if it had been her.

Leah had also noticed that Naomi made a special point in volunteering to help Anna with the bathrooms earlier, which had given the two of them time alone.

She had managed to get Miriam to sit in the *sitzschtupp* and have tea with her just after the noon meal; a feat they were all grateful for because keeping Miriam off her feet was *nee* easy task since she was determined to be active, despite the doctor insisting she must rest as much as possible.

Naomi had found time to chat with Ruth while they worked on the morning dishes. And she had helped Lillian entertain Anna's John when he woke up fussy from his nap.

The only one Naomi had not found a chance to corner yet was Leah—which left her wondering when it would be her turn.

. . .

Naomi looked up with a smile when she heard Samuel clear his throat. Her *dat* had used the same signal as long as she could remember. It had been his way of telling them the silent prayer was over and they could eat.

It warmed her heart to hear it and it was a great comfort to hear. It made her feel like she was already at home here. She looked at Samuel and smiled, hoping that her happiness was clear enough for him to see. He returned her smile as he passed a large bowl of biscuits to his right.

Naomi looked around the table at Samuel's beautiful family. How she had longed for more *kinner*. For more than ten years now, she had wanted more *kinner,* but it had not been in *Gotte's wille* for her then.

Was it in His *wille* now? *Could this family truly be mine soon?* Was it possibly in Gotte's wille for her? *Could it even be part of His wille for us to have more kinner?* She smothered the laugh that bubbled up in her at the very idea.

That was something she would have to speak to Samuel about. He had several *grandkinner* already. He might tell her he was not so old—but he might not truly want more *bopplin* of his own right now.

She certainly did not want him to do something only for her.

And that made her realize what a great many things they had to discuss. Truly they did not know each other well enough to convince a bishop to allow them to marry.

They would need to spend some time talking about their plans for the future.

She thought again of how insistent she had been when confessing to Samuel that she felt *Gotte* had brought the two of them together. She had been certain he would not believe her or that he would think she had taken leave of her senses.

He would have been well within his rights to be upset by her behavior, but he had seemed only to find it endearing—or perhaps even amusing. He was certainly not at all what she had come to expect of the typical Amish man.

Thinking about this—the typical Amish man—brought thoughts of Joel to mind. He would certainly be bothered by her brash behavior and he would most likely be angry with her. She would have to write him a letter, explaining her behavior and her choices.

She would also have to send a letter to her parents, asking them to send Rebekah here and asking them when they might wish to come out and meet her intended and his family. That would be a difficult letter to write, of that she was certain. But it must be done.

She very much hoped her parents would see in Samuel and his family the *wunderbaar* things that she did; she hoped they would be *froh* for her and not too upset that she would be turning down Joel's proposal. He had been expecting for some time that she would marry him and it did not seem to matter how many times she told him *nee*, he just kept asking.

When she felt tears at the corners of her eyes,

threatening to spill over, she shook off the difficult thoughts. They were much too dark to entertain while sitting here with this lovely family she hoped would be her own soon; she would not want anyone to notice her *schpassich* behavior.

. . .

Samuel watched Naomi as she looked around the table at his family. The smile on her face was so serene, it was almost breathtaking. He knew he should not be thinking of her in such terms since she was not yet his *frau*, but he couldn't seem to help himself.

Her smile was one of the first things that had captivated him, there was so much warmth, that it lit up her entire face. He looked forward to many years of seeing her beautiful smile.

However, when he looked back at her, he noticed she was *nee* longer smiling. She looked at first like she was considering something puzzling, but very quickly it looked as if her thoughts had turned troubling.

The light had gone completely out of her eyes and there was a cold darkness in their depths—almost as if a dark cloud was above her head and had cast her in its shadow.

What could be troubling her so that she looked so bereft, sitting here surrounded by the family that would soon be hers?

Equally surprising was his reaction to it all.

He found that he wanted to protect this delicate

woman with everything in him and the strength and ferocity of the thoughts that came to him and the unsettling way his muscles had already tensed—almost as if he were preparing for battle—shocked him.

He struggled to push them out of his head. It was not their way to do battle, not for any reason. *Gotte* called them to peace.

Besides, he could *nee* more fight his thoughts than he could have fought against *Gotte's wille* where Elisabeth had been concerned.

He sat there, dumbstruck at the realization that spread out before him with that thought. It was almost as if someone had turned a lantern on before him.

That was what had kept him locked up in grief all these years. He had been fighting his own nature. He'd not allowed himself to let go of Elisabeth, to give her over to *Gotte* and trust that His *wille* was best for her and for all of them.

Instead, he had been holding on to anger and pain, refusing to give it up to *Gotte*.

Right there at the supper table, looking at the woman he intended to marry, with his family surrounding them all, Samuel felt like he had been baptized all over again.

He felt as new and whole as he had the day he had vowed to live plain for the rest of his days. He felt as alive as he had when the Bishop announced he and Elisabeth would soon be married. He felt as full of love and joy as he had when Ella Yoder, who had served as the community's midwife for many years, put Anna into his arms for the first time.

He closed his eyes and allowed *Gotte's* love and healing power to wash over him, cleansing him of his anger, washing away his bitterness and sadness. As he gave it all up to *Gotte*, he felt like a new man.

. . .

Leah looked over at Naomi just then and noticed that one moment she was looking around at them and smiling, but in the next she looked almost like a different person.

There was a strange darkness in her eyes and she seemed to shrink in on herself, not an easy thing to do since she was already such a slight person.

Leah felt almost as if a cold wind suddenly blew between them and she found herself wanting to help somehow. Only a moment ago Naomi had been such a warm, peaceful woman, smiling and *froh*.

Now she looked lost and cold and alone and so sad, it nearly broke Leah's heart. She didn't know what to do for Naomi, but she knew she felt a desire to do something, so she reached out a hand and laid it gently over the tiny fisted hand lying on the table beside her.

Naomi looked up at Leah and it was almost as if she shook off an unseen barrier. And as it slid off, the warmth came back and Naomi was calm again. Leah knew she would wonder for a long time what it had all been about; at the same time she was not certain she wanted to know the answer.

EIGHTEEN

Samuel looked over at Naomi, sitting beside him in the buggy, wrapped in the blanket Anna had tucked around her. He had personally placed a hot brick at her feet, but he was especially thankful to Anna for her care of Naomi. She was still so fragile, it seemed as though a stout wind would knock her off her feet.

He wondered what he had seen in Naomi's eyes at supper. He wanted to ask her about it, but he also did not want to spoil their ride, so he kept silent as they rode along the dark road.

He was experiencing so many new feelings when he thought about Naomi, some he had never felt with Elisabeth. And before *Gotte* had healed his heart, he might have worried over it, but now he understood that was all part of *Gotte's* plan.

Gotte had led him and Naomi to this place and he had plans for them in the future; Samuel intended to see those plans fulfilled. And he would do that by following *Gotte's wille*. He had brought them here and He would lead them through the obstacles to come.

They would simply need to have faith and stand together.

Samuel thought of the sadness he had seen earlier. They would certainly need to stand together if they were to deal with whatever had caused such anguish. Perhaps that was another reason *Gotte* had brought them together.

Samuel knew he was blessed to have such a strong community who would stand behind him and he was thankful for his *wunderbaar* family who would welcome Naomi and her *dochder* with open arms and hearts.

. . .

Naomi sat next to Samuel in silence, wanting to speak with him about the things in her past, but unsure of how to begin. He would need to know all of it at some point. She felt it would be better to pour it out to him soon—if only she could find the words.

She wanted to fit into his family, his life and his community, but she was not certain that she was able to fit here, with all of the things she had fought against in her past.

Her own community had made her to feel that she alone was responsible for John's illness. The doctors had told her repeatedly that *nee* one could have done anything differently. John had become ill suddenly and it was not due to anything either of them had done.

She had worked so hard to care for her husband, sometimes even neglecting little Rebekah in the process. She had felt for some time; perhaps that was why *Gotte* had not seen fit to give her another *kind*. She had not cared properly for the one she had and so she would not have more.

Not that Rebekah had gone without attention. Naomi's parents had been *wunderbaar*; stepping in to help care for her.

For many years, they had spent more time in the *daudi haus* that was attached to the large farmhouse she had left behind in Ohio than they had in their own *haus*. And the more ill John had become, the more time they had spent with Rebekah.

Joel had assured her that it would all settle after they were married, but she did not wish things to settle if that was the only way to go about it.

Joel had never heard her; *nee* matter how many times she told him her reasoning for refusing him, he would just smile and say that she needed a bit more time and she would come to see *gut* sense.

She had remained firm for two years, but she had grown weary of having to stand her ground and she had *nee* idea how she would go about explaining to him now, that she had found precisely what she had been looking for all this time.

He would not accept it, that much she knew without

question.

She reasoned with herself that sending him a letter would suffice because going back to Ohio would only serve to cause more of a problem.

She knew *Dat* wanted the best for her; *Mamm,* too. She only hoped she could show her *dat* how important it would be for them to support her in the decision to marry Samuel Fisher, to show them that he was indeed *Gotte's wille* for her—and for Rebekah.

She realized that convincing them this was *Gotte's wille* for Rebekah might actually be the more difficult of the two. They were so attached to her sweet *dochder*, she was not certain they would be able to let go of her. And suggesting they move to New York would most likely be a bad idea. Without her *dat*'s support, there was *nee* hope of making Joel see reason and accepting the truth.

Naomi still remembered the *nacht* her life had changed forever and though she could see it now, at the time she had been too wrapped up in grief to understand Joel's reasoning or even his words.

. . .

Naomi sat there holding John's hand; his bruder Joel, sitting on the other side of his bed, held his other hand. She was whispering prayers over John with tears slipping slowly and silently down her cheeks.

She was supposed to pray silently, but she felt John might need to hear that she was praying over him, especially since he had not opened his eyes in nearly two days.

As John's breathing became more labored and shallow, her tears flowed more steadily and she felt a hand on her shoulder. She did not look away from John's face, but she could hear Joel's quiet voice just behind her. There was at least as much strain in it as would be in her own. His words came out a bit rough and broken. He was certainly grieving as she was.

"I will take care of you Naomi. You and Rebekah will always have a home with me. Do not fear. He will be with Gotte soon and out of pain."

She heard his words, but the meaning in them slipped right past her because she was so focused on John; she probably would not have noticed then what he was truly saying if Joel had proposed to her right then and there. She only knew that Joel was there with her, like he had been for so long during John's illness. Joel had been there with them all this time, helping them through this difficult time.

They had all been through so much in the past months. The truth be told, it had been more like the last ten years. Naomi felt like she had not taken a true breath in so long and it was wearing so much on her.

She was shocked to realize that, in that moment, she wanted to scream. She was just so tired—not only in body, but in mind and soul as well. And clearly Joel was feeling the same.

How much more could they take? Both of them were stretched thin and ready to snap.

Her breath hitched and her heart felt like it stopped a moment later when John did not take another breath. He lay there, silent and still. She waited for him to breathe in, leaning forward and reaching out to him with her other hand, but he did not take another breath. Joel's hand tightened on her shoulder and from somewhere far away she heard a chaos of beeps and other unfamiliar sounds and then the sound of soft-soled shoes against the linoleum floor.

She could not make herself look away from John's face, not when they checked him for a heartbeat, not when they turned off the machines, not even when she heard the doctor tell his nurse to note the time of death, although she could hear a faint scratching sound from behind her.

She just sat there, looking at him as she held his hand in hers. She felt somehow that if she kept her eyes on him and his hand in hers that he could not go, like she could somehow keep him here if she just kept him in her sight, kept a hold on him. Even when her vision was completely clouded with tears, she could not make herself look away. She dashed the tears away with her free hand, but did not let go of his hand.

After some time, Joel went out to fetch her mamm and it was she who finally convinced Naomi to let him go. She came gently into the room and spoke quietly to Naomi.

Naomi might never remember what exactly her mamm had said to her in those moments, but something in the words, or maybe just the sound of her voice had been enough to break Naomi's hold. She had slowly let go of John's hand and allowed her mamm and Joel to lead her from the room.

. . .

They had buried John a few days later and Joel had been there behind her, supporting her the way he had been for so long. And still, she did not realize fully what his words in the hospital room had meant. Even having so much time to prepare herself for John's death, she found that she was having trouble dealing with it. There were so many emotions rushing through her as she stood there by the plain wood box that held her dear husband.

The worst part of all of it was—as she stood there, looking at the large opening before her, she could not help feeling like she had lost him ten years ago. The disease had taken him from her then and he had slipped away from her a little more every day since.

They had sat in the doctor's office on that day so long ago, and heard the words that told them John's days on this earth were numbered. John had told Naomi every day after that had been a gift, a loan from Gotte of more time in this world and not the next, but now it only seemed like a cruel joke.

Naomi was unable to see Gotte's plan in any of it. There had been nee more kinner and for a time even John had been angry about that. He had kept the anger to himself, but Naomi was his frau and she had seen it. She knew it was there and it had built a wall between them.

It had been months before John had pushed a block out of that wall and reached through it to her. And she'd held on to it like a lifeline. He had finally begun to let her back in to his thoughts then—and his fears.

She had been shocked to learn that his fears were tremendous. She'd not realized a man could have so many fears weighing him down—but he did and when he had finally shared them with her she felt so much better herself, that she had shared her own fears.

That day had marked a new beginning in their marriage. They had a young dochder to care for and they had some time left together and they were both determined to enjoy every minute of it as much as was possible. She had joined him in stepping forward into the unknown and they had been blessed with almost ten more years together.

But standing there beside his grave, she did not feel blessed. She felt cursed. John was gone and she was left here alone. Jah, she had Rebekah and their dochder would always be a small part of John left here with her, but Naomi felt so alone in that moment, it felt as if the earth beneath her feet should open up and swallow her, too.

She stood there with Rebekah's hand in her own, Joel and her dat and mamm standing behind her, the community surrounding them, and felt as though a part of her was in the box with John. Even though she had cried much in the days since John had passed, more tears found their way out and slipped down her cheeks, mixing with the light rain that had been falling all day.

Mamm's hand had slipped into hers and Naomi had been surprised to realize it felt like an anchor instead of a comfort. She wanted to turn and walk away—do anything to get away from this place, from these feelings, from the chains around her that were holding her so tightly to her *grief.*

She remembered wondering when she would ever be able to rid herself of those feelings. Wondering when—or if —she would ever be able to live again, breathe again, without feeling so tied to John's grave?

. . .

Less than a month after John's death, Joel had asked her properly—to marry him. Actually he hadn't asked, not really. It had been more like he was reminding her of something they had already talked about.

Naomi remembered the shock more clearly than anything else about that moment. Try as she might, she could not think of a single time they had talked about getting married. They had talked for a long time and finally the memory of Joel standing behind her that *nacht* at the hospital came back to her.

She could remember him telling her he would always take care of her, but she had certainly missed the meaning behind his words. How could he have possibly thought this was a *gut* idea—how could he truly think she would agree? She had not even had time to process John's death, much less grieve.

She had been even more shocked when she discovered that her parents expected her to take his proposal seriously. They thought it was the best thing for her and, while they didn't push, they did encourage her to agree . . . the whole community encouraged her. Joel had been running their farm by himself for so long by then, even though she legally owned John's portion of it, she certainly would not have wanted to cause a rift that could affect their entire community.

She might own John's portion of the farm, but she was not about to suggest Joel sell it any more than she expected him to buy it from her. Nor would she marry him simply to make everything easier for everyone.

So she had put him off; for two years she had put him off. And when she'd grown weary of putting him off, she had packed her bags and gotten on a train. As she felt tears threatening again, Naomi reminded herself that this was *Gotte's wille* and He would see them through it.

She didn't have to know how—she only had to trust Him and believe.

NINETEEN

Samuel watched the emotions flickering over Naomi's face in the moonlight. He could see that she was thinking serious thoughts. He wanted to ask her about them, but she looked as though she was not ready to share them. He realized he had *nee* idea how to handle that.

This would be a very different relationship than the one he'd had with Elisabeth. He and Elisabeth had grown up together. He had known everything about her long before they were married. They had needed *nee* time to learn about each other, though the bishop had insisted on it due to the customs of their community.

With Naomi, he must learn everything about her, and she about him. There was much they would have to discuss. Since they had both discovered *Gotte* had brought them together, the decision to marry had appeared obvious. But now worries were beginning to creep into his thoughts.

Would she be *froh* to move here to be with him or would she expect him to pick up and go to Ohio? Would she want to escape the painful memories in her own community or would she wish to hold them tight to her, even as she stepped into a new marriage with him? There was so much they needed to talk about. Naomi would have to let him into her thoughts and worries, and he would have to let her into his.

. . .

While Samuel worried over whether Naomi and Rebekah would be willing to move to New York, Naomi was plagued by her own worries and fears.

After several long minutes, she looked over at Samuel's face and then up at the sky overhead. She was so tired of being worried, of having to put Joel off. She was tired of only being able to rely on herself.

"Samuel, there are some things I must share with you before you can be certain you wish to marry me." And she waited for him to respond, praying silently that he would be agreeable. Still, his words surprised her.

"We have both agreed that we are in *Gotte's wille*. He wishes us to be married. However, I do agree that there are things we should share with each other before we take that step." He looked at her with such tenderness; it almost brought tears to her eyes. It had been so long since she had seen such tenderness for her from anyone.

"You need not be afraid. There is nothing you could tell me that would make me turn away from you."

There was tenderness in his voice as he spoke. It almost undid Naomi, but she knew this had to be done so she pressed on.

"I lost John two years ago now." Her voice broke a little before she went on. "At times, it seems as if I lost him much earlier. He was sick for such a long time. Rebekah does not remember a time when he was well and there are moments when the memories escape me as well."

She took a deep breath and continued. "His *bruder* Joel was a true blessing. He took over most of the responsibilities and all the work of the farm as John became even more ill. I am grateful to him for all that he has done for us since John's death." She took another deep breath as her voice broke again.

"I understand that it is often expected for a young widow to marry quickly. And it was expected of me as well. John made certain that Rebekah and I would be taken care of when he could *nee* longer . . ." It took a second before she could go on and Samuel sat there, patiently waiting until she was able.

"Even though I had *nee* need of financial support, it was expected that Joel and I would marry. He made it clear to my parents and the community that we would be married soon after John passed—clear to everyone but me, it would appear." She looked up at Samuel, trying to gauge his reaction.

"I have put Joel off for two years now and the whole time I was praying for *Gotte* to show me the answers, to show me what he wanted for me and now that I have finally found it, I feel such a joy and relief."

She looked up at Samuel again, hopeful that he would understand how very relieved she was and not misunderstand. She wanted so much to leave it at that, but she knew she could not. She would have to tell him everything if they were to have an open, honest union.

. . .

Samuel listened to everything she was telling him, but he was also trying to listen to what she was not saying. There was a lot of sadness and even a little anger in her words. He knew from his own experience that some plain people were not opposed to applying pressure when they thought it was time that you did what was expected of you.

His neighbor Elias often made the joke that the old Bishop, Ezra Raber, had liked to see them all lined up two by two, but he had certainly not been the only one who felt that way. Many of Samuel's neighbors probably felt the very same way and his own *bruder* certainly did. He had escaped much of that pressure, at least in part, because of how much everyone in the community had cared for his Elisabeth.

Clearly that had not been the case for Naomi. He felt heartsick as he thought of the way she had been maneuvered by the very people who were supposed to take care of her. And he knew then that he would do everything in his power to make certain she would *nee* longer be within reach of such treatment.

He would marry her and convince her to move here to be with them. He would show her that it was the most sensible thing to do. She could have a fresh start here, with a new family and a new community—neighbors who were already becoming quite fond of her.

But before he could tell her of his feelings about the injustice of it all, she went on.

.   .   .

She began to feel guilt pressing on her as Samuel sat there waiting for her to speak again. She knew he must be wondering what she was about to say and she was amazed he could sit there and remain so calm. At last she took another deep breath and launched into the worst of it.

"After John's death I grieved, perhaps more deeply than anyone expected me to. We had known it was coming for some time and I expect that everyone thought I could have grieved already. The truth of it is, I spent all of my time trying to hold on to him, to keep him with me, to enjoy whatever time we had that I never even allowed myself to think about having to let him go."

"And then after he passed, I found myself grieving for him so much more than I had thought possible. It was a long time before I realized that I was grieving not only for his loss, but for the ten years we had together that were so full of sadness and exhaustion." Her voice was brittle now, but she forced herself to keep talking, spilling it all out to him—and he sat there listening; which gave her the courage she needed to go on.

"We both spent those years feeling as if there was an ax hanging over our heads. We were not able to fully enjoy our union or even our *dochder* because of his illness and how weak he was physically. And I found myself angry at John as well. I knew it was not his fault, but I felt as if it were somehow."

"He had not known that he was sick, how could it be his fault? And yet, I blamed him for having only one *kind*. I blamed him for being sick all those years and I blamed him for leaving me." She kept talking and Samuel sat there so quietly, she couldn't help, but feel compelled to go on. Perhaps if she let it all out, she would finally begin to heal.

"I know it is not our way, but I could not seem to help myself. I was angry for so long and I felt as if he had abandoned me—and our *dochder*. I was blessed to have my *mamm* and *dat*. If not for them, I do not know what would have become of me. I..."

She stopped for a moment. It was painful to even think the words, much less to say them. Finally she took another breath, a different sort of breath. This was a bracing breath. This secret would be the thing to turn him away from her and she must prepare herself for the possibility, *nee* matter how certain she was about *Gotte's wille*. She closed her eyes and at the same time, opened her mouth to speak.

"I went away for a time; I do not know how else to

speak of that time. I was right there with everyone, but I was—at the same time—very far away from everyone. I do not know how much of it Rebekah remembers or even how much she realized at the time, but my parents were there for her. She was grieving at that time so she may not have realized what I was going through or how different it was from her own feelings. It took me a long time to dig myself out of the pit I had fallen into; I did not think that I would ever again find the person that I was before. I have learned now to be content with the person I have become."

She paused for a moment before saying, "I was blessed to have my *mamm* and *dat*. They were the only thing that kept me from losing myself completely." And with that she stopped, waiting for him to react, or to say something. She had managed to bare her soul to him and now she could only wait to see what he would say.

She could never have anticipated his words.

. . .

"It is always difficult to deal with death. Our *freinden* and loved ones do not always react in a predictable way. I could never have expected the way my community rallied around me and grieved with me after Elisabeth passed."

Smiling, he added, "and *nee* matter how beloved Elisabeth was by the entire community, I have a feeling that I would have been in very much the same position you were in when she passed, had there been a single woman in our community near my own age at the time."

"We do tend to push our loved ones to do what we believe will be best for them—especially when they are heart-broken." He said, thinking of his dear *bruder*, Josiah. As he said it, he was thankful to realize there was *nee* bitterness in him now, only *lieb* for Josiah—who only wanted what he thought was best for Samuel.

"It is not always what is best for them; we just want them to be *froh* again." He looked over at Naomi and was not surprised to see the shock on her face.

She had most likely expected him to be upset by her intense confession. He hoped it was only that most of the people in her own community had been unsure how to help her and so they had ignored her grief and tried to push her into another marriage too soon. If it were anything else, the thought would be unbearable.

"You did not expect me to understand, did you?"

She only shook her head slowly back and forth.

Samuel watched her with a slight twinkle in his eyes. He tried very hard to keep the amusement toned down though. She looked like she had carried this heavy burden for such a long time and he did not want to hurt her by appearing to make light of it.

"You are right, I did not. *Nee* one else does or has, even my *aenti*—who I have always felt had an especially close relationship with *Gotte*." She shook her head slightly and then kept going.

"Now that I think on it again, perhaps she did and I simply did not see it. She certainly understood why I was here before I did. You should have heard her when Jacob came home talking about—" She stopped suddenly and ducked her head, a blush coloring her cheeks again.

. . .

Naomi felt the blush creep up her cheeks just as she heard a delighted laugh from Samuel. She really hadn't meant to say all of that. He truly did muddle her thoughts.

"There is something about you. I cannot seem to keep hold of my tongue when you are near." And by the time the words tripped out of her mouth, she was laughing along with him.

They laughed for several minutes as they drove through the moonlit *nacht*. And Naomi suddenly stopped when she realized her hand was on Samuel's arm. She was surprised and *verhuddelt* by the feelings that were rushing through her.

She looked up at his face, surrounded by the bright light from the large moon hanging low in the *nacht* sky. It gave him the appearance of having a halo around his head. She had come here to find an answer to her problem and instead she had found the answer to her prayers, and she just might have found her own personal angel.

TWENTY

Leah stood at the window, watching for *Dat* to return. As she watched the moon shining on the new snow, she thought about supper and Naomi Yoder. She had worried and prayed and wished for a new *mamm* and now she saw a real possibility of having her prayers answered; of having the *mamm* she had wanted for so long.

She still wondered about what she had seen in Naomi's eyes at dinner. What had she been through that was so terrible? And why did Leah feel such a strong compulsion to protect someone she barely knew?

Could it be the same thing was compelling *Dat* to feel a need to court her? Or could it be that they both felt such strong emotions because *Gotte* intended for Naomi to become a part of their family and they were already so attached—because *Gotte* was giving them the feelings they needed to bind them all together?

She thought of how much she had wanted a *mamm* she could talk to. For so long now, she had prayed and begged *Gotte* to send her a new *mamm*, someone who could understand all of the strange things going on in Leah's heart and in her head right now.

And that made her think of Jacob. Would he *kumme* to visit her tonight or would he be content to wait until tomorrow? Would *Dat* be home in time or would their courting be discovered tonight?

Before she could think of anything else she was distracted by a noise from behind her. She turned to see her *bruder* coming down the stairs. He was heading toward the kitchen, but he stopped when he saw her.

"You would not be waiting up for *Dat,* would you Leah?" He was shaking his head as he said it. "He is *nee* young man out past curfew." David sounded very serious, but there was a smile on his face.

When Leah shook her head, but didn't say anything, he walked over to stand behind her at the window. She felt his hand lightly rest on her shoulder and his support made her feel a little better.

"Leah, certainly you are not worried for *Dat*? It is a nice clear *nacht*; there is *nee* reason for you to worry." He paused a moment, still waiting for Leah to say something. "Or are you worried about something else?"

Leah nearly told David then, about Jacob. It would be *gut* to have someone to talk to. But would he understand?

Had he and Catherine ever snuck off in the middle of the *nacht* for a buggy ride?

Somehow Leah could not picture her steady *bruder* doing such a thing—so she decided to keep it to herself.

It was several long seconds before she came up with something else she could talk to David about, something that would explain her behavior.

"I am not really worried; or if I am, it is not what you're thinking." She turned from the sink and looked at her *bruder*; he was so tall and strong. Would he share her feelings about Naomi or think she was being *gegisch*?

"When we were having supper, did you notice Naomi . . ." she never got to finish because he interrupted her.

"Her face, *jah* I did. She was warm and open and friendly one minute and then the next, she looked very cold and sad. What was that all about? Did she say anything to you after?"

Leah shook her head before answering. "*Nee*, she did not. I think *Dat* must have noticed it though. He was certainly watching her throughout the meal. Perhaps he will find out and share it with us . . ." she allowed her words to trail off because she truly did not think *Dat* would share anything so personal with them. Still . . . she held onto the hope that he would find out and protect Naomi from whatever it was.

"You must let *Dat* take care of this, Leah. He will find out what he needs to know about Naomi." His next words made Leah feel as if he had heard her very thoughts. " . . . and if there is something she needs protection from, he will take care of it. Of that, I am certain."

He placed a hand on her shoulder again and squeezed lightly. "*Dat* will take care of this."

She nodded; she knew her *bruder* was right, but it was difficult to stand here and do nothing.

"You will understand some day, little *schweschder*; when you have a young man who wants to make you his *frau*." Leah nodded quickly and then ducked her head so David would not see the blush that spread across her cheeks.

If only he knew . . . but she kept her thoughts to herself. She only knew Jacob wanted to court her. He had not said anything that would make her think he wanted to marry her.

After another moment, Leah turned back to the window and the two of them stood that way for a long time before David spoke again.

"You are not worried about Naomi are you; about whether she is right for *Dat* or not?"

Leah quickly shook her head. "*Nee*—I thought I would be. But to be honest, I cannot help but feel that she is part of *Gotte's wille* for our family." She said as she turned back to face him before going on. "*Nee* matter how long I have prayed for a new mother, I do not know that I ever truly expected *Dat* to find one. I loved *Mamm* so much— we all did. And I know I am not the only one in the community who thinks *Dat* should have married before now. I think *nee* one pushed him because everyone loved *Mamm* so much."

"The lack of single women near his age may have been a factor as well." He interrupted, with a smile tugging at the corners of his mouth. And Leah couldn't help but laugh.

"That may have had something to do with it, *jah*."

"But you know what I mean David, do you not?" She looked up at him and waited for him to answer.

"*Jah,* I do not know how I know . . . but I do. Even though we were not expecting her, it feels as if she is meant to be a part of the family."

"Exactly." Leah said quickly. "I feel almost as if we have been waiting for her; only her—as if *Gotte* intended this for us all along. And now that she is here, it is almost as if the family is complete again. Does that sound *schpassich*?"

"*Nee,* it does not. It sounds like what I have been thinking as well."

Leah was surprised by how wise her *bruder* looked as he continued.

"I believe you are right. She has been *Gotte's wille* for us all along. It is sad to think of *Mamm's* passing being a part of *Gotte's wille, but* He knows what is best for us and he must have known it was time for her to *kumme* home. And now he has brought us Naomi." David looked over Leah's shoulder to the view out the window and then kept talking. "Perhaps she needs us as much as we need her."

"*Jah,* maybe whatever has made her so sad, is something we can help with. And so *Gotte* has brought them together now." Saying it all out loud made Leah feel much better and she realized she was even smiling about it.

. . .

Samuel rode along in silence through the brightly lit *nacht*. He thought of all Naomi had told him of her past. She had been through much since her husband died. He was surprised to feel anger rise up in him, for her community and her parents and even her church leaders.

How could they mishandle her so badly?

A central part of their faith was the community they were all a part of. Even though some things differed between communities, the support of *freinden* and family was a very important part of their faith and they should never have treated a grieving widow in such a terrible way.

The church leaders should not have allowed it.

It was the bishop's responsibility to take care of all the members of his community, especially one trying to deal with such a loss. And her parents, did they care nothing for their *dochder*?

Samuel found himself wishing that they were going to Ohio to fetch Rebekah so that he could have a word with the people who had treated her so poorly in her time of need.

And it was that thought which finally made him realize where his thoughts were headed. He was beyond anger now; he was far too close to malice—or even revenge—for his own liking. The realization frightened him. He had not experienced such strong anger since before he was baptized into the church.

His feelings for Naomi were clearly much deeper than

he had realized and it worried him. How was it possible to have such strong feelings for someone he had only known a matter of days?

And what did this mean about his relationship with Elisabeth? How could his feelings for someone he had only just met, eclipse the feelings he'd had for Elisabeth? He had loved her dearly—everyone had. She had been beloved in their community and her death had been difficult for everyone.

But he knew he had never felt this sort of anger over anything having to do with Elisabeth. Could it simply be due to the differences in the two womens' lives?

Elisabeth had been so deeply loved in their community, *nee* one had ever had cause to treat her the way Naomi had been treated—and he had never had a reason to become so angry over someone's treatment of Elisabeth.

Could it be this simple? And did it mean that he would have reacted in exactly the same manner if someone had treated Elisabeth in such a way?

Certainly it did—it must. He would have gladly given his own life for Elisabeth. He would have done so in a moment if it could have saved Elisabeth, as he would do for any of his *kinner*. They were his very life and without them . . . well, the thought did not bear dwelling on.

. . .

David had finally convinced Leah to go to bed, but *nee* matter how hard she tried, she could not get to sleep. She sat in her own rocking chair, wrapped in the quilt *Mamm* had made for her and looking out her window at the moon hanging low in the sky.

The next thing she knew, her head drooped and then jerked up sharply as she caught herself dozing off. She sat there for another minute, shaking her head and trying to wake herself up before she pulled herself out of the chair and turning toward her bed. Finding out if *Dat* made it home *allrecht* would have to wait until morning. She was too tired to worry about it anymore.

But when she lay down on her bed and snuggled under the quilt, sleep would not come. The body that had been so tired was now fully alert. She could hear every creak in the *haus* as it settled for the *nacht* and every gust of wind from outside.

A loose shutter banged against the outside wall and her favorite maple tree's bare branches scraped against the drainpipe.

She lay in bed for what felt like hours before she finally decided that she would not be able to sleep, not until she knew for certain one way or the other so she got back out of bed, wrapped a warm robe securely around her and went out into the hall.

She had left her door open slightly so that she would hear *Dat*'s boots on the stairs if she happened to miss seeing him out her window, but she had not counted on falling asleep so she could easily have missed him both ways.

She walked as quietly as she could down the hall, avoiding the creaky board *Dat* had never fixed as she went. She stopped just outside *Dat*'s room and listened as intently as she could, but she could not hear breathing or snoring through the thick wood door.

I could go downstairs and look for his boots by the back door, she told herself. But there were many times he came in and did not remove them by the back door so it would not truly tell her anything, unless they were there of course. She turned to go downstairs and gasped, covering her mouth quickly with both hands, when she saw *Dat* standing at the top of the steps.

"Leah, what are you doing still awake at this hour?" He whispered the words, which made it impossible for her to tell if he was angry with her or not.

She held a hand to her speeding heart, but could not think of a single thing to say in response.

"Leah, were you waiting up for me?" He laughed quietly when she nodded.

"*Kumme*, let us go down and talk a bit."

He turned to go back down the stairs and Leah followed, relieved that he did not appear to be upset with her.

. . .

Samuel thought over his *dochder's* behavior as they walked down the stairs together. He had been praying for *Gotte* to show him how to help her and he had hope now that perhaps a new *mamm* could be what she needed.

He had not considered how she might react to his earlier news. He had been so *eiferich* to finally feel that he was in *Gotte's wille* that he had perhaps rushed telling them all. He should have heeded his own advice to Naomi that afternoon and given his own family a bit of time to become acquainted with her before making such an announcement.

He made his way to the kitchen and Leah followed quietly behind him. Once inside the kitchen, she walked over to put on water and went about setting out things for tea before turning back to him.

"Would you like *kaffe, Dat*?" She asked, and her voice was so flat and full of worry, it nearly made him laugh.

Was he truly so frightening? He worked to control the lips that wanted very much to twitch with amusement, certain that Leah would feel he was laughing at her.

"*Nee Danki,* Leah, morning is early enough for that." He watched her as she moved from the stove to the cabinet to take out everything she would need for her tea.

Her movements were unhurried, but there was an air of nervousness about her that worried him.

He waited until she walked over to the table and sat down opposite him before continuing. "*Dochder*, are you under the impression that you are in trouble?"

Her head came up immediately and the look of surprise on her face was such that it was all Samuel could do not to laugh. She did not say anything and he imagined she was going over the words in her head, trying to come up with the best answer so he decided that he must find a way to quell the misery in her before the misunderstanding went too far.

"Leah, I am sorry if my announcement this afternoon

felt too sudden for everyone. I was so *eiferich*, it never occurred to me what a shock the news might be to all of you. I simply wanted to share it. I have been praying so long for *Gotte's wille* in all of our lives and I finally feel that I have found it." He stopped there, waiting for her to say something.

"*Dat*, I do have a worry, but it is perhaps not the one you are thinking." She stopped, but he motioned for her to go on so she did.

"I am sure you saw Naomi's face at supper tonight..."

Samuel let out a breath of relief and rushed to interrupt his *dochder*. "Is that all you are worrying over Leah, truly?" He asked and when she nodded, he went on. "Naomi and I spoke about that very thing as I drove her home this evening. She was quite concerned, just as you are, and wanted to make certain I knew all about the issues."

Leah started to speak, but Samuel held up a hand to her. She closed her mouth and he went on. "I do not feel that I should discuss all of these things with you myself, but I would like you to sit down with Naomi and have a talk with her. She will be able to explain them much better than I am able. I feel it is important that the two of you discuss these things together."

"But she has already explained to you?"

"*Jah*, she has and I can assure you that there is no need for you to worry."

"Then that is *gut* enough for me. *Danki Dat*."

He was much relieved to see Leah smiling now. He felt as though an enormous weight had been lifted from his shoulders.

"Now *dochder*, morning will *kumme* early and tomorrow is the Lord's day. I think we both need rest."

"*Jah, Dat*. I will just finish my tea and then I will *kumme* up to bed."

Samuel stood then, moving over to drop a kiss on his *dochder's* uncovered head before turning toward the stairs. "*Gut nacht* then Leah."

"*Gut nacht Dat*."

TWENTY-ONE

Sunday dawned on a beautiful morning. Fresh snow had fallen during the *nacht* and there was a lovely new blanket of white covering everything. Leah stood at her window, looking out over the snow-covered fields and said her morning prayers while her *naerfich* fingers played with the strings of her *kapp*.

Jacob had not shown a flashlight in her window last *nacht* . . . or tossed any pebbles at it. And, while she felt *eiferich* about the gathering this evening, she also felt *naerfich*. She would be meeting his *freinden* and at the very least, his *schweschder*.

What if they don't like me? The thought had kept her awake for much of the *nacht*. Once she *nee* longer had to worry about *Dat,* she had begun worrying about the gathering in Jacob's district.

Oh well, at least getting there is easily explained. She knew *Dat* would be so *eiferich* to see her going to a gathering—and she hoped she would return in as *gut* a mood as she had been in when Jacob had asked her to *kumme.*

She prayed that *Gotte* would give her the opportunity to talk with Naomi as well. If she was to be Leah's new *mamm*, there should be peace between them. She thought of *Dat's* face last *nacht* as he had said how *gut* he felt about Naomi. Leah could see he was already in *lieb*—or very close to it.

It was the same look she had seen on David's face whenever Catherine knocked at the door. Leah was not certain how she felt about watching her *dat* looking like a lovesick young person. And she had a difficult time accepting that he was truly lovesick after so little a time.

Don't two people need more time to get to know each other? Can it really happen so quickly?

Leah had many questions, but she certainly did not want to ask *Dat* and she was not comfortable asking Naomi yet . . . or David. Perhaps she could ask Catherine.

Leah was glad to see *Dat* so full of joy. She found herself thinking about having the same thing for herself. She didn't know if it was too soon to think such things about Jacob or not, but she could not seem to help herself. So she prayed.

Dear Gotte, please give me wisdom and understanding in this new relationship with Jacob. Lead me as you are leading Dat and Naomi; to know what is right and gut.

Help me know what to do and what to say when I see Jacob tonight and please let me not make a fool of myself in front of his freinden and family.

Ach, how I miss Mamm.

The thought came to Leah so unexpectedly, she felt tears stinging her eyes. She truly did still miss her *mamm*, but now she was beginning to look forward to having Naomi to talk to. She would just have to make every effort to find time soon to speak with Naomi. The quicker they got to know each other, the quicker Leah would feel comfortable asking her about things like boys.

Of course it might be a bit difficult still—what with Jacob being her cousin. And Leah nearly laughed at herself. It was *gut* to be able to laugh over such silliness.

.   .   .

Naomi walked back and forth in front of the kitchen window, looking outside every few seconds. Samuel was not due to fetch her for another fifteen minutes, but she could not seem to stop herself from worrying. She had told him so many things about her past on the drive back to her *aenti's haus* last *nacht*.

He had looked and sounded as if he understood, but was it possible that he had only been saying those things to keep her from making a scene before he dropped her off and could safely escape?

Was I wrong to go into so much detail? Or could I be wrong about his feelings? Had he returned home only to have his family convince him that she was not the woman for him?

Did I make a gut enough impression on them? Had she shown them that she could be a *gut mamm* to them, a *gut frau* to Samuel?

Could I have been wrong about Gotte's leading?

"Naomi, you must stop that pacing. You are wearing a groove in the floor. Your *onkel* will not be pleased."

Aenti Ida's voice surprised her and nearly made her jump with fright. There was a slightly disapproving tone to her voice, but when Naomi turned to look at her, she could see the twinkle in her *aenti's* eyes and the smile that tugged at the corners of her mouth.

Naomi put a hand to her heart in an effort to slow the frantic beating. *Aenti* Ida was absolutely right. She could not remember the last time she had been so *naerfich*. She was a grown woman with a nearly grown *dochder* and here she was behaving like she was still in the schoolroom.

"One might think you were a bit *naerfich* if they did not know you as I do." Her *aenti's* smile was full of mischief and Naomi couldn't help herself; she was soon smiling in return, and then she was giggling, and her *aenti* was giggling with her so she gave in to the feelings that had been rushing through her ever since she had looked up and seen Samuel's face clearly. If she was going to feel like a schoolgirl, she might as well enjoy it.

They both jumped at the sound of a team pulling into the yard and then they were giggling again. *Onkel* Ephraim walked into the kitchen to tell them that Samuel had just pulled up outside.

He stopped right inside the door, looking from one to the other and the seriousness of his face set off another round of giggles. After a moment, he turned to go right back out, shaking his head as he went.

It was several minutes before they both calmed down enough to stop giggling and Naomi had to admit that she had not felt so *gut* in a very long time. Even discovering her newfound feelings for Samuel, she had been weighed down with so much worry over telling him all the things about her that she had not yet been able to truly enjoy it.

But standing in the kitchen and letting herself giggle right along with *Aenti* Ida had given her such a *wunderbaar* feeling and she was grateful for it. She looked over and was not surprised to see her *aenti* wiping tears out of her eyes. Naomi felt a few on her cheeks as well, but they were *gut* tears, healing tears, tears of laughter and *lieb* and they were refreshing.

Her *aenti* was smiling and there was still a *gut* deal of mischief in the curve of her lips.

"Still *naerfich,* Naomi?" She asked and Naomi could feel her eyes widen in surprise.

Why, her *aenti* sounded as if she had planned to *kumme* in and start Naomi laughing.

Well if she did, it was a gut plan. I feel so much better now.

"*Nee Aenti, danki.* I do not know how long it has been since I truly enjoyed a *gut* laugh." And she walked over to fold her *aenti* into a warm embrace. Ida hugged Naomi back tightly for a few moments before letting go and they both stepped back.

"*Kumme* now, we must go out to meet your Samuel. There is *nee* telling what tales your *onkel* is telling him by now." She laughed again as she said it.

Naomi looped her arm through her *aenti*'s and they headed for the side room. *Aenti* Ida helped Naomi into the warmer coat she had insisted Naomi use while visiting with them and then Ida pulled on her own coat before they stepped outside into the cold, still air.

Naomi breathed deeply and found that the crisp, cold air felt different to her this morning. She wondered if it was the promise of what was to come or simply that she was finally beginning to relax and enjoy herself.

It certainly wasn't the weather itself. She had looked at the thermometer outside her *aenti*'s kitchen window several times as she had walked back and forth earlier and the temperature was a full ten degrees lower than the day before.

And I thought the drive back last nacht was cold. Though she had only felt cold last *nacht* when she sat there worrying over what she was telling Samuel.

Then he had told her he understood completely and she couldn't remember feeling cold after that.

Samuel turned to smile at her as he spoke with her *onkel* and she realized what the *wunderbaar* feeling was. The ice around her heart that had been threatening to destroy her since John died was finally gone. Samuel had melted it.

Onkel Ephraim was saying something to Samuel, but Naomi was much too distracted to pay any attention to what her *onkel* was saying. She felt her *aenti* shake with laughter beside her and decided she probably didn't really want to know. There was *nee* telling what her *aenti* and *onkel* were telling Samuel while she was standing here in a daze of *lieb*.

Just then she looked down to see Samuel holding out a hand to her. She moved quickly down the steps to place her hand in his. They moved to his buggy and it felt like her feet never touched the ground.

He helped her up into the buggy and then helped her tuck the extra blankets he had brought around her, before climbing up beside her. She felt *lieb* settle around her like one of the warm blankets; one she would happily leave there forever. She snuggled in for the drive and smiled up at Samuel, who clicked his tongue to the team before the buggy moved forward.

She waved to her *aenti* and *onkel*. She was pleased to see them standing there together waving, her *onkel*'s arm around *Aenti* Ida's waist, a smile on both their faces. She thought she might have even seen her *onkel* wink at her as the buggy moved off down the lane.

. . .

Samuel watched Naomi out of the corner of his eye. She looked different this morning—relaxed; perhaps more settled. He was glad she had decided to let the weight of her past drop off of her shoulders by telling him all about it last *nacht*. He was hesitant to mention Leah's worries for fear it might put some of the shadows back into her eyes.

For a long time they rode in a companionable silence. Even though the temperature had dropped considerably, the day was beautiful and the fresh layer of snow on everything made it even more so.

There was very little wind and that was quite rare. Their community was called Windy Gap for a reason. This season was usually the time of year for fierce winds to blow through their little valley, but for some reason even the wind had calmed today. It felt almost like a sign to Samuel that everything was as it should be.

He was content to enjoy the drive and the company as they rode toward what would soon be home and family for both of them.

He was surprised when Naomi turned to him and asked about the very thing he had been trying not to bother her with.

"Samuel, did anyone have questions or worries when you returned home last *nacht?*"

As he turned to look at her, he was once again struck by her smile. *Gotte* had truly blessed her, and him as well. He hoped to be able to enjoy her smile for many years to come.

He took both lines in one hand and laid his empty hand over hers before answering.

"Naomi, you have nothing to worry about where I am concerned." Somehow he knew she had been worrying herself over whether or not the rest of his family liked her and he must find a way to make her understand.

"Leah was awake last *nacht* when I returned home and she and I had a bit of a talk. It took some convincing to get her to tell me what was bothering her and I told her that I felt it would be a *gut* idea for her to speak with you about her worries." He looked at Naomi when he felt her tiny hand tense under his.

"Truly Naomi, you do not need to worry over this. Leah is much more concerned about what has hurt you in the past than whether or not you are a suitable *frau* for her *dat*." And he was very relieved to feel the tension in her hand ease a little.

"Truly?"

Naomi finally turned her face back to his and Samuel was not at all surprised to see a tear slipping slowly down her cheek. In the next moment, he determined to put the smile back on her sweet face though.

"Truly, Naomi. When she spoke to me, all I could sense in her words was a concern for you—not about you. Like me, she wants to protect you."

He slowed the buggy as they came to a large area that was typically used to pull off and allow a vehicle to pass. Once the horses were stopped and settled, he shifted to face Naomi.

"You are worrying yourself too much over this." He felt anger rise up in him again; anger at her community and even at her own family. They should never have allowed such treatment of this *wunderbaar,* gentle woman.

"I do not want you to worry about this anymore, Naomi. I am their *dat* and I can assure you, they have already accepted you into the family. I know my *kinner* well."

237

Samuel leaned in to pull Naomi into a tight embrace. He felt all of the weight that had rested heavily on him only moments ago lift away and as his tension fell away, he began to think about the woman in his arms—in the way of a husband.

He began to think of her in his home, in his kitchen, and in his bed. He thought of watching her sit in a rocking chair by the fire, quilting with Leah and Lillian. He thought of kissing her first thing in the morning, when he woke up to go out to take care of the morning chores. He thought of coming into the kitchen and moving in behind her, wrapping his arms around her as she prepared breakfast for the family.

He thought of snuggling with her on cold winter *nachts,* under soft flannel sheets. He thought of seeing her, as she grew round with his *kind*; and he thought of watching her as she nursed.

As those thoughts ran through his mind, Samuel realized this was the first time in ten years that he had truly thought about the things that went on between a husband and his *frau*; and suddenly he could hardly wait to be married to her.

He pulled back slightly from Naomi; saw her smile was as warm and beautiful as it had been a few moments ago. Though he knew he was toying with a very fine line, he could not help himself; he leaned in and gave her a very quick kiss.

At least . . . it was supposed to be a quick kiss; just a slight meeting of the lips to show Naomi how delighted he was with her and that he was *eiferich* to be moving forward with their plans.

But the moment their lips touched, it changed. They did not linger; he knew they did not. They nearly leaped apart like guilty *kinner* at the spark that ignited when their lips met! And Samuel was surprised the snow around the buggy did not melt into a steaming puddle as they sat there; so sudden was the blazing heat he could feel between them.

He watched Naomi touch her fingers gently to her lips, and while he wondered what she was thinking, he knew they should push on toward home. Even though he had not thought of it in many years, he had been married long enough to know just how quickly the passion between two people could lead them somewhere they had *nee* business going before they were properly wed.

He felt a smile spread across his face and he looked at her only long enough to make certain that she was settled firmly into her seat before turning back and taking hold of the reins.

He clicked his tongue at the team and signaled them to pick up the pace a bit.

TWENTY-TWO

Leah sat, trying to listen attentively to the bishop, but she was certain that later she would never remember a word he said. Now that she was sitting here in the service, with only a few hours until the gathering in Jacob's district, she was more *naerfich* than she could ever remember feeling before.

Nee matter how hard she tried, she could not seem to focus on what the bishop was saying. She was thinking of the coming evening; thinking of meeting Jacob's younger *schweschder* and his *freinden*.

She was nearly sick with worry that they would not like her and then Jacob would decide he did not want to court her anymore.

Leah was so intent on her worries that she very nearly

missed the singing. Fortunately, Ada nudged her with an elbow just in time. She dared not look around to see if anyone had noticed, because they certainly would then. She simply joined in with the singing and hoped *nee* one had noticed her distraction.

There would be time later to pray more.

. . .

Samuel sat on the hard bench and felt as if he were sitting on a thick cushion. He tried so hard to listen to the sermon, but he feared that he might only be hearing every third word, so distracted he was.

After a time, the bishop's words finally began to penetrate his thoughts. He liked Bishop Beiler's way of speaking. His voice and the enthusiasm in it made the words from their beloved Bible simply come to life.

Listening to the bishop's voice, Samuel could almost see the scenes playing out in front of him. It made the services move quickly; they almost seemed to be over too early.

Samuel was *froh* in this moment that he had listened to Elisabeth's council when the district had separated. He would not soon regret that. He also felt that the bishop's views might be one reason *nee* one had pushed him to remarry after Elisabeth passed.

He liked Bishop Beiler—as a leader, a person, and a *freind*. Noah Beiler was one who anyone in their community would feel comfortable talking with. Their previous bishop had not been that way at all.

Samuel was not certain if it was due to his youth or not, but Bishop Beiler had a very forward-thinking view of things. Samuel would not say it to just anyone, but he suspected it was one of the reasons most of the older members had gone with Bishop Raber when the community split into two districts.

Samuel had been inclined to follow Bishop Raber when the community split. His *bruder*'s family had followed Bishop Raber, but his other *bruders* and neighbors had stayed in this district with the new bishop.

When the announcement had been made during service that the district was becoming much too crowded and that they would be splitting up soon, he and everyone else in the community had begun to pray about which district to choose; to stay here with Bishop Beiler or to follow Bishop Raber.

He remembered that he and Elisabeth had spoken many times about the differences between the two bishops. Bishop Beiler was younger than Samuel by fifteen years so Samuel was immediately concerned about the issues that might arise with such a young man in charge of things.

Elisabeth had pointed out that he was young enough to still heed the council of his elders, but old enough to be past most of the foolishness that affected young men.

Samuel had been more inclined from the start to follow the Bishop he was familiar with; the man he had grown up listening to, the man who had wed him to his *frau*, the man he knew well already.

Bishop Raber had been over their community for

many years and Samuel was comfortable with his council. He was not certain he would be able to open up with a man who was so much younger than he; and Elisabeth had taken that opportunity to point out that it might not be many more years until that district would be getting a new bishop themselves and at least they both knew Noah Beiler fairly well.

He was also quite certain that his marriage to Naomi and her subsequent transfer to their church district would be a much smoother transition with Bishop Beiler. He just had to find the appropriate time to bring the subject up with the bishop. And the quicker he got to it, the quicker he and Naomi could be married and become a family.

Thinking of marriage and how he and Elisabeth had talked over things made him realize that he had rarely won an argument with Elisabeth. She had always been so determined in her thoughts and decisions and though he had sometimes done things the way he wanted and not the way she was sure they should, he could not help feeling that he had not truly won; he had only done it his way.

And, as he sat here thinking back to that last real argument with Elisabeth that he had lost, he wondered about Naomi.

Would she be the type to argue quietly, with logic and reason and scripture to back up her opinions? Would she be one to just quietly follow Samuel's lead, never arguing or presenting a different viewpoint? Or would she be one who argued passionately, fiercely, for whatever she believed strongly about, giving him the chance to argue just so that she could make her point?

Elisabeth's style had been the first and Samuel did not think it was possible that Naomi would share that trait with her. Many of the women in their community were very much of the second style and Samuel found himself hoping fervently that Naomi was not. He truly felt that her style was the third; she might be a quiet woman, but there was something about her that spoke of passion under the surface.

Knowing what he did about how her own community had treated her after her husband's death, he would understand if she were more like the women who submitted without question or argument. However, the fact that she had left that community and come here searching for something different, told him that it was much more likely that she would be more passionate about her feelings and beliefs.

Something about that idea made him very *eiferich*. He could hardly wait to have an argument with her, if only to see how she would react.

. . .

Naomi sat and listened to the singing around her. Out of respect to the bishop she had not looked around during the service, but she did look around for a few moments when the singing began. She was *eiferich* to get a look at the people in the community that she had not met. She was also *eiferich* to discover how much she enjoyed the services in this community.

She had enjoyed the services in her own community; the bishop was a very *gut* man and he had been a *gut freind* to John so he would always have a special place in her heart. He was a young man like the bishop here, but perhaps not quite as young.

When everyone had pushed for her to marry Joel, he had been one of only a few who had not pushed. She had never known if it was due to his own friendship with John or simply in his role as bishop. He knew how important it was to follow *Gotte's* leading and she had spoken with him about feeling that it was not in *Gotte's wille* for her to marry Joel.

She thought back to yesterday... meeting young Katie Beiler and her two small *kinner* yesterday had given her some insight into Bishop Beiler. She could tell simply by looking that Katie Beiler and her *kinner* were very *froh*. The *kinner* had been very well behaved even after their *mamm* had given them permission to run a bit and play with the other *kinner*. They had run through the kitchen a few times, laughter bubbling from them as they went, but they had never once been in anyone's way.

And Naomi smiled a little as she remembered that not one of the other women in the kitchen had even looked up at the chaos around them whenever one of the *kinner* ran through the room.

She had spent so much of her time watching the little ones playing. This community was simply full of families with small *kinner* and she knew that would be a tremendous comfort to her—even if it might also cause her some pain to see other women with their small *kinner* and *bopplin*.

The one thing she had worried she would miss here was the singing in her own district. In her own church, there had been such *wunderbaar* singing, so many beautiful voices being raised together to praise *Gotte*; she had worried that it might not be the same here.

She knew from the letters from her *aenti* that the singing was not the same in every community. Their own service had few voices that were truly a blessing to listen to and because of that the singing was very quiet and perhaps even a bit quick.

In this community, the voices around her reminded her much of her own district. It was *wunderbaar* to discover that there were things here that were much the same as her home community. It made her feel as if she was still very much at home and this was a comfort indeed.

She snuck a quick look around her again. These would be her new neighbors, her new community. She was glad to see the ones she had not met looked just as nice as the ones she had.

She would be truly blessed to become a member of this community.

She found herself wondering when Samuel would speak to the church leaders, how soon they could begin to communicate with her own church leaders. She was surprisingly anxious to get things moving along. It was surprising how *eiferich* and anxious she was. She could not remember feeling this way about a relationship in such a long time. It was *gut* to know she was still open to romance.

She had worried that her heart had broken in such a way that she could not open it up to anyone else. How else could she explain that she could not open her heart to Joel? He had been there for her for so long.

Even before John became so sick, he had been there for her, helping her and Rebekah, making certain that they had what they needed, making certain that the farm kept going.

It had never made sense to her that she could not open her heart to him and she had been worried. Now she didn't have to worry. She knew she was able to open her heart, simply not with a man who wasn't the man *Gotte* intended for her.

It was not likely to make the situation with Joel any easier. He would not understand, of that she was sure, but he was a *gut* man. He would let her go gracefully and perhaps one day he could perhaps even find it in his heart to be *froh* for her and Samuel.

TWENTY-THREE

Leah moved around the barn helping to get things ready to carry to the tables that had been set up for the afternoon meal. Anna was organizing and one of their neighbors had somehow maneuvered Miriam into watching the little ones in one of the upstairs bedrooms. Ruth was helping the other ladies carry platters of food back and forth to the *sitzschtupp*.

Standing next to Ada and Beth as they chattered, Leah set out disposable cups for the *kinner* and tried to look like she was interested in the conversation floating around her.

She did not think she'd truly heard one word, but *nee* one seemed to notice how distracted she had been all afternoon and she was glad of it.

There was only one thing on Leah's mind—Jacob. In a few hours she would be climbing into a buggy with her neighbors and heading to Jacob's district.

She let out a gasp of surprise when she felt a hand on her arm.

"Leah, your *dat* sent me to find you. He said you could help me find an extra tea pitcher."

Leah was amazed to find that she recognized the voice in her ear—but then, Naomi had such a quiet voice and the cadence of her words was very different from what she was used to hearing so it should not be too much of a surprise.

She took a deep breath, trying to calm her speeding heart and turned to answer Naomi. "*Jah* Naomi, I can help you with that." She looked around at the faces of her neighbors and was surprised to see several smiles that looked a bit embarrassed.

Had she been so deep in thought that she had not immediately heard Naomi?

She backed away a few steps before turning to Naomi. They moved together toward the *haus* and guilt tugged at Leah as their steps blended together on the snowy path. Only last *nacht*, she had told *Dat* how much she worried for Naomi and today she was practically ignoring her. She turned to Naomi as they walked.

"*Danki*, Naomi." She turned with a smile, but the look on Naomi's face was more confused than anything.

"My pleasure Leah. For what—if I may ask?" She laughed a little as she said it and Leah was surprised at how different Naomi's laugh was from *Mamm*'s. It was a light tinkling sound, almost like the wind chimes Leah had seen at the general store in town.

It was then Leah realized how little there was about Naomi that made her think of *Mamm*. What could that mean? And was it *gut* or bad?

"For seeking me out. I mentioned to *Dat* last *nacht* that I was concerned and it appears you have *kumme* to speak with me. You could easily have avoided me." She smiled again as Naomi let out another small laugh.

"I really do need an extra tea pitcher, though."

And Leah laughed with her.

"Well, we had best find one." And Leah led the way inside with Naomi following closely.

"Leah, I do not think this is the place to tell you everything that I have told your *dat* about my past, but I do want to share with you." When they stopped, Naomi took one of Leah's hands in her own and squeezed as she went on.

"I want you to understand and I intend to share it all with you—with the whole family." She stopped again for a moment, but before Leah could say anything, she kept going. "There is much about my life in Ohio that was . . ." she stopped and it seemed to Leah that she was trying to find the right word to use; it was several minutes before she went on again. ". . . difficult for me."

"I am so pleased that *Gotte* has brought me here and I feel blessed indeed to have found what I truly believe is *Gotte's* plan for me."

Leah felt herself nodding as Naomi spoke. *Dat* had said very much the same already and Leah knew it was not for her to question *Gotte's wille.* If they both felt that they were in His *wille,* who was Leah to argue?

"You do understand, don't you Leah?"

Leah nodded in answer and a moment later, Naomi let out a sigh of such relief.

"*Gut. Danki,* Leah. I promise you that we will find time to speak soon." She did not let go of Leah's hand, but turned and walked with Leah to the kitchen to find the pitcher.

"Be still and know that I am Gotte."

The words floated right into Leah's head as she moved through the *haus* with Naomi and she nearly stumbled in surprise. She was not certain where the words had come from, unless Gotte was speaking to her.

Does that mean I am supposed to simply trust you? Or are you reminding me that you know what is best for me?

Leah's steps had slowed, but she still strained to hear the voice again as she continued through the *haus.*

"Be still and know that I am Gotte."

The answer was *nee* clearer this time, but Leah was thrilled to know that Gotte was answering her. She would figure out what it all meant later.

. . .

Samuel stood there looking at the bishop. He could not believe what he was hearing. Bishop Beiler was laughing. What could this mean? Was he amused or did he possibly think Samuel was only joking? Samuel was not quite sure what to say now. Fortunately, he was saved from having to say anything.

"I apologize, Samuel. I assure you, I am not laughing

at you. To be honest, it is with great relief that I receive your request. I have been praying for news of this very event for some time now. It is a blessing indeed. Would this be the young woman from a neighboring district who helped to set up for services yesterday?"

Samuel almost asked the bishop how he knew about it before he remembered that he had seen the bishop's *frau* arriving with her young *kinner*. He had come out of the barn for only a moment and he had watched her walk up to the door holding a very large basket. He had marveled at the very well behaved *kinner* standing behind her, almost like little ducklings.

Elisabeth had also possessed an uncanny knack for drawing excellent behavior from their *kinner*. He did not recall their *kinner* ever having followed her around like ducklings, but he did remember they were always right by her side whenever they were in town or at a new place.

She had been the essence of calm and grace—always. There had been times, rare, but still, times that her calm had inflamed his temper. He could remember feeling anger claw at him that she was able to remain so calm when he was not. He had always taken himself off to pray when those thoughts came to him. He knew it was the tempter's influence and prayer was the only hope against such a thing.

In the years since Elisabeth had passed, with much prayer, *Gotte* had helped him to overcome his temper and many other things as well—which was why he had been praying dutifully about this very conversation.

He had never had much cause to speak with Bishop

Beiler and he had not been looking forward to this time. He had been ready to argue; he had several different arguments ready in fact, but he had not expected them to be unnecessary. He could not have expected the bishop to be so delighted and amused by his request.

Samuel had a very uncomfortable feeling that Bishop Raber would not have been as delighted by his request. And Samuel was again thankful that he had listened to Elisabeth's council. *Gotte* did indeed work in mysterious ways.

.   .   .

Nearly an hour after Leah's conversation with Naomi, she was sitting in a buggy beside Eliza and Sarah Yoder on her way to Jacob's district. She should have been *naerfich*, but she kept thinking back to the voice she had heard earlier today. For some reason, she did not think *Gotte* had only been speaking of Naomi.

Leah was convinced that He had also been speaking of Jacob. It truly did not matter how Leah felt about him, if he were not the young man *Gotte* had in mind for her— well then, she wanted nothing more than to find out quickly. And if he were the young man for her, then she had nothing to be *naerfich* about.

As the buggy bumped its way down the road, Sarah filled the silence with chatter and Leah began to realize why Eliza was so quiet. If Sarah was this way at home, it was a wonder anyone else had a chance to speak a word.

It made Leah thankful for her own *bruders* and

schweschders. There were times that Lillian would talk non-stop—especially when she was very *eiferich* about something—but never without giving anyone else a chance to speak.

Sarah had done that very thing, though. Ever since they had climbed into the buggy, Sarah had been chattering. Several times when she had taken a breath, Leah had tried to say something to Eliza, but Sarah had rushed back in to fill the silence each time—before Leah could say a word.

The second time it happened, Eliza happened to be looking at Leah and her expression answered the question Leah could not possibly voice without being rude. It was all Leah could do not to laugh out loud when Eliza grinned and rolled her eyes a little toward her talkative *schweschder*.

The ride took a lot less time than Leah would have thought. She realized it was most likely because of the constant distraction of Sarah's talking and she was thankful when she realized that she had not thought once to worry. She had been so distracted by Sarah's non-stop chatter and wild hand gestures that she had never had the chance to think about where they were headed.

When Eliza parked the buggy, two young men came walking out of the large barn a few feet from them and began unhooking the horses. One of them nodded to Eliza, but the other kept his head down, not saying anything at all and Leah wondered at it because a blush spread across Eliza's cheeks as soon as they walked away with the horses.

"*Kumme* on, let's go!"

Since Sarah was practically pushing them both out of the buggy, Leah turned to step down and she was surprised to see Jacob waiting to help her down. She hadn't seen him when they pulled into the yard so he must have walked up while she was paying attention to Eliza and the two young men who had taken the horses.

"You made it." His smile could not have been any bigger; which made Leah feel better right away. Clearly he was *eiferich* to see her.

"*Jah,* of course. I would not have missed it." She smiled as she spoke.

He reached up and placed his hands on either side of her waist, lifting her down as if she weighed *nee* more than a feather and her heart sped up at his touch.

Leah knew she couldn't possibly feel the heat of his hands through her thick dress and coat, but it certainly seemed as if she could. There was an unexpected warmth where his hands held tight against her waist—and it quickly spread through her. She smiled up at Jacob when he set her on her feet beside the buggy wheels.

He took hold of her hand, pulling her along with him as he walked around to the other side of the buggy where another young man was helping Sarah down.

Sarah was looking up at the young man with an expression that Leah imagined mirrored her own. It didn't take much to figure out that this must be the person who drew the *schweschders* to gatherings in this district.

Remembering her plan to get Eliza to open up a bit more, Leah looked around for Eliza, but she was nowhere in sight. Where could she have gone so quickly?

"Is everything OK?" Jacob asked, and his voice was right next to her ear, nearly startling her.

"*Jah,* everything is fine, Jacob. I was only wondering where Eliza had disappeared to."

He let out a low chuckle and nodded his head in a direction not far from them. "I do believe she is less shy than you may have thought."

Leah looked in the direction Jacob had nodded and her mouth dropped open in shock. Eliza Yoder was standing in the midst of a group of boys, talking and gesturing excitedly, her eyes bright and her features more animated than Leah could ever remember seeing them.

It took a moment for Leah to find her voice again. "Well I suppose she does not need my help with coming out of her shell, after all." Then she laughed with Jacob, as he led her across the wide yard, toward the group of young people.

After the first few feet, their progress was hampered by the dozen or more young people who stopped them, asking about her. There were *maedels* as well as boys and they all seemed very curious indeed; which left Leah wondering whether Jacob had ever brought someone from another district—or if he had simply never been so public with his attention before.

Even though every person she met was nice; she had to laugh at some of the antics of his *freinden.* Several young men even teased Jacob that they would like to steal her away for their own . . . at least she hoped they were only teasing.

As if he had heard her thoughts; Jacob said in a quiet voice, "They are only teasing . . . I hope you know that," and when she looked up at him, he went on, "If you had not noticed, we have an abundance of young men, but our district is low on *maedels.*"

He laughed then and a very strange feeling made its way through Leah at the deep, rich sound and the tickle of breath on her ear.

"Do not worry. I intend to keep a *gut* hold on you. Let them find their own *maedels.*"

His words sent another rush of warmth through her and she found herself holding his hand a little tighter as they continued walking toward the large bonfire that most of the youth had made their way to by now.

As they did, Leah noticed several other *maedels* from her district. She had never realized so many of her neighbors traveled this far for the gatherings of another district. Perhaps she should have been attending more of the gatherings in her own district. Then she might have noticed.

They made their way across the large open field, packed snow crunching under their boots, while Leah looked around her. There were nearly three boys for every *maedel* she saw. It was *nee* wonder that the other boys were teasing Jacob. He had done what many of them had not.

Before she even realized it, she found herself worrying about Jacob's reasons for wanting her here. Had he simply wanted to see her in the daylight hours or was he using her to make the other boys envious? After all, he had not *kumme* to any of their gatherings.

And who did you attend the last gathering with? A tiny voice in the back of her head whispered.

Right away she felt terrible. She had attended the last gathering with Zeke Hershberger—and she had never even told Jacob. She looked up at him then and forced herself to smile when he squeezed her hand.

She smiled as they walked over to a long table and picked up two large insulated cups filled with hot cocoa; she smiled as they moved closer to the fire and Jacob speared two hot dogs for himself before handing her a long stick with one stuck on the end, and she smiled while they roasted the hot dogs.

She kept smiling when they put their finished treats into buns and smeared on all sorts of toppings. She barely paid any attention to what she put on hers and she hoped he wouldn't notice how distracted she was, trying to think of how and when she could tell him about what had happened.

It was *nee* time at all before Jacob settled her on a *wunderbaar* wood bench that was close enough to the bonfire to keep her warm, but not so close that she would be too hot. As soon as she was settled, he went to get another cup of hot cocoa for them both and while he was gone, she began to worry.

Will he be angry with me? Will he decide he doesn't want to see me again? Ach! What will I do then? Thoughts were rushing through her head, making her feel dizzy, and when a hand dropped on her shoulder; she nearly fell off the bench.

"*Ach,* I'm sorry. I didn't mean to scare you." And Leah felt relief flood through her when she recognized Eliza's voice.

"I was going to ask if you are having a *gut* time, but now I think I will ask if you are *allrecht* instead . . ." her voice was full of confusion and Leah debated whether or not to share with Eliza what she was worrying about.

It would be *gut* to have someone else to talk to about this and she really didn't have anyone else she could ask about it . . . but she was uncertain if it was something she ought to share with someone she barely knew.

"Leah, *was iss letz?* You are white as a sheet." Eliza put her hand on Leah's arm and there was such concern in her expression, Leah knew she had to take the chance.

"It is *lecherich* and you will most likely think me a *gegisch maedel, but* I have to talk to someone about it."

"I would never think you *gegisch,* Leah. Tell me what has you so worried." There was *nee* judgment in Eliza's voice—which was the only thing that gave Leah the strength to go on.

"I only met Jacob a few weeks ago and in the most *schpassich* way. And I had *nee* idea he was interested in courting until he showed up outside my window one *nacht.*"

Eliza nodded, but said nothing, so Leah went on.

"The next day *Dat* announced that we were going to visit his *bruder* and we stayed there the *nacht.* After we returned, I went into town and met up with Jacob, but it was completely unplanned. We went to *Sew Sweet* and had hot cocoa and talked quite a lot." Leah could feel heat in her cheeks as she talked, but there was nothing to do now. She had started the story; she must finish it.

"Later that evening, Zeke Hershberger showed up to drive me to the gathering. I did not know what to say so I agreed to go with him." She allowed her head to drop into her hands as she said the last words and it was probably a miracle that Eliza even understood her. "I did not tell Zeke anything about Jacob and I have not told Jacob about Zeke."

"Zeke who? Not Zeke Beiler . . . Has he been over here bothering you?"

Leah's head snapped up at the sound of Jacob's voice and both hands flew up to cover her mouth. She looked at Eliza, but there was *nee* help from that direction and Leah hoped her face did not look quite as guilty as Eliza's did.

"I . . . I think I need to . . ." Eliza sputtered a little and then mumbled something that sounded like ". . . check on Sarah," before making her escape.

. . .

When Leah said nothing, only sat there with both hands over her mouth, Jacob walked around to face her and squatted down so that his face was level with hers.

"Leah, *was iss letz?* All you *allrecht?* Did someone say anything to upset you?" And he watched her face for any sign of distress.

She sat before him with both hands clamped tightly over her mouth and her eyes were nearly as big as saucers and full of fear, but she said nothing in answer.

"Please, Leah, tell me what is going on. I want to help, but I cannot if I do not know what has happened." He reached up and tried to gently pull her hands away, but he soon realized he would have to wait until she was ready to speak.

Finally, after what had begun to feel like an eternity, she lowered her hands, but the fear did not leave her eyes. "Jacob, I do hope you will not be angry with me. I really did mean to tell you about this."

She stopped a moment, took a deep breath and then launched into an explanation that was much longer than he had expected.

He listened to her words, trying to figure out what about it had upset her so. She mentioned that first *nacht* they had taken a buggy ride, went on to talk about how her *dat* had surprised them with the announcement that they would be visiting his *bruder*, went on to talk about how she had met him in town that day nearly a week ago now.

It took several minutes for her to get to it but she finally did. And when she did, her forehead dropped back into her open hands and he thought he might have heard tears in her voice. He thought of her words and realized she thought he would be angry with her over this Zeke Hershberger who had driven her to the gathering in her district.

"Leah," he waited until she looked up at him before going on, "You think I am angry with you because you rode to the gathering in your district with a boy you have known your whole life, but have *nee* interest in otherwise?"

Her "*jah*" came out somewhere between a squeak and a whisper and he smiled at how terrified she sounded.

"Leah, you have *nee* interest in this Zeke Hershberger, *jah?* He is just a *gut freind, jah?*" He asked, and she answered with a nod—her eyes still nearly the size of saucers.

"Why would I be angry with you about that? If you were trying to make me jealous or you were seeing both of us at the same time or you lied to me about it, I might have a reason to be angry. But it sounds to me like you had very little choice in the whole situation."

She nodded but said nothing, so he kept going. "You had *nee* way of knowing then that I was serious about wanting to court you, and you might have hurt your *dat's* feelings or he might have thought you disrespectful if you had refused with *nee gut* reason . . . *Jah?*"

She nodded again but still said nothing.

"Leah do you wish me to court you?"

Her eyes finally relaxed and her face lit up in the most brilliant smile he had seen from her yet.

"*Jah,* Jacob, I would like that very much." And the stiff posture of her shoulders finally relaxed.

He felt his own posture relax when she did. She had really had him worried for a minute there.

"When would you like to tell your family about us?"

She opened her mouth to speak but instead tucked her bottom lip between her teeth and the smile fluttered away.

Jacob was immediately torn between the rush of

warmth that filled his gut when she started chewing on her lower lip—and the tug of worry that he had caused the smile to leave her face.

"*Ach* Jacob, I do not know." She reached out and took hold of his hand when he started to speak. "I want to tell them. Truly I do—but I am not certain it is the right time. *Dat* has just announced that he intends to marry your cousin Naomi and there is so much to be done still for David and Catherine's wedding, and Naomi's *dochder* is coming in on the train soon."

She worried that lip some more and it took all of Jacob's willpower to look away from her mouth.

"I just do not know that they need anything more to think on just this minute."

As she looked at him, her lower lip was caught again between her teeth. He tried to think of what she had just said.

She does not think now is the time to tell her family we are courting. Jah, that was it.

Well, as long as they could keep spending time together, he did not particularly care when they told her family.

"Whatever you think is best, Leah," and then he added in a rush, "but we can continue to court in the meantime, *jah?*"

Leah nodded and her smile returned, but she caught her lip between her teeth again. It was all he could do to tear his gaze away from it.

"Hey, how about we go make some s'mores?" He pulled her up from the bench and headed toward the bonfire, hoping that the heat of it would help disguise the heat he felt in his own cheeks.

TWENTY-FOUR

Leah woke the next morning with a smile that felt as if it would never fade. She had never before imagined just how *wunderbaar* it was to be courted. She could barely contain her excitement as she went about her morning chores. She found herself singing as she rolled out the dough for biscuits.

It could not have been more than two minutes after she put two pans of biscuits in the oven, that she heard a knock on the front door. Knowing that *Dat* and her *bruders* were in the barn, she wiped her hands on the apron she wore and headed for the front hall.

What greeted her at the door was such a surprise, she simply stood there, mouth agape—until Ruth laughed and threw her arms around Leah.

"*Schweschders*, I do believe Leah has forgotten what today is." She turned to Anna and Miriam, who smiled at her and then they all three spoke together, their voices full of *lieb* and excitement.

"Happy Birthday, Leah!"

Leah stood there, staring at her *schweschders*, trying to think what today was.

Is it really my birthday today? How could I forget my own birthday?

But she knew how—she had been thinking of nothing but Jacob for weeks now.

Leah stepped forward and hugged each of her *schweschders* in turn and then stepped back to give them room so they could *kumme* in out of the cold. As they made their way in, Leah realized they were all carrying large baskets.

Without hesitation, she stepped forward to take the one from Miriam but her *schweschder* pulled it back and tucked it behind her back, out of Leah's reach.

"It is not that heavy, little *schweschder*." And then she fluttered her empty hand in Leah's direction. "You go find something fun to do; go back to bed for a bit or read a book. Relax and let your *schweschders* get to work."

The three of them headed off for the kitchen and Leah was left standing there by herself, trying to think of one thing she could do that would make her *schweschders* content that she was not working.

When nothing came to mind, she marched into the kitchen and pulled out a chair. The conversation stopped and three pairs of eyes turned to land on her as she sat down in the chair and crossed her arms over her chest.

"What . . . you told me to relax and enjoy my day. I would enjoy nothing more than to spend time with my *schweschders.*" She said as she smiled at the looks on their faces. Clearly they had not thought of this. They must have some sort of special plans for breakfast. Otherwise, why would they want to keep her out of the kitchen?

Ruth was the first to speak and there was a definite sound of laughter in her voice as she said, "She is too *schmaert* for us, *schweschders.*"

After only a moment, Ruth and Miriam were laughing. Anna held out a bit longer than her *schweschders,* but it wasn't long at all before she joined them.

Leah watched as her *schweschders* laughed and knew this was going to be her best birthday yet.

. . .

It took most of the morning, but Miriam finally convinced Leah to go into town. Leah laughed all the way to the barn, and then laughed again when she discovered Benjamin had already hitched up the small buggy for her. They truly wanted to get her out of the *haus.*

So she went to town.

She drove through the gently falling snow and snuggled into her warm coat. She was glad Benjamin had placed a warm brick at her feet after helping her up into the buggy. The snow was not coming down hard, but the wind was blowing and there was a cold sting to it that Leah knew meant colder weather would be on its way soon.

When the town came into her view, she wasted *nee* time pulling into the gravel lot between *Sew Sweet* and *Sew Nice*. She tied up Matilda as quickly as she was able and headed for *Sew Sweet*. Hot cocoa would be just the thing to warm her up on such a cold day.

The window was frosted over so she couldn't tell how busy the shop was—so she pushed the door open and then nearly tripped backwards as several people jumped out and yelled,

"Surprise!"

She put a hand to her chest and breathed deeply, trying to slow her speeding heart, as she recognized Margaretta at the front of the group. She should have suspected something like this from her sweet, energetic, *Englischer freind.*

Margaretta was busy laughing and Leah knew it must be at the stricken look on her face. Leah could not help herself, and after a moment she joined in, and then she playfully punched at Margaretta's arm when her *freind* moved over to give Leah a hug.

"I couldn't help myself. You looked like you'd walked in on a murder or something." Margaretta laughed again as she hugged Leah.

"Well, did you have to frighten me half to death?" Leah answered with another laugh but she was surprised to realize how warm and loved she felt. Margaretta might be a bit *schpassich,* but she was a *gut freind.*

In *nee* time at all, Leah was surrounded and while she wished there were some way Jacob could be here too, she enjoyed having the special time to spend with her *freinden*.

Margaretta even brought out a cake; though it was not fancy on the outside, it tasted so *gut*—Leah wished there was some way she could take enough home to share with her family, too. The other young people must have felt the same though, because the cake disappeared very quickly.

Ada, Margaretta and several other *freinden* had made Leah presents and they were eager to have Leah open them.

I am blessed indeed to have such wunderbaar freinden. To think of the time they must have spent on these. Leah would have thought Margaretta's gift was the cake but *nee*, she brought Leah a beautiful scarf. Leah was certain she must have bought it somewhere but her *freind* shook her head and smiled at Leah.

"Ana has been teaching me to knit." Leah could not figure out why Margaretta looked embarrassed when she said it but she ducked her head and something in her *freind*'s expression told Leah to let it go.

"Well she has done a *gut* job with her teaching. This is *wunderbaar*, Margaretta. I was certain it was store-bought." Leah knew the compliment would be lost on many of her plain *freinden*.

Leah didn't completely understand it, either. She only knew that, for an *Englischer*, saying it that way was a compliment—and she was rewarded with a brilliant smile from Margaretta so she knew it was the right thing to say.

Not every young person who had *kumme* presented her with presents, but several of her other *freinden* had brought her something special to mark her eighteenth birthday.

Ada presented her with a heavy package, wrapped in simple brown paper. Leah tore into it, and then puzzled over the strange cookbook her *freind* had given her.

"Tob . . ." she stopped suddenly and Leah looked up; she was surprised to see her *freind* was blushing. "A *gut freind* told me that these cookbooks are very popular. I thought you might like it." And she surprised Leah further by saying nothing else about it.

Normally, Ada was something of a chatterbox but Leah thought it must have something to do with what she had started to say before stopping herself. It has sounded very much like Ada had been about to say "Tobias."

As she turned to the gifts her other *freinden* had brought for her, she thought about her dear *freind* Ada who was suddenly very quiet and *naerfich*. Leah thought back to that last gathering.

Did Ada's behavior mean that she and Tobias were courting? If they were, they were certainly keeping things quiet—just as quiet as Leah and Jacob were. That was a tremendous surprise to Leah, since Ada had never been known for keeping secrets.

. . .

Naomi looked over at Samuel as he brought the buggy to a halt. "Are you certain Leah will not feel as if we are intruding? It is her birthday; perhaps she wants to spend it with only her *freinden*." Even though she and Leah had gotten along very well since their talk on Sunday, she did not want the young woman to think that she was pushing too hard.

"Nonsense Naomi, she has already had a special gathering in town with her *freinden*. Though Miriam said they nearly had to shove her out of the *haus* to get her to go." He chuckled at that.

Knowing his stubborn *dochder,* he had not been at all surprised when Miriam had told him how difficult it was to get Leah out of the *haus*.

However, her *Englischer freind* who worked at *Sew Sweet* had assured him that she was having a *wunderbaar* time when he had stopped by to pick up the special cake she'd made for Leah. And her *freind* Ada had promised to keep Leah occupied until he'd had time to bring Naomi, her *aenti* and *onkel,* and their *kinner* to the *haus*—where her *schweschders* would be ready with a special supper.

With that in mind, Samuel was surprised when he realized there was a buggy coming down their driveway. It could be Naomi's cousin, who had *kumme* behind them but it looked to be about the same size as the small buggy they had sent Leah to town in and it was still far enough away that he could not tell who was driving so he jumped down and rushed around to help Naomi down.

Naomi's *onkel* was helping his *frau* out of their own buggy but he did not appear to be in any hurry so Samuel relaxed a little; perhaps he recognized the rig and it was their son. As it moved closer, Samuel could see that it must be; the driver was clearly wearing a black hat, not a bonnet.

Samuel knew Leah would still be along soon and they all needed to move into the *haus* so he turned to Naomi.

"I am going to get the horses put away before Leah *kummes* back. Could you take everyone inside?" The smile on her face could have lit up their whole *haus*.

Samuel swung himself back up into the driver's seat and drove over toward the barn and smiled when he heard the rig behind him moving too. Looking over his shoulder, he realized the small buggy was nearly to the end of the driveway and he was heading straight for the barn.

Once all of the horses were settled with fresh hay and warm blankets, the three men headed for the *haus*. As they walked, Samuel thought about the two men who would soon become his relatives.

Several times now when he had arrived to fetch Naomi, her *onkel* had stood talking to him. He was easy to talk to and Samuel felt blessed that they would soon be related. However, he was very close to Samuel's age—one of the few things that made him feel a bit old when he thought of marrying Naomi, even though she was old enough to have a teenage *dochder*.

And then there was Ephraim's teenage son, Jacob. From the first time Samuel had seen him, sitting at the table across from Benjamin and inhaling Leah's biscuits, he had liked the young man.

If only Leah would find a nice young man like him. . .

.   .   .

Jacob watched Leah across the table. She had the most *wunderbaar* smile on her face. He enjoyed seeing her here among her family, smiling and *froh;* it gave him a *gut* idea of how important family was to her and it was giving him ideas about his feelings for her.

He had never truly considered just how quickly he would fall in *lieb.* He had always thought he would attend the gatherings and eventually one of the *maedels* he had grown up with would become interesting to him, they would date for some time and then he would propose at the proper time.

And for years, he had attended the gatherings, hopeful that one of the young women there would catch his interest—but none ever had. Oh, he had driven home plenty of *maedels* over the years, but he had not been able to imagine wanting to spend much time with any of them, much less the rest of his life.

He had nearly given up hope. He had even considered moving to Ohio in the hopes of finding a suitable *maedel* there. Quite a few of his *mamm's* relatives still lived in Hope Springs and they had invited him to *kumme for a visit.*

He had been giving the idea a lot of thought until he had knocked on the Fisher's door that morning nearly a month ago now. Almost from the moment he had laid eyes on Leah Fisher, he had known she was the *maedel* for him. Although it had been a bit of a shock, he had not been able to *kumme* up with one *gut* reason why he should not court her.

So he had.

And now he was sitting here across from her, enjoying a *wunderbaar* meal her *schweschders* had prepared especially for her birthday. And though everything tasted *wunderbaar,* he could not help but think about how much tastier Leah's cooking was. . . or at least what he had sampled thus far anyway.

He had not even known it was her birthday; it was one of the many things he had not thought to ask her yet.

Naomi had *kumme* into the *haus* yesterday and told them that they were all invited to a special dinner for Samuel Fisher's *dochder* and he had been *eiferich* about it ever since.

On the way here, he had stopped in town and bought what he hoped was an appropriate gift for the *maedel* he hoped to make his *frau* one day soon.

He had wanted to stop into the cafe she liked so much and buy her some of the sticky buns his cousin had mentioned that she liked, but Naomi had also mentioned that her *freinden* were having a special party for her that was also meant to be a distraction and he didn't want to give anything away, so he had avoided even walking in front of it.

TWENTY-FIVE

Leah looked across the table at Jacob and felt a blush creep up into her cheeks. She had been hoping to see him today. She had hoped he would be at her window later, but this was even better—although she was more than a little *naerfich* to be meeting his family.

She looked around the table at her family and his. It was *wunderbaar* to see how well everyone was already getting along. She had met his *schweschder* Beth at the gathering in his district on Sunday, but their younger *schweschder* Eva and their *bruder* Levi were both still too young to attend the youth gatherings.

Levi reminded her of her youngest *bruder* Matthew. In fact, the two of them had paired up immediately. Eva, however, was much more quiet than Lillian and had stuck to her *mamm's* side so far.

Beth had gravitated toward Leah, sitting beside her and peppering her with questions. Leah had worried that she would say something about seeing them together at the gathering on Sunday, but she never even mentioned the gathering, except to mention that she knew their neighbor Sarah. Instead, she asked Leah about the youth in this district and about the shops in Windy Gap they had passed on their way here.

She had already asked Leah when they could go shopping and when the next gathering here would be and if she could attend. She was at least as much a chatterbox as Ada, but she had drawn Leah into her excitement and it had made for a *wunderbaar* mealtime conversation.

Everyone took their time with supper and there was much joyful conversation that floated around the table. Leah enjoyed the entire meal and she could not help wondering if a lot of it was thanks to Naomi.

In the years since her *schweschders* had married, they'd not had many meals where the entire family came together, but in the weeks since *Dat* had announced his intentions, they had already *kumme* together for two meals and she had heard Anna and Ruth mention that they should make this a regular event.

Everywhere she looked, there were smiling faces and friendships forming. Naomi had brought their family closer together than they had been since *Mamm* passed and it was a *wunderbaar* blessing.

When the meal finally began to wind down, Anna disappeared into the kitchen. Leah was very surprised when her *schweschder* brought a cake from the kitchen that looked just like the one this morning at *Sew Sweet*. It tasted just as *gut* as the one she had shared with her *freinden* earlier; Leah was *eiferich* to be able to share it with her family, just like she had wanted to earlier, but there had been none left over.

She looked over at Jacob again as Anna cut the cake and passed slices around the table to each person and found herself wondering if they would be able to find a way to spend even a few minutes alone while he was here or if he would *kumme* back later that evening.

She hoped they would find time while he was here, but the idea of seeing him without her entire family—and his—all around them was appealing, so she kept trying to catch his eye.

After the cake had been reduced to crumbs, *Dat* announced that the animals needed tending to, so he and the boys headed to the mudroom to put on their boots and head out to the barn. Naomi's *onkel* and his sons followed *Dat* and her *bruders* out. Leah stood, and began to gather up the dirty dishes.

"*Nee,* Leah, you just stop that right now." Anna took the plates out of Leah's hands and stacked them on top of the ones she had already gathered.

"Not on your birthday, you don't." Then she waved her hands at Leah in a little shooing motion. "Go. Find something fun to do."

Leah looked at her other *schweschders;* Miriam was smiling, but in her sweet, quiet way and Ruth was trying not to laugh. Naomi smiled at Leah too, but there was a hint of mischief in it and Leah could see that she was enjoying their family dynamic.

As much as she wanted to stay and tease her eldest *schweschder,* she also wanted to see if she could find a way to snatch a few minutes with Jacob, so she walked into the mudroom and shrugged into her heavy coat.

As she tugged her boots on, she listened to the *wunderbaar* sounds coming from the kitchen. She could hear laughter and *froh* voices from her *schweschders* and Naomi. Then she heard Jacob's *mamm* and *schweschders* joining in and she smiled. It was *gut* they were all getting along so well, since they would soon be family.

It was a comfort to her, for sure and for certain; their *haus* was beginning to feel like a home again. She snuggled into contentment like a warm blanket and the crisp, cold air that greeted her when she pushed through the side door felt more invigorating than shocking.

.   .   .

Jacob listened to his *Dat* and Samuel as they went about the chores in the barn.

It is gut that they get along so well, since I hope to make Leah my frau soon.

The thought should have frightened him, but he only felt excitement and impatience when he thought of asking Leah to marry him. The only thing that worried him was her reaction to the question.

Will she think I am moving too quickly or is it at all possible that she feels the same as I do?

He didn't know the answer to either question, but he knew he wanted to ask her as soon as he possibly could so that he could speak to Samuel about it and they could begin planning. It would most likely be too late in this season, but having a year to prepare would give him plenty of time to find a home for them.

There were so many things they would need to talk about. Would they live close to her parents or his? Would she want to be married at the beginning of the season or near the end to give them as more time to prepare?

And then there were all of the things they did not yet know about each other; things they would need to know.

Thinking of those questions made Jacob *naerfich*. Was he being *lecherich;* was he rushing into this? Would she think he was rushing too much?

He forced himself to take several deep breaths when he realized how hard he was gripping the handle of the bucket he was carrying. The thing to do was to go and find Leah. That was the only way he would ever know how she would react to his questions.

Jacob finished what he was doing and then he looked to where his *dat* and Samuel stood and he could see they certainly had *nee* need of his help, so he made his way to the small buggy he had driven and retrieved the box he had found to put Leah's birthday gift in.

With a last look at his *dat* and Samuel, to be certain they did not need him, he headed for the large doors.

As he closed the barn door behind him, he looked at the warm lights that lit up every window he could see. It was such a *wunderbaar* home. He would have to work extra hard, but he wanted Leah to have a home like this one. She was such a *wunderbaar maedel* and he wanted nothing more than to see her *froh* all the time.

Just as he turned at the corner of the large *haus*, on his way around to the side door, he rammed into Leah and they both went sprawling in the snow. He gripped her around the waist and turned so that his body would cushion hers as they fell. He ended up with snow down his collar and she let out a small grunt as she bounced off his chest, but he kept her from hitting the ground; which was much harder, for certain.

"Are you *allrecht*, Leah?" He was surprised to hear how breathless he sounded.

"*Jah,* Jacob, I am *allrecht* . . . just a bit surprised. I suppose I was not watching where I was going." She let out a little laugh then; which made him feel better.

She would not be laughing if she were hurt.

"*Nee*, it's my fault. I was not watching where I was going."

Leah pushed at him, trying to move, but her hand slid off his coat and she dropped back onto his chest with a small "oomph".

When she landed, he realized he *nee* longer felt the cold of snow at his neck. In fact, he wondered at how there was any snow left beneath them because it suddenly felt very warm inside his thick coat.

Taking matters into his own hands, he fumbled a bit, but finally managed to pull himself up, bringing Leah with him. And when they were both on their feet, he stepped back a little from her.

They both stood there for several moments. He was surprised to find that he needed to catch his breath. As his own breathing slowed, he noticed that Leah sounded a bit winded as well. For some reason, knowing that made him feel very *gut*.

After what felt like hours, but was most likely only a few seconds, he knew he needed to say something. He looked around for the box that had slipped out of his hand when they collided and was relieved to see that it was right next to where they had fallen.

He breathed a sigh of relief as he moved over to it; he could see that it had not opened and it didn't look wet. He picked it up, swept the snow off of it and moved back over to Leah, holding it up to her with a hopeful smile.

"I think it may be OK."

Leah took the box from him.

He sucked in a breath when she looked up at him. He could see her face clearly in the bright moonlight and the smile on her face caused his heart to beat a little faster. She had such a *wunderbaar* smile; he was really beginning to enjoy finding ways to see it.

"Jacob, you did not have to get me a present." She looked down then and he thought he could see a bit of a blush on her cheeks.

"I know I didn't have to. I wanted to." He didn't push. He wanted to see her open his present, but he was enjoying the moment, just standing here with her in the moonlight.

She looked up at him again and he felt the words he had meant to wait for, pushing their way up his throat.

"Leah, would you . . ." but he never managed to get the words out because at that moment his *bruder* and Leah's came barreling around the corner of the *haus* and slammed into his back.

It was all he could do not to crash into Leah again. As it was, she jumped back and nearly dropped the box with his present in it. He managed to catch her by the elbows and keep her from smacking into the porch rail behind her as the two boys mumbled an apology and then rocketed off again.

"Perhaps we should get you inside." He reached up then and brushed away the snow that was in her hair. Even though the front was still neatly parted over her face and tucked back into the complicated twists that he had never been able to figure out, her *kapp* was hanging crookedly.

He looked down at the rest of her then and he could see snow on her coat and the bottom of her dress. His landing must have sprayed snow all over her.

"If you don't get inside and into some dry clothes soon, you'll end up sick and I'm certain that's one birthday gift you don't want."

He said it with a smile that she returned, along with a little laugh—but she moved back toward the porch and he followed her up the stairs.

"I haven't opened your present." She said as they moved up the stairs.

"You can do that anytime." He told her; then he moved to open the door for her.

She moved through the door ahead of him and he

could see then that she was shivering. He sent up a prayer of thanks that he had noticed the snow covering her. She started to pull off her boots but after a second she stopped and looked up at him.

"You aren't going to be at my window later, are you?"

He had not thought of that. *Can I chance it?* He asked himself—but he knew the answer.

"I think after the full day you have had, you need your rest. Tomorrow *nacht*?" And he left the words a question.

But before he had finished speaking, she was nodding her head. He started to speak again, but Naomi chose that moment to walk into the mudroom.

"Leah, are you *allrecht*? I saw the boys and they muttered something about knocking you down."

She looked over at Jacob next, almost as if she had not seen him before.

"Did they knock both of you down?" She looked very concerned and he was surprised to realize he felt very much like he was standing before his own *mamm.*

"*Nee,* cousin. They ran into my back and I nearly knocked Leah down but managed to catch her before she fell." He laughed then. "However, I did knock her down earlier. I was walking around the corner of the *haus* and so was Leah. I was not watching where I was going and we collided."

And at Naomi's fierce look, he went on quickly. "I did manage to keep her from hitting the ground, but my landing must have sprayed snow all over her."

Naomi looked at him for nearly another minute before she hurried Leah away toward the stairs.

And Jacob stood there only a moment before turning back to go outside. Maybe he could find something else in the barn to do to help.

TWENTY-SIX

Leah looked up from the cookbook in front of her when she heard the sound of a knock. One of her neighbors must have come to visit—it was the right time of day for it.

I certainly could use a break from deciphering the crazy recipes in that book, she thought as she moved into the hall, heading for the door. *What was Ada thinking when she gave me that book?* Not one recipe in it made any sense to Leah and she had been reading over them all morning.

Leah was certain her *freind* had meant well, but she had some strange ideas about cooking. Leah was not sure she would ever understand the recipes Ada seemed so fond of.

But perhaps her feelings about the book have more to do with the young man who suggested it. Leah laughed a little to herself, thinking of her *freind* and the young man who had clearly captured her heart.

I hope that isn't Ada at the door, kumme to see how I like the recipe book . . . she thought to herself as she headed for the door. But she was surprised to find Naomi instead, standing on the porch.

Her first thoughts were relief.

"*Gudemariye,* Leah, you look to be in a very *gut* mood today." There was a hint of mischief in the smile playing around Naomi's lips and Leah was certain she saw right through the smile on her face.

Still, she could try and get away with it . . .

"*Jah,* Naomi, I am in a particularly *gut* mood this morning. It is a beautiful day and everyone is well." And she kept smiling, hopeful that Naomi would not press her further.

Naomi smiled back at Leah as she turned her head a little, "While I am delighted to see you so *froh* to see me, I think perhaps you are more *froh* that I am not, in fact, someone else." And she laughed as Leah's mouth dropped open.

"This would not have something to do with the look I saw on your face the other *nacht* aimed at the cookbook your *freind* Ada gave you, would it?"

Leah laughed then; clearly there would be *nee* fooling Naomi. "*Jah,* you are right. I don't know what Ada was thinking when she gave me this crazy cookbook."

The sound of a shoe moving across the boards brought

Leah's attention back to Naomi. She was standing out in the cold. She was such a little thing; Leah still found it difficult to believe this woman in front of her was old enough to have a *dochder* Leah's own age.

"*Ach*, I am sorry to leave you standing out in this cold. " Leah said as she moved aside. "Won't you come in?" Leah waited for Naomi to step into the warmth, but she didn't move an inch.

"Actually Leah, I was hoping you would want to come into town with me." Naomi looked down at her feet for a moment, before squaring her shoulders and looking back up at Leah.

"Truth be told, I need to do a bit of shopping and I thought it might be a *gut* idea to do it here. I was hoping you could come and perhaps show me around."

Leah was surprised and delighted. And even though she had been to town only the day before, she had not exactly gotten any shopping done of her own, so she could take care of that at the same time.

"I think that sounds like a *gut* idea. Let me just get my coat and write a note for *Dat*." The look on Naomi's face caused a strange warmth to spread through Leah.

. . .

Samuel looked at the *haus* in front of him. David had done a fine job building his new home. David and Catherine would have a *gut* home to come to when they were wed. Samuel could scarce believe his son would be married in only one more week.

Where has the time gone? It seemed only yesterday that David had been a wee *boppli*—and now he was going to be married.

And soon he will have bopplin of his own. That thought brought Naomi to Samuel's mind. He had so hoped they would have news from her church leaders by now. There did not seem a reason for their decision to take so long. Perhaps he needed to have more patience on this matter.

Gotte had his hand on them both; of that, Samuel was certain. He felt sure that he and Naomi were in *Gotte's wille.* He only had to trust that *Gotte's* timing was better than his own. It had gotten them both to where they were and Samuel was not about to start thinking that he knew better.

At least, Naomi and Leah were getting along very well. Naomi had said laughingly, that she did not expect they were finished getting to know each other, but she did feel they had made a *gut* start.

It was a load off Samuel's shoulders, and off his mind as well, to know that his *dochder* was so accepting of Naomi.

He and Naomi would be married, he was certain of it; he only had to be patient. Having patience was proving to be mighty difficult and that was a bit *schpassich* for him. He had always felt that he had too much patience, or at least he had in the past.

He had certainly taken his time with Elisabeth. It was a *gut* thing she had set her sights on him or they might never have gotten together. With Naomi, he had waited ten years after Elisabeth's death. So why was he suddenly struggling so with patience? It was a puzzle to him; one he would need to solve soon. He did not want to worry over it.

He turned his attention back to the *haus* before him. Even with the help of their community, David had built it in a short amount of time. Samuel remembered all the evenings David and Catherine had sat at their kitchen table, looking through catalogs and books and samples of things, trying to decide on things that would grace their home.

David had become a very fine man and Samuel was glad to be his *dat*—though he knew that most of who David was had nothing to do with him and everything to do with *Gotte*.

It was one more thing Samuel was grateful to *Gotte* for. David had never been close to leaving their faith, as far as Samuel knew, but he had come to Samuel many times with questions. Samuel had tried to answer them, but it had not always been easy. David was also a very *schmaert* young man.

But through it all, *Gotte* had kept a hand on David and on Samuel; now David was a fine young man, an important part of their community. He was a *gut* man and Samuel felt blessed to be his *dat*.

. . .

Leah stood in *Sew Sweet*, delighted at Naomi's reaction to one of her favorite places in Windy Gap. Naomi stood there just as Leah had so many times, looking at the treats behind the large glass case in front of them as if it were impossible to pick a favorite.

It always took Leah a long time to order; Margaretta was well used to this, so she had not yet come over to take their order. However, it was *nee* more than another minute before she caught Leah's eye and then made her way over to them.

"Leah, it is *gut* to see you."

And Leah smiled at her *freind*. The look of interest on Margaretta's face was full of curiosity. Leah could tell she was near to bursting to ask questions, but she just stood there, looking at Naomi and Leah.

Leah looked over at Naomi then, too. She had worried about Naomi's feelings about the tiny town of Windy Gap, but she needn't have.

From the moment they had driven into town, Naomi had shown only delight at the shops that lined the main street—and the cafe as well.

Leah looked down at the selection available for the day then and her attention fell on a plate of sticky buns. A smile spread across her face slowly. She had been waiting for this.

"You finally talked Ruth into it, then?"

Margaretta was already nodding her head and her smile could not have been any wider. She had told Leah so many times how much she wished Ruth would let her make some of her own recipes for them and Margaretta made the pastries sound so *appeditlich*, Leah had found she nearly licked her lips at just the mention.

"*Jah!* And it is so right that you're here today. You just

have to try these." Leah saw then that Margaretta was holding two plates already. Leah looked over at Naomi to see that she was also grinning while nodding her head.

"*Danki,* Margaretta, that is so sweet of you." She moved to take the plates from her, but the young woman was having none of it. She motioned to one of the small tables by their front window.

"I was hoping you would be in soon. They've been going so quickly, I worried they'd all be gone before you came in. I was about to go hide one in the back room, just in case." She shrugged her shoulders as she said it, but Leah noticed that her smile had gotten even bigger.

Margaretta stood beside the table, hopping from foot to foot, while she waited for Leah to take a bite. Leah laughed a little at how *eiferich* her *freind* was. And when she looked over at Naomi, there was a look of such happiness and contentment on her face that Leah began to see just how much of a kindred spirit Naomi might be; that made Leah very glad that *Gotte* had brought Naomi to them. Clearly, she was exactly the person their family needed.

"*I know the plans I have for you.*"

The words came to her from nowhere. Leah was not certain if *Gotte* had spoken it or simply brought it to mind, but she could feel her smile getting bigger, and in that moment, she felt as if so much heaviness lifted right off of her.

She felt like jumping and shouting and telling every single person in town about how blessed she was to have such a *wunderbaar* Heavenly Father and an Earthly *Dat* who obeyed their Heavenly Father. And now she would be blessed with a *wunderbaar* new *mamm* who clearly listened to *Gotte's wille*.

Leah felt happier than she could remember feeling since before *Mamm* had become ill. As she sat there smiling across at Naomi, who was enjoying her sticky bun and chattering away with Margaretta, she felt almost as if she could feel *Mamm* telling her that everything was going to be *wunderbaar gut* now and she just knew that it was *Gotte's* way of allowing her to know that *Mamm* approved.

She reached for her sticky bun and took a big bite. The flavors exploded on her tongue and she thought nothing had ever tasted so *appeditlich*.

Margaretta had done a *wunderbaar* job with these. Ruth would be very *froh* that she had added these to the menu. For sure and for certain, they would sell a lot of these.

Naomi had stopped talking for a moment and was looking at Leah with a look that she couldn't quite figure out. It felt very warm and loving, so she smiled at Naomi, then turned to Margaretta to tell her how *appeditlich* the sticky buns were.

. . .

She and Naomi spent the rest of the day in town. Leah took her to each store and introduced her to the owners— Amish and *Englisch* alike. Naomi spent a *gut* amount of time in each store, looking over the items sold there and talking to the people Leah introduced her to.

The weather was even on their side. This time of year would usually mean strong winds and heavy snow, but the day was clear. The wind barely moved the flags and holiday decorations that graced almost every storefront they walked past.

Leah was glad she had *kumme* with Naomi today. She was having great fun introducing Naomi to everyone as her *dat's* fiancé and she and Naomi talked about so many things as they walked through town.

Leah asked Naomi about the differences between Windy Gap and Hope Springs. Naomi told Leah about her community in Ohio and how *wunderbaar* they had been while she had been mourning the loss of her husband.

She also told Leah about the way they had pushed her to marry his *bruder* Joel. She cautioned Leah to make her own decisions about *lieb*.

"Never let someone else decide what is best for you when it *kummes* to marriage, Leah. The community may worry about you, but they are not the ones who are making that commitment. You are. And you need to be sure."

Leah wanted so much to ask Naomi about Jacob, but she was still uncertain of his feelings herself and she did not want to say the wrong thing. While she tried to think of a way to ask Naomi without giving anything away, Naomi kept talking about marriage and her words mostly answered Leah's questions, so she let it go for now.

"The best thing you can do is pray. *Gotte* will direct you; believe me. He has a plan for your life and He wants you to follow it because His plans are what are best for you. You are the only one who can make decisions for yourself and you should always turn to *Gotte* first if you need help with those decisions, especially the big ones like marriage."

Leah took all of that in and thought about it as they walked. She would pray about Jacob. That would be the best idea. *Gotte* certainly knew better than she did whether he was meant to be with Leah or not. So she would put her trust in Him and wait to see how things went.

Later that afternoon as they headed back home, Leah realized how much better she felt about everything. She was not worrying about Naomi anymore. She was clearly just what their family needed and Leah was grateful that *Gotte* had sent her to them.

She wasn't worrying over Jacob anymore, either. *Gotte* would show her what to do; all she had to do was trust Him and wait.

The more she got to know Naomi, the more *impatient* she was for her to become *Dat's frau* and her new *mamm*.

Is this how Dat feels? Impatient and eiferich at the same time? Nee wonder he could not wait to tell us about Naomi . . .

TWENTY-SEVEN

Naomi looked at the faces of each person who stepped off the train. It was a surprise to realize how *eiferich* she felt. It had not been very long since she had seen her *dochder,* but there was much to tell her and Naomi had high hopes that Rebekah would rejoice with her.

She squeezed Leah's hand, marveling at how *Gotte* worked. Only the work of *Gotte* could explain Leah's quick acceptance. Naomi had once despaired of finding a way to even talk to Leah and now she and Leah were *gut freinden* and quickly working their way to more.

Looking over at Leah, who was bouncing a little as they stood there waiting, Naomi only hoped her *dochder* would be as welcoming and loving as Leah had been in the past few days. There was much to be *froh* about, but there was also much to worry about.

What if Rebekah did not like it here? What if she insisted they return to Ohio? Would Naomi be able to refuse her *dochder* anything after what Rebekah had sacrificed over the years due to her *dat's* illness?

Nee, I will not do that to her. She has been through enough already.

Naomi assured herself that she would not have to worry about any of that. Rebekah would be *froh* to have new family, not only a *dat* but also *bruders* and *schweschders.*

At least Naomi hoped she would.

When she felt Samuel slip his hand into her empty one, she was relieved that he and Leah had accompanied her to the train station. They had even hired a driver to bring them. Samuel had laughed as he reminded her of the accumulation of new snow.

"We would not want Rebekah to start her time here in the same way as her *mamm,* would we?" And she had laughed along with him. The thought that they would share that joke for years to come warmed her considerably.

Already they had a history. It was comforting and Naomi found herself anxious to begin building even more. She hoped Rebekah would feel the same way.

After nearly every other person must have stepped down from the train, Naomi spotted a neat white *kapp* among the crowd. She lifted up on her toes, but the small heart-shaped top of the white head covering was swallowed up by the crowd. And then Samuel was moving forward slowly. He was much taller than Naomi; therefore he would be able to see above everyone's head.

She clung tight to his hand, pulling Leah with her as they followed his lead through the thick crowd. Bodies brushed and bumped her as they passed and she heard more than one person grumbling under their breath as they pushed past.

There was even one person who seemed to be speaking with someone, but when she looked around for who, there was *nee* one nearby that gave the appearance of listening. Naomi shook her head at that.

Who could understand *Englischers*.

And then she forgot all about the person because they had finally reached Rebekah. She stood before them, looking very *naerfich* as she twisted her hands back and forth over the handle of the plain black bag she held. She looked at Naomi, and the bag dropped to the ground with a thud, as she launched herself toward her *mamm*.

Naomi caught Rebekah as she nearly flew through the air. She was surprised to see that her *dochder* was thinner than she had been when Naomi left. She eased Rebekah back and held her at arm's length, so she could get a *gut* look at her.

She was much thinner, but she was also taller. She must have grown several inches in the last month. *Nee* wonder she was thin—her body was stretching to adjust to her taller frame.

Naomi was *froh* to see that, other than being taller and a bit thinner, Rebekah looked much the same as she had when Naomi had left Hope Springs only a month ago. Rebekah's cheeks were a bit pink from the cold, but she looked healthy.

Knowing Mamm, it is probably a miracle Rebekah has not gained twenty pounds.

Naomi almost laughed at the thought of her *mamm.* She remembered well how often she had been forced to push her plate away before it was empty while growing up.

Mamm had meant well, but she had never understood why Naomi couldn't handle the same amount of food as her *dat.* And Naomi could see from the twinkling in Rebekah's eyes that she knew just what her *mamm* was thinking.

Naomi pulled Rebekah in for another hug. Oh how she had missed her *dochder.* She noticed that Rebekah held on to her tightly as well, which helped ease her guilt about bringing Rebekah so far from her grandparents.

"*Ach!* Before I forget . . ." Rebekah eased back from Naomi's arms, looking around for her large black suitcase. She jumped when she saw Samuel standing there holding it and looked back at Naomi.

"Rebekah, this is Samuel Fisher." Naomi stopped, unsure of how to go on. But she needn't have worried. Samuel took over from there.

"I am most pleased to meet you, Rebekah. I came to make certain you have a proper introduction to our community. And to see you and your *mamm* safely to your *aenti's* home." There was a look of such mischief in his eyes, Naomi nearly laughed out loud and she was *nee* longer even a little *naerfich*.

"Is this all you brought with you?" He motioned to the suitcase that he had set down by their feet and Naomi could have kissed him right there. He'd dissolved her nervousness and introduced himself to Rebekah without being at all awkward.

She closed her eyes and offered up another prayer of thanks. *Gotte* had truly known what he was doing when he had brought them together.

Rebekah looked from Samuel, back to Naomi, and then back again to Samuel, before she looked at Naomi with understanding in her eyes. They had always had a sort of silent communication and Naomi was very glad to see that she would not have to explain more to Rebekah. Now all she could do was hope Rebekah would be as *eiferich* as she was.

"This is all I brought . . ." Rebekah's words trailed off and she looked back at Samuel before speaking again. "*Grossmammi* is sending . . ." Again her words stopped abruptly before her head turned back toward her *mamm* and Naomi could see that Rebekah was truly beginning to understand.

"She is sending the rest." Naomi said, nodding her head as she answered the question in Rebekah's eyes.

"*Grossmammi* knew about this?" Rebekah asked. Naomi was trying to decide what she could say when her *dochder* went on.

"You told her before you told me . . . *Mamm?*" Rebekah's words took Naomi completely by surprise—she hadn't considered Rebekah being hurt by that.

Ach! Why didn't I think?

Why had she been so worried about Rebekah getting angry and never once considering that her feelings would be hurt. She looked back at her *dochder* and was surprised to see the hurt was gone. Rebekah had put a smile on her face and she was turning to Samuel again.

"It appears that congratulations are in order."

Naomi could see the surprise in Samuel's eyes, but he controlled it quickly and dipped his head a little.

"*Danki,* Rebekah. It is *gut* to hear you say that. I admit we have been worried you would not feel that way."

He looked over Rebekah's head at Naomi and she tried to convey her own surprise at how quickly Rebekah had figured it all out. Naomi was struggling to find something to say, when Rebekah turned her attention back to her suitcase.

"I nearly forgot again, *Mamm. Grossmammi* sent this for you." And she reached into the small pocket on the front of the plain black case, pulling out a large envelope and then handing it to Naomi.

"*Danki,* Rebekah." She took the envelope, but didn't open it. This might very well be *Mamm's* way of telling Naomi the Bishop's decision. She was still awaiting his letter, but perhaps *Mamm* had other news to share. Either way, Naomi knew she would need to read this later in private.

Rebekah didn't say anything. She turned back to get her case, but Samuel had already lifted it and was smiling at the two of them, waiting patiently for them. Naomi wrapped Rebekah into one more hug, before leading her toward where their driver had said he would be waiting for them.

. . .

Hours later, Naomi sat beside the fireplace with *Mamm's* letter on her lap. Despite the warmth of the fire, she was shivering.

How will I tell Samuel? What will I tell Samuel? What can we do? How can this be Gotte's wille?

The thoughts crashed over her like waves, each one bringing a new round of emotion. If it was *Gotte's wille* for the two of them to marry, this would have to work out —somehow.

Naomi lifted her eyes to the ceiling and cried out to *Gotte,* then slipping out of the chair and onto her knees. She gripped the letter in her hand as she fell forward onto the rug and continued to pray. All of her worries and fears poured out with her tears.

She prayed about everything she could think of, offering her worries over fitting into Samuel's community, over bringing Rebekah so far from everything and everyone she knew, about what her *mamm's* letter said about Joel's reaction to her letter, about her own bitterness over John being sick for such a long time and then dying so horribly.

She poured it all out to *Gotte.*

Afterward she felt better than she had in years. She felt lighter; she knew that she was in still in *Gotte's wille.* She had *nee* reason to worry about how everything would work out. She only needed to trust that *Gotte* had it in hand. He would work everything out according to His *wille*.

TWENTY-EIGHT

Leah sat by the window in her room, gently pushing with her foot to keep the rocker moving back and forth as she prayed. She didn't know why, but she felt like *Gotte* was telling her to pray for Naomi.

She wasn't praying anything specific, just normal things she would pray for someone when she didn't know what they needed. Then she spent a while thanking Him for sending Naomi to them. Not only would they all have a *mamm* again, *Dat* would not be alone anymore.

He had been so much happier in the last few weeks than Leah could remember ever seeing him. Her *mamm* had been sick for so long before she died, Leah couldn't really remember things being any other way. But then, she had only been seven when *Mamm* had passed.

She was so thankful for the time now. She had thought she wanted a new *mamm* but *Gotte* had known the timing better than any of them. He had known the proper time to bring Naomi into their lives, and for this, Leah was thankful. She was especially thankful that she had managed to let go of her misgivings and discover a *freind* in Naomi. And somehow she knew they would have a *gut* relationship.

And she would have a new *schweschder,* too! That news *eiferich* Leah. She had wanted to go with *Dat* and Naomi to the train station to meet Rebekah, and she was so glad when Naomi had agreed. *Dat* had looked like he wanted to argue, but one look at Naomi's face and he had just nodded his head and went out to wait for the driver.

Leah thought about her first look at Rebekah—and how exciting it was to have a *schweschder* so close to her own age. Not that she didn't *lieb* her *schweschder* Lillian; she truly did. It was just nice to think of having a *schweschder* she could truly share things with.

Ach, if only she had been here weeks ago, I would have had a schweschder to share all these worries over Jacob with, instead of having to keep them to myself or share them with near strangers. She thought of it and laughed at how *gegisch* she was being. *Gotte* knew the proper timing in that as well and she certainly should not question it.

Leah thought again about how *wunderbaar* it would be to have Rebekah here. Why it would be like having her best *freind*—right here in this *haus*. Surely they would be the best of *freinden*.

With her prayers done and her excitement giving her

plenty to think about, Leah left the rocking chair and slipped quietly between her cool sheets. With thoughts of what she would make for supper and excitement over introducing Rebekah to all her *freinden,* it was a long time before Leah fell asleep, but she did so with a wide smile on her face and joy in her heart.

. . .

It felt as if Leah's eyes had only just closed when she heard a familiar rattling sound. She nearly jumped out of bed before remembering to be quiet. She had been hoping Jacob would *kumme* tonight. There was so much to tell him.

She rushed over to the window, waving until he saw her and smiled to her. Then she slipped back into her dress and stockings, pinning her hair as quickly as she could under her *kapp* while moving down the hallway.

She was so intent on seeing Jacob, she nearly forgot about the noisy step. Just in time, she dropped a pin and when she leaned down to pick it up, she realized which step she was on and moved carefully to avoid the next one.

Jacob met her at the back porch edge, with the smile she loved so much on his handsome face. It had become their practice already for him to help her down from the porch.

As he lifted her off the porch, Leah became aware of his hands on her waist. Ever since they had collided with each other the other *nacht,* she had been thinking about how it felt to be sprawled over his strong chest. She had found herself wishing her *dat* and Naomi were already married, so that she could talk with her about these feelings. It was very confusing and Leah was not at all certain what to do about them.

She looked at Jacob's face as he set her down. It was difficult to be certain, but it looked as if he was struggling with the same sort of feelings. He took a long time to set her on her feet and move his hands away from her waist. They stood there for several, long seconds before he gently placed a hand on her face, sliding it slowly up her cheek as his head moved toward hers.

Is he going to kiss me? The thrill that rushed through Leah at the very thought of it, brought heat to her cheeks and a strange tightening to her stomach. The emotions that were rushing through her in the wake of the it were very confusing, but she knew that she wanted nothing to stop him, so she didn't even dare breathe as he closed the distance between them.

He stopped moving when his lips were only a breath away from hers and looked into her eyes. The emotions in his eyes were so raw, so intense, that it was a little frightening. Leah was glad she had already been holding her breath; she might have gasped and stopped him from kissing her. She was surprised how the look in his eyes affected her.

And then he smiled as he closed the distance, and all Leah could think of was the feel of his lips on hers. She tried to pay attention to everything, but there were so many feelings and emotions rushing through her, it was impossible to keep anything straight.

Leah could feel her knees weakening and she reached up to grip Jacob's sleeve. He was so strong; she knew if she could just anchor herself to him, he would hold her up. As soon as her hand wrapped around a part of his sleeve, she felt him move his free arm around her waist and she almost sagged against him in relief.

When Jacob took a tiny step back, the shock of it was almost too much for Leah; she felt herself staggering until Jacob moved his other hand to her waist and held tight.

She looked up into his face, trying to figure out why he had stepped back, but all she could see in his face was confusion. She would have worried about whether he had enjoyed kissing her, except that both of his hands were still gripping tightly to her coat and his breath was coming in the same short, hard bursts that matched her own.

"Are you *allrecht*, Leah?" All she could do was nod at him.

"I won't apologize for kissing you—but I am sorry if I frightened you." He said, and his voice was low and fierce.

It took a few seconds for Leah to find her voice. "Oh Jacob, you didn't frighten me." She felt his hands tighten their grip on her and before a single thought came to her, he had closed the distance between them again.

This time his lips were even stronger on hers and his hands had fisted tightly around her coat; pulling her up against him. She took the opportunity to reach up and wrap her hands around his neck.

All too soon, he stepped back—again.

"Leah, we have to stop now. As much as I am enjoying kissing you, we have to stop!" His words were a whisper in her ear, but there was such a firm tone to his voice, it was nearly as if he had shouted.

He moved back again, but both of his hands were still gripping tightly to her coat.

She nodded and then leaned her head against his chest as she tried to calm her speeding heart.

"Let's go for a ride."

She must have made some sound of assent because he was moving them quickly away from the *haus*, with her hand caught tightly in his.

All the way down the driveway, Leah thought about the kisses they had just shared. Should she tell him that those were the first kisses she had ever received from a boy? Should she ask him about how many other *maedels* he had kissed?

She put a finger to her lips and thought about the strength of emotions that had rushed through her when their lips met.

I really don't think I want to know.

When they reached the buggy, Jacob took her completely by surprise again and leaning forward and placing a quick kiss on her lips, before taking hold of her waist and lifting her up into the buggy.

She gasped in surprise and then laughed as a smile spread over his face.

. . .

Jacob jogged around to the other side of the buggy and climbed up into the buggy; then . . . before he could let himself get distracted again, he released the brake and directed the team down the remainder of Leah's driveway.

He would have to work very hard for the rest of the evening to control himself. All he wanted to do right now, was to pull off the road and kiss Leah again—and again—until it was time to take her back home, but he knew that would not be a *gut* idea.

He may not have kissed any other *maedels*—and he certainly had not gotten into some of the things his *freinden* had done during their *rumschpringe,* but he knew enough about what went on between a husband and his *frau* to know that it would be far too easy for them to get carried away.

He had certainly watched enough of his *dat's* stallions going crazy over a mare to know that it didn't take much to flare up passions.

They rode for a long time in silence. Jacob used the time to think about the intense feelings he had discovered tonight. He had wanted to ask Leah to marry him before, but now he knew without a doubt that he wanted to spend the rest of his life with her.

He was also more than a little worried about how impatient he felt when he thought of being married to her.

With that in mind, he knew he would have to wait to ask her. If he asked her now, it would only sound as if he was allowing those emotions to rule him. He would also have to give her time, because if she felt anything like he did now, she would need to process her own emotions and feelings.

They rode along in silence for quite a while. Every few minutes, he glanced over at Leah. She had a kind of half smile on her face and he found himself worrying about what she must be thinking right now.

Had she felt the same things he had? Would it be rude to ask her? For the first time, he regretted his limited experience with dating.

"Jacob . . ."

Her voice was very quiet. He worried about what she might be about to say, but he turned to her and answered as calmly as he could. "*Jah?*"

"Is that..." she paused and he looked over at her, only to discover that she was chewing on her lower lip. It was nearly more than his recently assaulted system could handle so he forced his eyes back to the road quickly and waited for her to go on.

"Is that normal . . . for kissing, I mean?" The question came out in a timid voice, but he could hear the excitement underlying her words and it was exactly what he needed. As relief flooded through him, he wanted to jump up and shout out his excitement.

However, he knew that would be a bad idea, so he took another moment to calm himself before answering her. "Truly Leah, I would not know, but I imagine that is how it should be between two people who—" he forced himself to stop before he said too much.

She looked up at him, her eyes wide and full of emotion.

"Do you mean that was your first kiss, too?" Her

words told him something he had wanted to ask, but hadn't dared, for fear it would be a bad idea.

He had been the first boy to kiss her.

The knowledge sent a strong surge of excitement rushing through him again.

It has been a very gut nacht indeed.

"*Jah* Leah, those were my first kisses, too."

Her smile bloomed and for the first time tonight, he felt peace. This was exactly where *Gotte* wanted him—there was *nee* doubt about it.

All too soon, it was time to turn the buggy around and take Leah back to her home.

TWENTY-NINE

Samuel stood at the kitchen sink and looked out over his snow-covered fields while he drank his *kaffe*. He had spent hours in the barn this morning, working on a Christmas gift he was making for Naomi.

The project was coming together nicely; the wood was almost shaping itself under his hands. He had only taken a short break to come in and warm up.

It was early yet and he had not lit a fire in the wood stove out in the barn yet. He would go back out in a few minutes and do so, to give the barn time to warm up before David and Benjamin came out to start their morning chores.

He felt such peace—unlike any he had ever known before. He *nee* longer worried for Leah.

She and Naomi spent time together talking every time Naomi was here. Naomi was spending almost as much time with Leah as she was with Samuel when she visited, but Samuel was not the slightest bit bothered by it. He was relieved that they had found a way to connect. He felt such a peace about Leah now, he could not have been jealous if he had tried.

He felt as if all of his prayers had been answered. It was less than four weeks until Christmas and their family Thanksgiving had been a *wunderbaar* day for all of them.

Naomi's *dochder* Rebekah was a very quiet *maedel* but she had appeared to feel at home with the family. Samuel was glad she had arrived in time for the holiday season.

He remembered how *eiferich* and *naerfich* Naomi had been as they drove to the train station together. He had taken his large buggy to Naomi's *aenti's haus* and then he had surprised her with a driver who had picked them up there.

A chuckle escaped his lips when he thought of Naomi's reaction the first time he had mentioned her somewhat unconventional arrival here. He enjoyed his joke, and after a moment he could see Naomi was enjoying it, too. It was such fun to have this little joke between them. It felt as if they had known each other forever, instead of the month it had been since he'd found her stranded on the side of the road, dressed much too lightly for their weather.

But he didn't want to take a chance on anything happening when they picked up Naomi's *dochder*, so he had called for a driver. Besides, it just made sense to leave the buggy there, so he could stay and visit for a time after the driver brought them back from the station. Afterward, he could drive himself and Leah home.

He and Naomi had agreed that it would be too much excitement for Rebekah to meet his family right away, so they had only brought Leah to the train station. That had given Rebekah a day to get settled with the news they would be sharing with her, before introducing her to the rest of the family.

Thanksgiving had been full of noise and food, as usual, but this year the entire family had gathered under the Fisher's roof. Even his *bruder* Josiah had *kumme* with his family.

Samuel had worried that it would be too much for Rebekah, but she had blended right in with the family. She'd been quiet, but he had seen her talking to different members of the family throughout the day; either they had sought her out or she had made a point to speak to each one of them.

Everyone had gotten along well and Samuel knew it had been the best holiday their family had spent in many years.

His older *dochdern* had even stayed until very late in the evening. Daniel and Anna had been the first to leave; arms full of sleeping children.

Miriam had surprised him by being the last to head home with Joshua and little John. Ruth had also surprised him by giving *nee* objection at all when her David had said it was time they headed home, just after Anna and her husband had towed their three sleepy *kinner* out to the waiting buggy.

There were only a few days left until David and Catherine's wedding and Samuel knew their *haus* would be taken over by the ladies in the community to prepare everything. He was glad to know that Naomi and Rebekah would be included in that as well. What better way to become *freinden* with all of their neighbors—than to help prepare for a wedding?

Every prayer was being answered and Samuel had felt all of his worries over Leah fading away. She and Naomi had such a *wunderbaar* relationship now; it was impossible to see it had ever been any other way. Clearly *Gotte's wille* was directing them all.

. . .

Naomi stood in the front hall, waiting to hear Samuel's team. She had the letter in her hand, but a smile on her face. Samuel needed to know what was going on back at home, but he didn't need to worry. They both had to remember that *Gotte* was in control. His *wille* would come to pass, *nee* matter what barriers appeared in front of them.

She had not been able to bring herself to show him the letter before Thanksgiving. It had been such a *wunderbaar* day for them all. Even Rebekah had told Naomi later that evening how much she had enjoyed herself.

Naomi had not expected that. She had thought Rebekah would be angry with her for a very long time. It had been a great relief to find that she was not.

Now she just had to face this current situation. Samuel was on his way to pick her and Rebekah up so that they could help prepare for David and Catherine's wedding. Naomi knew that even though she did not want to spoil the wedding for him, he needed to know what was in the letter Rebekah had brought from Ohio.

She didn't have to wait long before she heard the crunch of gravel under horse's hooves. She pulled on her coat and hat and pushed through the door quickly. She was certain it would be better to speak with him away from everyone else.

Samuel parked the buggy, setting the brake; and—instead of stepping down—he sat there and simply looked into Naomi's eyes as she stood waiting for him.

A delightful warmth crept through her entire being. She expected her knees to feel weak, but the opposite happened. She felt stronger than she ever had and she knew in that moment that they could handle anything as long as they did it together.

She felt her smile warm for Samuel and she could *nee* longer feel the cold temperature. They could have been standing in a baking hot desert.

After what felt like hours, Samuel finally stepped down from the buggy and rushed up the steps in front of her, taking them two at a time.

She felt a giggle bubble up and trip from her lips at his obvious hurry. She felt like a young woman again.

He was certainly looking at her like a young man would. For the moment, it was only the two of them and nothing else intruding on their private, little world. Even the letter in her pocket was forgotten.

It was several moments before the sound of footsteps from inside broke into the moment and Naomi remembered why she was standing out here in the cold, waiting for Samuel. She was hesitant to mention it now, with such a wondrous feeling of *lieb* crashing over them both, but she knew she would have to bring it up with him at some point, and it would be much worse if she were to wait any longer.

"Samuel," she began but her voice broke and she was forced to stop and start again.

When she did, she noticed the warmth drain out of Samuel's eyes. He could already tell something was not quite right. She must hurry or she would worry him too much.

"Samuel, you remember the letter Rebekah gave me at the station?"

He nodded his head, and she went on. "*Mamm* sent it with Rebekah so we would know a bit of what was going on at home." It was all she could do to go on, but she leaned into Samuel and his strength gave her the strength she needed.

"The church elders have not made a decision yet, but *Mamm* felt it was only fair to tell me what she has discovered." She paused for a moment and gathered all of her courage.

"According to what she has heard from neighbors, and how Joel reacted to my letter, she believes their answer will be *nee*. Joel has made it plain to everyone that he spoke to me after John's passing and that I promised to be his *frau*. The bishop—"

She stopped speaking, as tears ran down her cheeks. She looked down at the snow-covered boards under their feet then, waiting for him to say something. She didn't have to wait long; after only a moment, his hands lightly gripped her arms and he lowered his head until he was looking her in the face.

"Naomi, you should not worry yourself over this." His words surprised her and she looked up, nearly hitting his chin as she did. That was the last thing she'd expected him to say, but it was somehow exactly what she needed to hear.

Gotte must be guiding his words. Ach, why am I worried? Gotte is clearly in this. I am such a gegisch woman.

"Naomi, we both know that we are in *Gotte's wille.* When it is His *wille,* there is nothing that can stop it. We need not worry over this. We must leave it all in His hands. We have done our part and now we must leave the rest up to Him."

His words sent warmth flooding back into her, chasing away the cold that had crept into her hands and feet; she felt even better than she had only a moment before, when she had remembered the letter.

Before she had time to think about her actions, she threw her arms around Samuel, leaning into him as his arms came around her, reveling in the strength she felt in his arms. In that moment, it was like they were back in their own world—and everything around them blurred and disappeared.

They stayed just like that—for a very long time.

THIRTY

Rebekah watched from the window as her mother stepped into Samuel's embrace.

I should have known. Mamm wouldn't send for me like this without a gut reason, and getting married is certainly that.

Rebekah wanted to be angry. She should be angry with her *mamm,* but if she were honest, it wasn't as much a surprise as she was making it out to be. *Mamm* had been lonely for a long time—even before *Dat* had passed, Rebekah had known her *mamm* was lonely.

But somehow Rebekah had convinced herself that *mamm* would marry *Onkel* Joel and she could stay in Hope Springs with her grandparents.

But it's not like you have many freinden you would be

leaving. The words were right, but they didn't make the reality any less frightening. She didn't exactly have any hope of finding *freinden* here, either.

Ach, the whole thing is so frustrating! Why didn't she just tell me before she dragged me out here! But she knew the answer to that one.

I would not have kumme so willingly. Rebekah knew herself well enough to know that she would have been stubborn about it. She would have insisted that *Mamm* was moving too fast, that she needed to come home and think about it, that she needed to speak to their community in person.

And all of those would have been excuses to cover up Rebekah's own fears. It had taken a train ride for Rebekah to finally admit that she was terrified of forgetting her *dat.*

For so much of her life he had been terribly sick; he had gotten worse and worse as she grew up. She had never felt like she had a *dat* like the other young people in their district and too many times she had been angry about it.

Now she was just sad that she had not spent more time with *Dat,* even if it had just meant sitting by his bedside. She should have held on tight to what little time she'd had with him.

Instead, she had been off with the other young people and spending time with her grandparents—avoiding the sickroom. She had even been angry with her *mamm* for a long time because she hadn't left *Dat's* side more often to be somewhere else—anywhere else—with her *dochder.*

Too late, Rebekah wished she had sat there with *Mamm* and *Dat,* just to be with them. But there was nothing she could do about any of it now. She could only start fresh with *Mamm* and hope they could make up for the past.

Which means . . . I'm going to have to accept this marriage and the move and not make any problems for her. I have to do everything I can to be froh for her.

Rebekah knew her *mamm* well enough to know that she would call the whole thing off if Rebekah asked her to.

But she also knew that *Mamm* would be miserable if she did that, and she was determined not to be the cause of any more sadness for *Mamm—nee* matter what it took.

She turned from the window, and quietly padded back to the kitchen where *Aenti* Ida was making bread for them to take with them to the Fisher's *haus.*

.   .   .

Samuel stood at the kitchen sink, looking out over the snowy fields while the cup of *kaffe* he held was steadily growing colder. The ladies of the community had only just left a few minutes ago. The Stutzman *schweschders* had insisted on taking Naomi and Rebekah home, since they lived at the very edge of the district and her *onkel's haus* was only minutes from theirs.

He thought about what Naomi had told him earlier this afternoon. His first thoughts had been panic, but of course, he had not wanted to upset Naomi further, so he had pushed aside his own worries and called out to *Gotte* to give him the right words. Words that would help calm Naomi's fears and give him the strength to stand with her against the obstacles they were clearly going to encounter.

As he prayed, calm had spread through his entire being, and he knew that *Gotte* was reminding him that He was in control. His *wille* was more powerful than anything on this Earth. And with that, Samuel knew exactly what to say to help calm Naomi.

The hug had been very unexpected—and very nice. That one embrace had given Samuel a glimpse of his future with Naomi and he truly enjoyed the picture he saw. He could easily imagine the years to come with Naomi by his side. When Elisabeth had passed, he had been lonely, for certain, but he had never truly thought of marrying another woman.

It was a surprise to find that he was very *eiferich* about marrying Naomi and spending the coming years with her. He would never have known to ask *Gotte* for someone like her, but He had known what Samuel needed and sent her along, putting her right in Samuel's path.

And if it had not happened just as it had, Samuel was certain he would never have looked at Naomi as a potential *frau*. Even if they had met at some point, he would certainly have discovered that she was from a community so far away, which would have made it difficult for them.

But *Gotte* knew what needed to happen to bring the two of them together and he had set in motion the perfect events. It was truly a testament to how great *Gotte's* plans were. And Samuel was thankful for them.

Since Leah had accepted Naomi, the entire family was simply besotted with her. They included her in the family as if she had always been a part of it. And Rebekah had been pulled right into their large circle this evening as well.

Throughout the day, each one of his neighbors had found time to tell him what a blessing Naomi and Rebekah were certain to be to their family. It made him feel *gut* about the whole matter. And that reminded him that they truly were in *Gotte's wille.*

There was *nee* reason to think that *Gotte* would not work everything out in the right time. He certainly knew the timing much better than Samuel could. Over the years, Samuel thought he must have forgotten some of that in his loneliness and sadness over Elisabeth's death, but he was remembering now and he was so grateful for it.

He thought back to the flurry of activity that had taken over his entire *haus* today. He had watched Leah as she talked with Rebekah, until one of their neighbors had shooed him out of the kitchen. Given how Leah had initially felt toward Naomi, Samuel had been concerned that she would be resistant to Rebekah as well, but that had not been at all the case.

The two of them had been easy with each other and they seemed quite comfortable—almost as if they were already *schweschders.* Rebekah had blended right in with the ladies of their district, somehow knowing what needed to be done before anyone had to tell her. Leah had joined her and they had worked in a beautiful harmony.

He remembered the look on Naomi's face when he'd

looked over at her. She had looked at him with such *lieb* in her eyes, it had stolen away his breath. Even now, he wondered what he had done to deserve such *lieb*. He had asked her later, but she had only said that he was a *wunderbaar Dat*, and that his *kinner* were so blessed to have him. Then she had put her hand in his and said that she was blessed to have him, too.

And as she had stood there looking up at him, her hand in his, he had felt a tightness in his chest that he did not remember feeling since his days as a young man.

.   .   .

Samuel looked at Bishop Beiler. He almost could not believe what he was hearing. He knew they were in *Gotte's wille,* but he had begun to worry that they might have to endure a season of prayer and separation before the church leaders in Naomi's community would allow them to wed.

It had been less than two weeks since Naomi had received the letter from her *mamm,* warning her that the church elders might not be sending them *gut* news about the request to transfer Naomi's membership here so that they could marry.

Something must have happened there, between the time Naomi's *mamm* wrote the letter, and whenever the church elders had sent their own response.

Samuel was more than a little surprised by his bishop as well. Noah's smile was as wide as Samuel had ever seen it. He looked to Samuel almost like a mischievous *kind,* with Samuel as his co-conspirator. He clapped Samuel on the shoulder and laughed, a rich deep laugh that did not sound at all like the young, thin man he was.

Samuel found himself joining in. And why shouldn't he? It was very *gut* news indeed. Now he only had to go and tell Naomi.

"Would you like to come in for some *kaffi* or some of Leah's pumpkin bread?"

In truth, Samuel wanted to be on his way to share the news with Naomi, but he was not about to send off the man bringing such *gut* news without even a cup of *kaffi* on this cold December day. Bishop Beiler only laughed again.

"I would be glad to; Leah's pumpkin bread is not something I like to turn down. But I must be getting home." He turned to leave, then turned back and with a slight tilt of one thick eyebrow, he added.

"You have things to do as well, *jah*?"

Samuel laughed out loud as Noah descended the steps and headed for his buggy. He did indeed have things to do. He found he was even more *eiferich* than he had been only a moment ago.

He ducked back into the *haus* for a moment to let Leah know where he was headed.

. . .

Naomi was glad she was standing by the table. She felt as if her legs would not hold her. Had she truly heard Samuel say they could be married now?

It was nearly impossible to believe that her church elders had given their permission, especially since Joel was one of the elders. And *Mamm's* letter had made it sound as if they would never give permission. What could have happened between then and now?

She thought about the letter she had received from him only today. It had been nothing like she had expected. If she had not recognized his familiar handwriting, she might have wondered if it had come from someone else.

His words had been vague, but he had told her he truly wanted her happiness over anything else—which was just like him. She had been praying for him to accept that she would not marry him, but she could never have expected it to happen this quickly. She had also been praying for *Gotte* to help him move on without being hurt by her decision.

Gotte had certainly been at work in Joel's heart. Perhaps *Gotte* had his hand in everything here, with Leah and her *bruders* and *schweschders*—they had accepted her much quicker than she would have thought possible, even Leah. She and Samuel must truly be in *Gotte's wille*.

"Naomi, are you well?" Samuel's voice was so near her ear, she jumped a little at the sound of it.

"*Jah* Samuel, I am well. Truly, we can be married now?"

He was nodding before she even finished speaking.

"And your family is *allrecht* with all of this—with me?" She looked up at Samuel; feeling *gegisch* for needing him to tell her again that everyone was in complete acceptance of their marriage.

"Truly, my *lieb*." The sweet term of endearment made Naomi's heart fill with warmth and chased away every other fear and worry.

"Leah is so *eiferich* when she speaks of it." He stopped only a moment before adding, "and she tells everyone she sees. All of our neighbors have heard the news by now, and most of the people in town." He laughed as he said the last.

Naomi knew that he was laughing because Leah had made extra trips into town, using this as a reason.

"It truly is a miracle. *Gotte's* hand is upon us all." Samuel's smile could not have been any bigger; his face would not have held it.

And Naomi could feel that her smile was at least as wide as his own. She felt a warm glow spread all through her. She had not realized it until now, but without knowing it, she had been doubting *Gotte's wille*.

Even though she had been certain of what *Gotte* had spoken to her about Samuel, that she had finally gained acceptance from Leah, and Rebekah had been *froh* about the news . . .

Knowing that Joel would not want her to marry Samuel was the strongest fear that had held her in its grip since John had taken a turn for the worse.

The relief that flooded through her made her glad that she had lowered herself into a chair only moments before.

They could be married now.

THIRTY-ONE

Leah wiped a tear from her eyes as Ada lightly nudged her. She smiled over at her *freind*, so she would know Leah was crying tears of joy.

She felt as if an abundance of blessings had been poured out over her. Today Catherine would become her *schweschder* and her *bruder's frau*. Leah could not be happier for them.

Dat had told them last *nacht* that the church in Hope Springs had given their approval. That meant in another week Rebekah would also become her *schweschder;* Naomi would be her new *mamm*.

She had been praying for so long; it was almost too much to believe that her prayers were finally being answered. Naomi truly was the perfect *mamm* for them and the perfect *frau* for *Dat*. She was just what their family needed.

Of course she is, Leah thought, *Gotte sent her to us*.

She felt Ada press a handkerchief into her hand and she smiled as another tear spilled over and ran down her cheek. It was a *gut* thing Catherine had not asked her to stand up with her today. Leah feared she would have embarrassed Catherine with her tears, and today would not be a *gut* day to embarrass her new *schweschder*.

Leah watched Catherine's face as she spoke the words of her vows after Bishop Beiler. Her face was lit up with joy. Leah looked over at her *bruder*'s face and his was a mirror of Catherine's.

Leah had seen him that way quite often since he and Catherine had announced their intent to marry. They made each other *froh* and Leah was *nee* longer bothered by it—even a little. She had a whole new appreciation for their *lieb* now.

It was much easier now for her to think back to the start of their courtship as a bright point in time since *Mamm* had died. How David and Catherine had met and then fallen in *lieb* was one of the family's great stories, and it was quickly becoming one of Leah's favorites. She begged them to tell it so often, they were probably sick of repeating it.

The one bit of sadness was how much she would miss him—miss them both. When they had announced their engagement, *Dat* had announced that David would, of course, take a portion of their own land to build his home on. From there, he could decide if he wished to continue working with *Dat* or start his own crops.

David had decided to continue working with *Dat,* but he had begun almost immediately building a *haus* for his future *frau* and *kinner,* and he had asked *Dat* for help and advice every step of the way.

Leah could remember listening to them as they sat at the kitchen table, looking over catalogs and paint samples. David had made it a point to involve Catherine in every step of building what would be their home. It had only made Leah that much more determined that if she were ever to marry, he must be someone just like David and their *dat.*

Of course, the thought of courting brought Jacob to mind. She had not seen him yet that morning, but she knew he was there somewhere, since Catherine had made a point to invite all of Naomi's family.

She looked over to where the men were sitting, trying not to be noticed as she did, and was surprised that it only took a moment to find his familiar face in the crown of young men sitting near the back of the room.

He turned his head just then and their eyes met. She could not quite figure out the expression on his face, but he looked very serious and the intensity in his eyes might have frightened her if it had not been for the look of *lieb* in them as well.

She thought back to her birthday. There was a moment when he had been about to ask her something. Her romantic heart could not help but wonder if it was possible that he had been about to ask her to marry him, but her little *bruder* Matthew and Jacob's *bruder* Levi had chosen that moment to run around the corner of the porch, ramming into Jacob, and nearly knocking him down.

The mood of the moment might have *kumme* back, had Jacob not seen that she was covered in snow. He had rushed her into the *haus* and said *nee* more on the subject.

Only two nights later, he had shown up at her window and they had shared some pretty incredible kisses. In the evenings she had seen him since, he had said nothing more about whatever he had been about to ask, but she was trying very hard to give her worries over to *Gotte* and wait for His timing.

. . .

Samuel watched his son as he exchanged vows with Catherine. She was a fine young woman and he was pleased his son had found such a *wunderbaar frau*. He felt certain they would be *froh* together for many years to come. Their *lieb* was a beautiful thing, so pure and unselfish—it brought to mind the love Jesus had for the church.

He looked over to where Naomi sat and saw that she was looking at him as well. Only one more week and he would be standing before the bishop pledging himself to Naomi.

He thought back to the week before he had married Elisabeth. There had been excitement in him, but it had been far outweighed by fear. He had been worried that he was making a mistake or that he would make her unhappy.

He felt none of those things when he thought about Naomi—only an excitement and a calm certainty. He knew that he was in *Gotte's wille* and he was certain that *Gotte* would guide their steps in the union.

Gotte had already shown Samuel that Naomi was the perfect *frau* for him in so many ways. Every one of his *kinner* had told him many times that she was truly *wunderbaar*. Even Leah, who had been worried about their courtship in the beginning, had come around.

Naomi had sought Leah out and they had talked about Leah's fears and worries, and since that talk, they had been nearly inseparable whenever Naomi was in their home.

Samuel found himself glad he always went to fetch Naomi and then return her home. It was the only time he had to be alone with her lately.

But in another week, he would not have to worry about those things any longer. Naomi and Rebekah would live with them and he could find plenty of time to be with Naomi, and his family would still be able to take command of her time as well.

. . .

Naomi watched as Catherine and David pledged themselves to one another, and she could not help but shed a few tears of joy for them. She could clearly see how much in *lieb* they were and she was certain they had many years of happiness before them. She was glad to have so many new *kinner* to care for and *lieb*. She would at last have the large family she had wanted for so many years.

She dared not hope for any more. *Gotte* had blessed her so, just with Samuel's family; it would be selfish to want for more. Still, she could not help the tiny voice within that hoped *Gotte* might have it in his *wille* for her to have another *boppli* of her own.

She and Samuel were still young. It was not impossible—nothing was impossible with *Gotte*. She would simply have to be patient and see what was in *Gotte's wille* for them.

And even if there were *nee bopplin* in her future, she would certainly have many *grandkinner* to *lieb* and even spoil a bit. With three of Samuel's *dochdern* married, and now his oldest son, there would be plenty of *bopplin* to come. And she would enjoy every single one.

It would not be too many more years until Rebekah would be falling in *lieb* and be getting married and having *bopplin* of her own. The thought suddenly made Naomi feel much older than she had felt only a moment before.

Perhaps it was only in *Gotte's wille* for her to spoil her *grandkinner*.

.   .   .

In typical fashion, even though there was *nee* dancing or any of the things their *Englisch* neighbors seemed to expect at a wedding, the celebration following was a joyful one that lasted well into the evening. Fortune had smiled on them with a break in the weather. The temperature had climbed into the mid-thirties today and some of the snow had even evaporated.

Leah made her escape to the front porch when her throat began to feel as if her voice had been replaced by a fat bullfrog. She was bundled up in her warm coat, with a thick scarf wrapped around her neck and tucked right up to her chin, sitting on the wide, porch swing that had graced their home for as long as she could remember.

Mamm had told her once that *Dat* carved it for her as a gift to celebrate their first wedding anniversary. It had been one of *Mamm*'s favorite stories. *Ach,* how she had fretted for weeks about what to get for him. She had finally settled on knitting him a new scarf because his own was becoming worn and frayed in places and she wanted to make something for him.

She had worked so hard to hide her work from him, knitting furiously whenever he went out in the morning to do chores—and then hiding it as soon as she heard his boots on the porch. It had never occurred to her that he might be doing the very same thing.

He had been careful to hide his work. He had done such a fine job of it, that *Mamm* had begun to think he had forgotten and ended up spending most of that day feeling sad . . . and even a little angry. After a supper of *Dat*'s favorite foods, he had suggested they take a walk in the cool autumn evening and *Mamm* had protested. There were dishes to do and she was cross with him, but he had eventually charmed her into going.

And what had been the very first thing she had seen when they walked out onto the front porch, but the swing, delightfully carved, lovingly polished and carefully hung where they could sit and watch the sunset together for years to come.

.   .   .

Leah looked at the big *nacht* sky as she gently moved her feet back and forth against the smooth boards beneath them. There was not one cloud in the sky; it was just full to bursting with stars. A prettier *nacht* sky Leah could not remember ever seeing in all of her seventeen years.

She turned to the door when she heard it open and *Dat* was walking through the doorway. Only a moment passed before he walked over and sat on the swing beside her.

"Hiding out here is sure to save your voice, but your *bruder* and his new *frau* are going to notice that you are missing at some point." There was *nee* rebuke in his voice, just a gentle reminder. She took a deep breath and let it out slowly before answering him.

"I know, *Dat*. I just needed a few minutes. It has been a *wunderbaar gut* day, *jah*?"

"*Jah*, it truly has." His voice sounded almost sad to Leah and there was a bit of worry there too, if Leah had not completely missed the mark. She looked at his face. There was a tear on his cheek. It had clearly not been there for long, but there it was, glistening in the moonlight. Somehow it made Leah feel better to know that *Dat* was just as sad about this new step in their lives.

Catherine would be a *wunderbaar gut* addition to the

family and they would all welcome new *bopplin,* but it comforted Leah to see that *Dat* would miss David just as much as she would. As they sat there, he pulled her to him for a quick hug.

"Promise me you won't get in too much of a hurry, Leah." His words took Leah by surprise. His voice sounded entirely too shaky.

"I won't, *Dat.* I promise." She tried to shrug it all off, but she felt *Dat* stiffen when she said it. Could he hear the wistfulness in her own voice? Could he hear the worry? The worry that she had somehow misjudged Jacob's feelings for her? Could he tell that she was wishing and hoping for a declaration of some sort of her own very soon?

"Trust me *dochder,* there are boys interested." Leah looked at him as he said it, but she could only see his profile. He looked serious, very serious.

She wanted to ask if he knew of anyone, but she knew it would not be a *gut* idea. He would only be upset to be reminded that she was eager to begin her own family. And if the boy he knew of was Zeke Hershberger, she really did not wish to know it.

It was not more than a minute later, before Anna swept out to the porch and found them. She pulled Leah to her feet and headed for the door, calling over her shoulder that cake was being served and he had better get a move on if he wanted a piece.

Leah was laughing when Anna pulled her back into the *haus.* It was a very *gut* day indeed.

. . .

It was several hours later before Leah had a chance to really talk to Jacob. She was standing at the edge of the barn by herself, when he walked over to her. She looked up at the smile on his face and thought of how *froh* she had felt all day. It was *gut* to see he looked *froh,* too.

"You've heard the *gut* news . . . *jah*?"

"About your *dat* and Naomi?" Leah nodded and he went on.

"Oh *jah.* I was coming in from evening chores when your *dat* arrived to give her the news." He laughed then and smiled.

"It's a *gut* thing they're in a hurry. They remind me of two young people; the way they look at each other when they think *nee* one is looking."

Of course, before he had finished talking, Jacob was looking at her in much the same way and she could feel her heartbeat speeding up at the intensity in his eyes. It was the same look she had seen earlier and she bit her lip to keep from asking him what it meant.

A moment later she could feel heat flooding her cheeks because his eyes had shifted to look at her mouth and the expression there had changed again. Something in his eyes made her feel the need to blush, and brought the feeling of his kisses to mind.

Before she realized what he was doing, he had taken her hand and was pulling her through the large barn doors and away from everyone else. Once they were all the way around to the back area of the barn, he stopped and took both of her hands in his.

. . .

"Leah," He started, but stopped when he saw her lower lip was tucked between her teeth again. He couldn't help himself—he leaned forward and kissed her—hard.

For a second, he could feel the bump of her lower lip where it was caught before her mouth opened on a gasp of surprise and then her lips met his as she leaned into him.

He still held both of her hands between them and he forced himself to stay that way. It would not be a *gut* idea to get carried away here.

Still, they stayed connected for much longer than was probably *schmaert* before he was able to pull away from her. He didn't even look to see if anyone was around. He just leaned in for one more quick kiss before deliberately taking a step back.

Leah's cheeks were a *wunderbaar* pink and she was smiling the way he loved so much. Before he could think any more about his words, he blurted out.

"Leah I *lieb* you and I want to spend the rest of my life with you."

He was rewarded with two surprises. First, her smile bloomed even bigger and more beautiful. Second, she kissed him.

It was the first time she had made the gesture herself and warmth spread throughout him as she leaned up to him and gently pressed her lips against his.

"Does that mean your answer is *jah,* then?"

Leah laughed, but did not get a chance to answer him.

THIRTY-TWO

"Leah, kumme! Quick! Ach, where are you, Leah?" Ruth appeared at the corner of the barn, nearly shouting. "Leah, thank heavens. You must *kumme.* Miriam has gone into labor." She took hold of Leah's hand and turned, pulling her along.

Leah stumbled a little at the word "labor", but managed to keep her footing and followed a bit quicker, looking over her shoulder at Jacob—who had a wide smile on his face.

"I will go see if there is anything for a young man to do to help out, *jah?"*

Leah smiled, but Ruth didn't even seem to hear him as she hastened her pace, still pulling Leah along behind her.

Across the yard and up the porch steps, into the *haus*

and upstairs, Ruth never slowed down. She pulled Leah with her past neighbors and family alike, stopping only when she reached *Dat's* room.

Miriam was leaning against Joshua, moaning a little as she rocked back and forth. Leah could not help but notice that Joshua was exceptionally calm as he rocked with Miriam.

She must be in the middle of a contraction.

Before Leah had a chance to think or say anything, Ruth was propelling her to the other side of *Dat's* bed.

"Here, Leah. Help me with this." All business, Ruth tossed the end of a thickly woven sheet over the bed. Leah caught it and tucked her side in tightly, patting it down smoothly so the thick material wouldn't rub against Miriam later and chafe her skin.

A moment later Naomi rushed into the room, moving immediately to Ruth's side.

"What can I do? Is there anything I can do, Ruth? How can I help? I want to help somehow." She wrung her hands the entire time she spoke and it only took a moment for Leah to realize she was *naerfich*—very much so.

I have never seen her so naerfich. Has she never done this before? Only a moment later, Leah remembered that she had not. Naomi had only the one *dochder* herself. *And she must have been so busy taking care of her husband; she had nee time to help out with the women in the community.*

Leah wanted to go to her, comfort her somehow, but her *schweschder* must have given Naomi some quiet instructions because she rushed right back out of the room.

Leah went back to the business of preparing for the *boppli's* arrival, moving around Miriam and Joshua, who were slowly walking back and forth now. Together, Leah and Ruth moved around the room making preparations in quiet harmony.

Not every one of the new Fisher *kinner* had been born here, but Leah had been present for each birth so far.

Miriam, with the help of several of their neighbors, had set things up for Anna's first and Leah had been much too involved in amazement and awe to pay attention to any of it, but apparently Ruth had taken note of everything they'd done because the very next time, she had set up and after watching her just the one time, Leah had been able to help and the work went much quicker—which had been handy since the next *boppli* to arrive had been Miriam's . . . so, of course, she was unable to help Ruth, and Anna had been involved in a very different capacity, so she was unable to help much at all.

Leah had talked her through as much as she could, but mostly Anna had followed her around, asking questions until the local midwife arrived and then she had taken to following her around until Eva sent her off to boil water—a task usually reserved for *naerfich dats,* shaking her head and doing her best to stifle a laugh.

Just as Leah and Ruth finished arranging the pillows into a cradle of sorts—to support Miriam later, Reba Hershberger walked in the door with her young apprentice Dora.

"Ruth Fisher, if I did not know better, I would think

you are after my job."

Ruth responded with a laugh, as she usually did, before answering, "Don't be *gegisch*, Reba. I plan to have my hands full with all the *kinner* David and I will soon have. We plan to keep you busy enough—until young Dora takes over, that is."

Reba let out a hearty laugh of her own in reply.

"True enough. Why I believe the Fisher family alone will keep me plenty busy over the next twenty or so years. And by the time I am ready to retire, your *kinner* will be having their own *bopplin.*"

"And then we'll be keeping Dora busy."

Leah watched Dora's eyes get a little bigger with each proclamation and could not help but feel a little sorry for the young woman. For sure and for certain, her *schweschder* and Reba were teasing, but you wouldn't know it to look at Dora. She was positively white.

She needn't have worried though. Within a minute or two, Reba began giving her young apprentice instructions, which wiped the fear from her features, replacing it with the look of concentration as she went about each duty Reba gave her.

Leah let out a laugh as Ruth slipped an arm around her shoulders and said quietly in her ear, "Got that one well-trained already, hasn't she?"

The two of them giggled as they turned to give Reba and Dora space to work.

"*Kumme,* Leah. Reba has things well in hand here. I believe we can take a bit of a break." Ruth said.

Leah took the subtle hint her *schweschder* was giving.

Reba would need to examine Miriam and she would certainly want privacy for that. The two *schweschders* made their way downstairs. Much of the celebration was still underway.

Having *bopplin* was certainly *nee* mystery for plain folk and though most of their neighbors had cleared out by now, Leah was certain their extended family would stay over to welcome the new arrival. And, of course, someone must mind the little ones while the adults went about the business of welcoming the next *boppli*.

Leah searched for Jacob's face as they made their way through the crowd in the *sitzschtupp,* but didn't spot him anywhere among them.

Perhaps he is still in the barn, cleaning up. She would wonder if he had gone home with his parents, but she saw them talking to Naomi, so clearly that was not it.

Ach, well, he must be around here somewhere.

Leah watched Naomi as she moved through the room with Ruth. Naomi stood there with her *aenti,* still wringing her hands and looking very *naerfich* indeed. Leah felt a moment's amusement, but quickly pushed it aside. It was certainly not Naomi's fault that she hadn't been present for as many births as they had in the Fisher family.

It was then that she spotted Jacob. He walked over and pressed a steaming mug into Naomi's hands. He stood there a minute, loosely holding onto it.

He must be making certain she has a gut hold of it.

When he stepped back, he looked up, right into Leah's eyes. The smile that blossomed suddenly on his features had butterflies dancing in Leah's stomach and she had to turn away so she could concentrate on her feet, as they nearly came out from under her.

"Leah, are you *allrecht*?" Ruth asked, slowing down to give Leah a chance to get her footing back.

"*Jah*, Ruth. I'm just fine." She looked back at Jacob and he looked suspiciously like he was smothering a laugh— and at the same time, he looked nearly like a cat that had swallowed a canary whole.

She looked away again before he had another chance to mess her around, shaking her head at the whole thing. *Boys are so schpassich.*

When they reached the kitchen, Leah breathed a sigh of relief. Her dear *freind* Margaretta had taken charge of the kitchen, it seemed. She had cocoa, *kaffe* and hot water for tea brewed and set about the stove for the steady stream of people who were wandering in and out. Leah moved over behind her *freind* and enveloped her in a hug.

"Margaretta, you are such a blessing. Do you know that?"

She laughed, before turning to Leah and answering. "Well, I was already here and all the great cooks of the Fisher family were a bit occupied, so I figured I would put myself to use so no one thinks to send me off."

Leah waved her words away. "What nonsense. *Nee* one would send you away. You are a dear *freind* and we are *froh* to have you here. You do not have to work just so that you can stay."

Margaretta laughed again. "Oh, I know that, Leah. I was only kidding anyway. I just figured . . . someone had to do it. It may as well be me. You know how everyone is about Ruth's cocoa." She pointed a thumb back at herself then before adding, "Lucky it is only me who knows the recipe."

Leah laughed with Margaretta as her *schweschder* wandered off to fix a plate of food. Thinking of how long it had been since she had eaten—and thinking of the long *nacht* ahead, she moved away to make her own plate of food.

"Have you eaten, Margaretta?"

"Oh yeah, I ate before I got all this going." She pointed to a plate that was sitting at the back of the small table beside the stove. "In the meantime, I have a few tidbits to tide me over while I keep the cocoa going. You know how it is. If you don't keep it moving, it will scorch."

"Sorry we don't have one of those fancy contraptions Ruth has in the cafe."

Margaretta laughed in return. "Oh yeah, I think my tennis elbow is starting to flare up. Remind me what your homeowner's policy covers again?"

"It only covers injuries. Pre-existing conditions do not count." Leah answered in the most *Englisch* accent she could manage, trying to sound a bit nasal at the same time. And then she and Margaretta were both laughing.

"Seriously, that contraption is pretty handy. If there weren't so much to it, I just might consider purchasing one."

"I would agree with you, but I've looked them up online. They're ridiculously expensive. Honestly, if Ruth hadn't found that one at an estate sale, I'm certain she wouldn't have it, either."

"*Gut* thing she does, though. It saves your poor elbow." Leah laughed again and Margaretta joined her. Then, after a minute, Leah moved away again to fill her plate with the various foods still spread out across the kitchen table and counters.

"At least there's *nee* shortage of *wunderbaar* things to eat."

Leah smiled at her *freind*'s words. "*Jah*, we have some *gut* neighbors."

Over the next several hours, Leah and Ruth made trips up and down the stairs to *Dat's* room. Miriam progressed well and Reba sent them on errands to fetch her tea or warm blankets. Leah worked alongside Margaretta mostly, rotating blankets that were warming by the kitchen fireplace.

Benjamin had brought one of the metal washtubs in so the blankets would stay clean and not catch a spark from the embers. Leah would hand off the blankets to Ruth whenever she arrived for a new one, exchanging it for one that had cooled.

They all knew how important it was to keep Miriam warm during this time. Joseph had stoked the fire in *Dat's* hearth right away, but the warm blankets were necessary as well. At one point, Ruth arrived with a stack of fresh blankets and Leah knew Miriam must be getting close then.

If her waters have broken, she is nearly there. Leah smiled at the thought of welcoming the new *boppli*. *Bopplin* were always a cause for celebration in the Fisher household and they couldn't have much time left.

Several times Leah had seen Jacob *kumme* and go with plates of food and cups of tea. She wondered if he was delivering food to anyone specific. *For sure and for certain, he cannot be eating all of it himself . . . can he?*

She was certain the tea was for Naomi. *Tea will give her something to keep her hands busy, at least.* Leah struggled with her laughter any time she thought of the only flaw she had yet to find in her soon-to-be stepmother.

Who would ever have thought it?

"Leah, it's time. *Kumme.*" Dora rushed into the kitchen and took hold of Leah's hand. Leah had the presence of mind to reach for the smaller stack of blankets in the enormous tub before Dora pulled her away.

We will need these for the boppli.

Margaretta nodded to Leah as she moved through the kitchen. "I'll keep an eye on them."

"*Danki.*" She called out to Margaretta, just as they left the kitchen. *I certainly am being pulled around an awful lot this evening.*

Still, they would be welcoming a new *boppli* in moments. It was a very exciting time.

As they moved through the *sitzschtupp,* Leah caught sight of Jacob standing next to Naomi and *Dat.* He winked at her and smiled wide. She had a feeling there was a somewhat *gegisch* smile on her face, but she really did not mind one bit.

Then, just as they reached the creaky step, Leah heard a loud wail of protest.

"My, what a set of lungs." Dora said, before looking over at Leah with a wide grin of her own.

Then they were both racing up the stairs to welcome the new *boppli,* as the family gathered below began to laugh and cheer . . . and then resumed their chatter—a bit louder this time.

EPILOGUE

Leah looked sideways from under her lashes at the young man sitting near the back with the other single men. She thought about how *schpassich* it all was, that he had shown up at their door asking for help and now *Dat* was marrying his cousin. *Gotte* truly did work in mysterious ways.

As she looked at him from across the room, secretly hoping he would turn his head and meet her gaze, but also content to look him over while he was completely unaware of it, she felt a strange fluttering in her stomach.

She found herself hoping she could have an opportunity to speak with him today at some point, but she knew how difficult that would be. He might be here as a guest, but she certainly was not; she would be kept busy with so many things today, she would hardly have time to breath.

As she stood there, trying to be unobtrusive in her glance, her *bruder* Elam caught her eye. She turned her head back toward the preacher as Bishop Beiler led *Dat* and their new *mamm* in their vows. There was such warmth in Leah's heart. She had received precisely what she had been asking *Gotte* for all along. And, as a bonus, she had gained a new *schweschder*.

She looked at Rebekah, standing just in front of her. She was so tiny. Leah had inherited her *mamm's* slight build. She had always thought of herself as small, but Rebekah was even more so.

She and her *mamm* both were so tiny and delicate they looked more like life-size dolls than women. Leah had first-hand knowledge though, that there was nothing delicate about her new *mamm*.

She had not had the same experience with Rebekah. She felt like she was beginning to get to know her, but she had been here such a short time and she was very quiet— even more so than Miriam, who was the most quiet and reserved person Leah had known . . . before meeting Rebekah.

Leah hoped they would get to know each other better soon. Now that Rebekah was becoming a part of their family, they would have time to learn all about each other. She had certainly begun a *wunderbaar* friendship with Naomi, her new *mamm*, and she hoped Rebekah would be just as easy to get to know.

One thing was for certain. Leah was so *eiferich* about

her new *mamm* that she was going to do everything she could to make Rebekah feel as if she had always been a part of the family.

She was also *eiferich* to have the chance to become acquainted with her new grandparents. She had met Naomi's parents for the first time when they had come to Windy Gap for the wedding. They had actually arrived a few days after David's wedding and they were staying with Naomi's *Aenti* in Clearview, but they had spent each evening so far with the Fisher family, visiting and going over wedding plans.

Leah could remember how delighted she had been to be included when Naomi and Rebekah had headed upstairs to where Naomi was sewing her new dress. She had stood and reached out a hand to Leah with a smile and then waited until she joined them. They continued upstairs together, Naomi walking arm in arm with Rebekah on one side and Leah on the other.

As Leah thought about Naomi's family, she also found herself looking forward to spending a few minutes alone with a certain cousin of her new *mamm's*.

Jacob.

This relationship she had not prayed for—not specifically anyway. She had always known the day would *kumme* when she would need to think about such things, but never could she have imagined that the young man who would show interest in her would be someone who happened upon their farm completely by chance. That was what her *freind* Ada had said, that it was unplanned—serendipity, she called it.

Leah wasn't sure she agreed. She chose to look at it somewhat differently. She was convinced that all of this was simply a part of *Gotte's wille*. He had a plan for her life—and for Jacob's—and this was the way in which He had found a way to bring them together.

Ada never came right out and said such things were stuff and nonsense, but Leah felt it was how she truly felt. Leah never pushed much to change her *freind*'s mind, because she did not want Ada to try and change her own. It was far easier to simply hold on to her precious beliefs and leave well enough alone.

But just wait until her rumschpringe kummes. She just might have a different outlook then. The thought made Leah smile.

. . .

In front of Leah, Rebekah stood, looking at her *mamm* and at the man who would be her new *dat*. He had a very nice face and he had been most welcoming to her already. She only hoped to fit in with the rest of his family as well.

She knew it was going to be quite an adjustment since she had grown up with only herself, her *mamm* and her grandparents—and this man had eleven *kinner* all his own.

Granted, four of them are already married and living in their own homes now, but with so many people about every day, it is sure to be an adjustment.

Still, she was determined to do everything she could to help keep the peace. She had not seen her *mamm* so *froh* in such a long time. She would do anything to help her stay that way, even if it meant pretending she was *froh* as well . . .

WATCH FOR BOOK TWO

COMING IN 2018

A Suitor For Rebekah

After their parents marry, the Fisher kids must find a place within the family for Rebekah, who is not at all used to such chaos – having grown up with a father who was ill most of her life, a mother who spent her days taking care of a sick husband, and grandparents who doted on her to the point where she felt more like their daughter than their grand-daughter.

Rebekah must find her place in the loud, rambunctious, sometimes nosy Fisher family and the community of Windy Gap.

Could love be the thing that will make her stay or will she turn her back on even that to return. . . to the place she calls home?

DISCUSSION QUESTIONS
WARNING - SPOILERS AHEAD

1) Family is perhaps the most important part of a person's life. They pick you up when you fall... they make us who we are... Would you let pride come between you and a family member—especially a father or mother?

If you happened to answer yes to the question above, you might consider examining your life and deciding whether the sacrifices you have had to make in that case are worth your pride... or not.

2) In plain communities, widows or widowers are generally encouraged to remarry quickly. This stems not only from their tendency to produce large families, but from their strength of community. Do you consider this to be a good practice?

In the same situation, would you be happy to have neighbors and loved ones trying to rush you into another relationship?

3) Have you ever been in Leah's shoes—feeling that the loss of a loved one has left an enormous gap in your life? Was there a point when that gap was filled by someone—perhaps a stranger? How did you handle the situation?

4) Have you ever been in a situation where someone misunderstood your intentions. . . like Joel did with Naomi? He was certain she would marry him after a suitable amount of time. . . but Naomi, in her grief, had no memory of Joel's intentions. If someone expected you to follow through on an agreement you don't remember making, would you?

Or would you do the same sort of thing Naomi did. . . go in search of your own solution?

5) What time of the year do you consider to be the best for marriage? Do you have a date already in mind or do you prefer to wait until you are in a serious relationship so that you can schedule your wedding date for an important date for the two of you?

ABOUT THE PUBLISHER

Publishing for HIS Glory!

S&G Publishing offers books with messages that honor Jesus Christ to the world! S&G works with Christian authors to bring you the best in "inspirational" fiction and non-fiction.

S&G is proud to publish a variety of genres:

inspirational romance

young reader

young adult

speculative

historical

suspense

Check out our website at

sgpublish.com

MORE FROM

S&G PUBLISHING

DON'T MISS NAOMI MILLER'S
AMISH SWEET SHOP SERIES